GUARDING HIS PRINCESS

YAHRAH ST. JOHN

OLIVERHEBERBOOKS

MORE IN THIS SERIES

Look out for the first two books in the Mitchell Brothers trilogy:

Claimed by the Hero

Seducing the Seal

Available now!

PROLOGUE

Six months earlier

"I'm sorry, Cameron, but you'll never fly again," the doctor said, looking across the desk into Cameron's hazel eyes. "The injury you sustained changed your vision and there's no way we can get you back to the twenty-twenty vision you'll need in order to fly for the Unites States Air Force."

Cameron sighed audibly. He wasn't surprised by the expensive ophthalmologist's statement. He'd met with three eye specialists, but he'd been hoping against hope they were wrong and that somehow, someway he could go back to doing what he loved. But the injuries he sustained from the plane crash several months ago effectively ended his career as a pilot which meant he wasn't fit for duty and would be honorably discharged.

Cameron was still in disbelief. All his life, he'd wanted to serve his country as his grandfather, Carter, father, Cal, and his brother, Caden, had done in the Army and his brother, Cage, in the Navy Seals, and, for a while, he had. Cameron had put on the uniform for eight years, but it was all over now, and he would be getting his walking papers.

He was bitterly disappointed and didn't know what do with all the anger he had growing inside him. One person, however, came to mind. His mother. He'd been stunned to learn she'd cheated on his father, or at least the man he'd always thought of as his father. Apparently, when Cal had been deployed, she'd gotten pregnant with another man's child and passed Cameron off as his son.

His ancestry made sense now. Growing up, he always wondered why his complexion wasn't brown or dark chocolate like his father, or brothers, Caden and Cage. Cameron thought he favored his mother with her smooth vanilla skin, but the eyes, he'd never known where his hazel eyes came from because they didn't run in the Mitchell family. Now, he knew. He must have inherited it from his paternal side of the family. Sometimes, Cameron thought about finding out more about them for health reasons if nothing else, but learning his entire life was built on a lie was like a fresh cut that hadn't quite healed over. Cameron wasn't ready to pull off the scab to delve in deeper.

Maybe one day.

Since he'd been released from the hospital, he'd had no interaction with his mother, despite her repeated calls and texts. Today, however, she was standing outside of the specialist's office waiting for him in front of her custom Mercedes Benz.

"I can't talk to you, Mother," Cameron said, walking past her to his Jeep. "Not today." He'd heard the most devastating news of his life and needed time to lick his wounds, *in private.*

His mother didn't take the hint. Instead, she followed him toward his Jeep, putting herself between him and the driver's side door.

"Cameron, I know you're upset with me, but it's been months. Months of me, patiently waiting for you to give me a chance to explain."

Cameron's brows furrowed into a frown. "And say what?

What exactly can you say that will make knowing the man I have looked up to my entire life is not my *real* father? You allowed him to raise me for three decades and never said a word to either of us. Instead, you kept this dirty little secret to yourself."

"I know, I know, baby and I shouldn't have." His mother sniffed. "I should have told you, when you were older and would have understood."

"Understood what?"

"How lonely I was when your father was deployed," Camilla stated. "I never intended on having an affair. I loved your father, I love him still though I know he finds that hard to believe, but I do. I made a mistake, a terrible mistake, but that doesn't negate how much I love you and want to care for you during your time of need."

"There is no time of need," Cameron replied. "Because there's nothing that doctor..." he pointed to the building behind him, "or anyone else can do to put me back together again and give me the vision I need to fly a plane. Are you happy now? Now you know everything."

"Oh darling," His mother sighed, "I'm so sorry. I know that's not the news you were hoping for and I can see that you're hurting."

"Wouldn't you be?" Cameron yelled. "My career, the life I planned for myself, is over. I don't have a back-up plan. The Air Force was it for me."

"And it can still be, just because you can't fly... "

Cameron held up a hand. "Just stop right there. I don't want to hear that. I *can't* hear it right now. Will you just please move out of the way and let me leave!"

Tears welled in her eyes, but Cameron felt nothing. He just felt despair.

"I know you don't want to talk to me, but you have to talk to someone. You can't keep this rage bottled up inside."

"Anger is all I've got right now," Cameron replied. "And if I want to hold on to it. It's my right. You don't get to tell me what to do, not anymore. You, who have always held yourself up as some paragon of virtue and esteem, but you're nothing but a liar and a cheat. Stop calling. Stop texting. I don't want to see you."

His mother covered her mouth with her hand and wept. Quietly, she stepped away from the Jeep and tearing his gaze away from her, Cameron climbed inside and turned on the ignition. He drove away leaving her standing alone in the parking lot.

Cameron knew he was being unconscionably cruel, but he couldn't help himself. She was in the wrong place at the wrong time. He wasn't in the right headspace to have that conversation, but she'd forced his hand. Now they would all have to live with the fallout.

KNOCK. *Knock.*

Cameron didn't want to answer. After leaving the doctor's office, he'd stopped off at the liquor store and picked up a twelve-pack of beer along with his favorite whiskey. Hours later, Cameron was well on his way to tying one on and that was just fine with him. He was wallowing in self-pity and recrimination.

He was so far gone; he didn't notice that his father, Cal Mitchell, had used his spare key to enter his bachelor pad. The two-bedroom apartment was an investment property, a place he could hole up after finishing one of his tours. It was roomy enough and had all the essentials, a large reclining sofa, entertainment center, and the cocktail table Monae convinced him to buy way back when.

Cameron's eyes rolled back in his head. He didn't want to think about his ex-girlfriend who was now in love with his brother. He'd made his peace with it, but he couldn't think about how happy they were, not tonight.

"So, you've decided to drown your sorrows," his father stated, sitting on the opposite end of the sofa from Cameron, who was sprawled out on the other end. At least half a dozen empty bottles of beer were strewn across the floor.

"What's it to you?" Cameron was spoiling for a fight and didn't care with whom.

"I'd like a beer if you have one to share."

Cameron reached into the cooler by the sofa and pulled out a cold brew and handed it to Cal, the man he'd thought for the last thirty-two years was his father.

"Thanks." Cal twisted off the top and took a long pull. Then he turned to look at Cameron.

Cameron knew he must look a mess. The last time he'd bothered looking in the mirror, his eyes had been bloodshot and he had several days' growth of beard. If he'd been on duty, it would have been a big deal. Being clean shaven was expected in the Air Force.

"How long are you going to keep feeling sorry for yourself?"

Cameron snorted. "As long as it takes."

His father cocked his head and stared at him. "I get it, Cam. You got a raw deal. First with Cage stealing your lady and now losing the ability to fly, but..."

"Enough about Cage, Dad," Cameron sighed. "I've made my peace with him and Monae. You need to, too. She and I were over long *before* they got together. Should they have told me they wanted to pursue a relationship? Hell yes, but it's water under the bridge. They love each other, so if they're happy, who am I to hold a grudge?"

"You're a better man than I am, son," Cal responded. "If I'd discovered your mother's infidelity back then, I don't know where we'd be."

Cameron glanced at him sideways. "Where are you now?"

"Honestly?"

"That's all I can take right now."

"I'm not sure. On the one hand, I want to divorce her because my life has always been about duty, honor and loyalty, but yet... we have forty happy years together. Do I throw the baby out with the bath water? The same applies to you too, ya know."

"How do you figure?"

"I know I may not be your biological father," his father said, "But you *are* and will *always be* my boy. You're my son and no DNA test is going to tell me otherwise."

Tears sprung to Cameron's eyes. He hadn't known he needed to hear those words. Hadn't known how he might feel, but they were exactly what he needed most in the moment when he felt like his entire world was falling apart.

"Dad..." His voice broke and Cal instinctively moved closer until he was pulling Cameron into his arms and holding him tight, just like a father would a son.

CAMERON APPRECIATED Cal making it clear in no uncertain terms *he* was his father. However, after he left, it brought Cameron back to the present.

What was he going to do with his life?

His grandfather, Carter Mitchell, was a retired three-star general in a high-level position at the Pentagon and owned a security firm. He could easily offer him a job like he had Cage, but Cameron wasn't ready for that. He had to get away. Re-group and figure out his next move. The phone call he received later that evening couldn't have come at a better time.

It was his good friend, Khalil Naseer, a former Air Force Academy friend. Khalil had an American mother with blond hair and blue eyes, and his father just so happened to be King of Bahara, a small country in the Middle East. Khalil didn't have much of a relationship with the king because his parents divorced when he was young. His younger brother Malik was the Crown Prince because Khalil's father re-married and took a native wife who came from royal blood.

The king put all of his efforts into Malik while Khalil, although the eldest and should have been next in line for the throne was left to his own devices. Khalil was able to do as he pleased. After four years of serving in the US Air Force, Khalil had gone on to acquire great wealth after investing in several lucrative business opportunities. He was now a self-made millionaire.

"Khalil, it's been a long time," Cameron said, answering the call.

"Yes, it has, my friend," Khalil said from the other end.

"How are you?"

"Shouldn't I be asking you that?" Khalil inquired. "I heard from Brett that you were injured during a routine flight."

"Yeah, I was."

"And? What of your injuries?"

If Cameron could be honest with anyone, it was Khalil. He'd been in the trenches with Cameron and understood the struggle it took to become an Air Force pilot. "I won't ever fly again."

"Damn! I'm sorry to hear that, Cam," Khalil responded. "I know how much flying means to you."

It meant everything and without it, Cameron was floundering. "It's a shock I haven't really come to terms with yet."

"So that means you haven't made any decisions about your future?" Khalil inquired.

His question surprised Cameron. "That's right. Why?"

"Well…" Khalil sighed heavily and there was a long pause.

"Whatever it is, you can tell me, Khalil. We've never kept secrets from each other."

"No, no, we haven't. And this will come out soon enough although the palace has tried to keep it under wraps, but the Crown Prince's plane carrying him and his mother went down in the desert a few hours ago. There's a rumor, it was a planned attack against the royal family."

"Ohmigod, that's horrible, Khalil," Cameron replied. "Did they find the wreckage? Did Malik survive?"

"That's the thing, Cam. The Crown Prince is presumed dead much like I might have been if you hadn't risked everything to find me when my plane went down while I was in the Air Force. The assumption is I'm next in line to rule Bahara. A member of the royal council showed up to my office and demanded my immediate return to Bahara to take my rightful place as heir to the throne."

"What?"

"As you know, my father died a few years ago from a stroke. There's no one else. I'll have to step in, but I'm woefully ill prepared for this role. Malik was the Crown Prince. He was groomed to be king one day, not me."

"Not anymore," Cameron stated quietly. "You're the next king of Bahara." His statement was met with silence. "What do you need from me, Khalil? How can I help?"

"I need someone I can trust to stand by my side. Someone who can look after my sister."

"Sister?"

That's when Cameron recalled Khalil had a younger sister, nearly a decade younger.

"Yes, Amani," Khalil answered. "We have to be sure this wasn't an attempt on the royal family, until we do, I need to keep her safe at all costs. Can you come? I need you."

"Of course," Cameron replied. He could help a friend in need and distract himself from the wreckage of his own life. "I'll be there."

1

———

Six months later

"**P**rincess Amani, are you excited to be opening the new girl's school in the country?" one of the reporters asked Amani as she exited the limousine surrounded by four bodyguards, including Cameron Mitchell, the one man she wished would look at her like a woman, rather than a job.

Amani gave a small smile like she'd been taught during her decorum classes. It was never a good idea to smile too brightly or reveal too much teeth for the cameras, her instructor always said.

"This way." Cameron moved their convoy onward and Amani waved at several spectators as they swiftly passed through the halls.

Amani was used to Cameron's high-handed nature because he was the head of her security team. It had been that way for the last six months since her brother Malik, the Crown Prince, and her mother, had been killed in a suspected attack against the royal family. Since that time, her older brother Khalil

Naseer, the true heir to the throne had come home to Bahara and taken over as King.

Amani was still filled with grief. Losing her mother in such a fashion was traumatic, but they'd never shared a close relationship. Queen Fatma had always doted on Malik, her father's second son and raised him to be the crown prince. Malik was stoic in front of others, but with her, he'd always been fun and lively. Growing up in the palace with him had been a delight. Despite her station as a woman in a predominantly male-led country, Malik never made her feel unimportant, but Khalil was different. He was serious and rarely smiled.

Though Amani doubted he had much to smile about these days. Since Malik's death, he had to overcome hard odds. There were some members in the royal Bahara council who thought of Khalil as an outsider because his mother was an American and he hadn't been raised here. Amani remembered his visits when she'd been younger. Her mother would be in a fit of jealousy if their father spent too much time with Khalil. Eventually, Khalil's visits became less frequent, until eventually Amani no longer saw her older brother at all.

And now that he was King, there was a rift between them that Amani had no idea how to overcome. It didn't help that he'd brought an outsider into their midst to oversee her every waking minute and ensure no harm came to a hair on her head.

Cameron Mitchell.

From the day he'd arrived, Amani had been mesmerized not just by his tall stature at six-foot-two which equaled Khalil's own six-foot-three, but because he was by far the most gorgeous man she'd ever met. Smooth, butterscotch skin with hazel eyes and a slim, yet athletic figure, Cameron spelled Hunk with a capital H.

Whenever she tried to make eye contact with Cameron or engage him in any sort of conversation, he kept her at a distance. Why? Did he sense her attraction to him? Did she wear it on her skin like a bad cologne? Amani thought she was doing a good job of hiding her interest in the dashing bodyguard who right now wore a custom all-black suit with a Baharan insignia on his left lapel which showed he was part of the royal guard.

One time, when she'd been on a rare holiday weekend for a few days last month, they'd gone to the beach and it was so blazing hot in the desert, Cameron had to take off his usual suit gear and wear comfortable clothing more suitable to the desert. When he'd put on light fitting pants and a white t-shirt, he'd looked every bit the dashing rake Amani imagined him to be in her fantasies.

And she fantasized a lot. She'd been raised in the palace and although she'd gone to finishing school in Switzerland, she'd had a sheltered upbringing and was never allowed to see inappropriate things. She was a princess, after all, and was supposed to remain a virgin until the day she married a man her family deemed a suitable match.

Amani understood her obligation, but she didn't have to like it and so she rebelled against the grain a bit. She snuck romance books into her finishing school and the stories she read made her more than a little hot and bothered. What would it be like to have a man like Cameron kiss and caress her like the men did in the pages of one of her romances?

She desperately wanted to know, but she doubted she would ever find out. Cameron was always stone-cold and unfathomable. Amani wondered what or *who* had made him become so impervious. Perhaps one day she would be able to sneak through his defenses and learn more.

~

DAMN HER! Cameron thought.

The little minx with her long, thick black hair cascading in soft waves down her back. Those full, bee-stung lips. Almond skin. Dark, caramel brown eyes surrounded by lush lashes he could lose himself in. Amani Naseer was one gorgeous-ass princess. Every time Cameron was around her, he had to remind himself of his position. Khalil had brought him to the small island country because he needed someone he could trust. After the death of his father and now the Crown Prince, Khalil was worried about losing his remaining family. He was keeping Amani, and his mother in America, heavily protected.

How would it look if he got involved with Khalil's sister? It was wrong on every level and was why Cameron protected Amani with a long-handled spoon. He couldn't let her get too close. Yet, as he watched her hips sway as she walked ahead of him, Cameron couldn't deny she was sexy as hell.

Focus, Mitchell, Cameron told himself. He mustn't let himself get sidetracked from his goals. Khalil brought him here to find out who was behind sabotaging his youngest brother's plane. Six months later, they still had nothing. Despite going over the evidence and the wreckage, there hadn't been anything to confirm or deny Malik's death wasn't accidental, but Khalil still wasn't sure and asked him to stay on. Cameron would do everything in his power to protect Amani, but her beautiful smile and sweet perfume sometimes made him want to throw caution to the wind and sample her.

The entourage paused in front of the computer lab where the girls in the country would be given access to top-of-the-line computers and formal education. He'd been stunned when Amani informed him that, for years, she hadn't been given access to any sort of technology let alone a computer, phone or even a television. Cameron would never understand a country's reluctance to allow women the same sort of freedoms men had. He was glad Khalil was changing that. In the meantime, he had to keep his wits about him where Amani was concerned.

Once they arrived at the auditorium where she would give her speech, and after Cameron and his team had checked the room, Amani went to the small podium. "I'm so honored to be here today for this momentous occasion. Women's education is very important to the King. He's determined to bring Bahara into the future, so this will not be the only school of its kind."

After her remarks, Amani took a few pictures with the principal, along with several students in hijab before leaving the school. Cameron was right there waiting for her. Instead of going to the front door, he had an alternate route.

"Where are we going?" Amani asked when he led her away from the entrance.

"We have to do the unexpected. Everyone anticipates you'll exit through the front and someone could stage an attack. This way gives me more control."

"And control is important to you, isn't it?" she quipped.

Cameron turned and stared at her. Her dark brown eyes were alight with amusement. She knew she'd struck a nerve.

Control was important to him. Now more than ever and not just because he was her bodyguard, but because everything in his life upended the last year. He'd loved being a pilot. It had been part of his makeup for so long, but he'd found a new dream and a new purpose. He was focusing on that and not looking back on what could have been.

He and his team quickly moved with Amani and her maid, Nadia, down the hall until they came to a series of corridors. When he found the one he wanted, Cameron opened the door and led them down to a secret back entrance where the limo was waiting.

"Very covert," Amani said as he helped her and Nadia inside.

Cameron didn't respond. He couldn't because he was too busy reminding himself not to think about the sexy curve of her bottom.

"Aren't you coming?" she asked.

"No." He closed the door behind her. There was no way he was sitting in the back seat with Amani. The smell of her perfume was too intoxicating and would drive him wild. Spending too much time in her company spelled danger and this was a surefire way to remedy the situation.

"Why does he continue to ignore me, Nadia?" Amani wondered aloud once they were alone in her quarters. It was opulently decorated with a bedroom, ensuite bath, living room area, kitchen and a private terrace which faced the desert.

"Because he's here to protect you, Amani."

Nadia wasn't just her maid. She was her assistant and confidante. Half Baharan and half African American, Nadia had come to live in the palace after her parents were killed in a car crash. Five-foot-five, slender, with long dark brown hair, big brown eyes and warm vanilla skin, Amani had liked Nadia instantly and they'd been friends ever since.

"Urgh!" Amani fell forward onto her bed in a heap and then spun around to sit upright. "You have no idea how hard it is living in this gilded cage. I'm supposed to marry someone suitable that my *brother* chooses for me. I don't get to choose. And before it happens, all I want is to live a little."

"Perhaps you'll get that when you attend Soraya's upcoming wedding," Nadia commented.

Amani nodded. "Oh, yes, the wedding festivities are going to take place over several days in Faharat, a neighboring kingdom. Maybe I can have some fun then."

She was surprised Khalil agreed to allow her to attend her best friend Soraya's wedding. Amani could only ascertain it was because Soraya was marrying Sheikh Jamal Syed from Faharat, a country Khalil wanted to do business with and would be seen as a gesture of goodwill.

Plus, Amani and Soraya grew up together and had attended the same finishing school. During their time in Switzerland, they'd seen other young women fall in and out of love, but because they both were watched over so strictly, there had been no room to take chances like kissing a boy. Soraya understood what it was like to be in a gilded cage.

All Amani wanted was some real-life experience. She didn't even know what it was like to kiss a man. Soraya told her stories of the passionate attraction she and the Sheikh shared. It was something Amani wanted to experience one day along with a little freedom like other young women her age. She understood her country's customs and traditions, but she also yearned for more. However, it was going to be hard to shake her bodyguards, especially Cameron.

"With the wedding only a few weeks away, we should think about what you're going to wear to attend the festivities so if you need a few new items, we can have them made," Nadia responded.

"Yes, let's do that." Amani needed something to look forward to other than this desert life.

"Come in." Khalil waved Cameron forward when he decided to join him in the fitness center on the lower level of the palace. Four bodyguards were strategically positioned on either side of the room, ready to defend Khalil should someone strike.

"Thanks," Cameron replied. Earlier, he'd changed into his normal workout gear of t-shirt and shorts before coming to the two-thousand square foot, fully equipped gym with treadmills, rowers and ellipticals as well as weights, kettle balls, and a boxing bag which Khalil was giving the business to.

"How was your day?" Cameron asked.

"Arduous as always," Khalil responded, giving the bag a punch. "I had no idea how many irons the Crown Prince had in the fire. None of which he'd followed through on. There's much work to be done."

"Do you resent having to do it?" Cameron inquired, holding the punching bag.

Khalil dealt the bag another harsh blow. "Yes." He punched it again. "I was never supposed to inherit the throne. So all of this," he motioned around the room, "my brother was groomed to lord over. It's all very disconcerting to find myself king of the castle."

"But nothing you can't handle. You started your own company for Chrissakes. You've got this."

"Building my empire from the ground up was one thing, but leading a country is quite another, especially a country so set in its ways as Bahara. And the royal council? I've never met more traditional men. They still think a woman's place is at home. In my company, I employ thousands of women."

"You'll change their minds, but it won't happen overnight."

"And my sister? How is Amani behaving?"

"I've no complaints," Cameron replied. Other than the fact, she was all cheekbones, velvety brown eyes, sexy curves, and full, pouting lips.

"I'm surprised," Khalil responded. "I heard she gave her former bodyguards a tough time and had given them the slip the odd time or two. They had a hard time keeping up with her."

"I keep a tight rein on her."

Khalil snorted. "She's no horse, Cameron, but she is a feisty one. When we attend Sheikh Jamal's wedding, I'm going to need you to be extra alert. That weekend could prove a prime opportunity for an enemy to make a move since we're not on our home turf."

"I understand and I've been making arrangements with the Sheikh Jamal's security team as well as coming up with some contingency plans."

Khalil sighed. "I knew I could trust you, Cam. After Malik died, I feared for Amani and my mother's safety."

"How is your mother?" Cameron replied. He hadn't talked to his own since arriving here six months ago. He wasn't ready to put her deception behind him, if ever.

"Doing good. She left Bahara behind her a long time ago because she couldn't live this life. She worries about me," Khalil said and moved away from the bag to walk over and look out at the mountains from the floor-to-ceiling windows.

"As most mothers do."

"I'm fine," Khalil responded, spinning around. "In any event, I need you to look after Amani and be on your guard because she'll give you some resistance once we're no longer within the confines of Bahara."

"I can handle Amani," Cameron replied. He would take control of the situation from the start and let Amani know he wouldn't tolerate any impulsive behavior. She would follow the rules he set or there would be consequences.

2

Nadia knocked on Amani's door when it was close to dinner time. As usual, she helped Amani select a dress, did her hair and makeup and often bathed her and Amani needed her assistance tonight. She wanted to look her best because Khalil, Cameron, and several other heads from the Royal Council, were coming for dinner.

As the only female in the household, Amani often played hostess and greeted them when they arrived. It was a new role she'd taken on after her mother and Malik perished in the plane crash. The fact Khalil allowed her to be involved was a big deal because when Malik had been alive she had been merely an adornment at the table.

Nadia was a great help and ensured Amani found the perfect dress that showed off her slim waist but revealed a hint of cleavage, as benefitting a princess. As for her long, dark tresses, Nadia arranged it in an intricate hairstyle that would take some undoing later on. Amani didn't care. Looking in the mirror, she felt as beautiful as one of the peacocks strutting their stuff first thing in the morning.

And that's how she walked down the hall until she saw

Cameron striding toward her from the entrance to the former parlor. "I'm sorry I was delayed in meeting you."

"I'm perfectly capable of walking down the corridor in my own home."

Cameron grinned, giving her a brilliant smile that made her tummy flutter. "Of course, you are. But I need to be here. You should always know you can count on me."

"I wonder what other things I can count on." She gave him a wink before walking inside the room.

Amani paused at the entrance and, with a nod, one of the servants then opened the double doors. Her brother Khalil was standing in the middle of the room, surrounded by several men in different modes of dress. There was Asad Fakhoury, the prime minister, dressed in a dark suit and several men from the royal council, all in traditional thobes of different colors.

"Amani, you're looking as beautiful as ever," Asad replied.

"Thank you." Amani didn't care for the man or the way he looked at her as if she weren't wearing any clothes. She made sure to endeavor to never be alone with him or sit next to him at a meal. She swiftly moved away.

"Everything all right?" Cameron whispered so that only she could hear him.

How was he so in tune to her feelings? "I'm fine."

"I'm here if you need me." And then, he was gone. In the shadows, as if Amani imagined him when she knew she hadn't.

The evening went on as many of the state dinners hosted by Khalil and even Malik before him. Matters of importance were discussed over the meal. Most of the time, the men at the table ignored Amani as if she had nothing valuable to add to the conversation because she was a woman.

Despite the fact, she had a degree in business administration and economics from her finishing school, which was also a college. She was certain everyone assumed the school focused solely on etiquette, manners, and how to find a husband, but she'd selected the school because it also had a stellar reputation for education.

Eventually, when the men retired for cigars, Amani left their circle to go the gardens. She walked down a complicated series of sweeping marbled stairs and then beneath soaring ceilings and through halls inlaid with beautiful mosaics to finally reach her happy place. She was permitted solitude within the confines of the palace and didn't need Nadia with her. Amani chafed at the confines she was placed under since returning to Bahara. She'd had more freedom when she'd been abroad with Soraya.

She wished Bahara weren't so conservative especially toward her, a *female* offspring to a Middle Eastern king. Amani was thinking about how she could ditch Cameron and the other bodyguards at the wedding in a few weeks. It wouldn't be easy. Cameron stuck to her like glue, but surely there was a way?

As if he sensed her thinking about him, Amani turned and found Cameron watching her from a short distance away. He was always observing her as if she were some specimen in a lab experiment, when she was, in fact, a real woman. A woman with needs and desires which had never been met. What she wouldn't give to know what it was like to kiss a man like Cameron Mitchell. The craving was so strong, her lips twitched.

Cameron came toward her. "Are you all right? Is something wrong?"

Amani nodded.

"Did something happen at dinner?"

She shrugged. "What always happens? I'm ignored. Dismissed as if I'm of no importance."

"And that angers you?"

"Wouldn't you be mad if everyone in the room ignored you as if you didn't exist? As if you didn't have a brain or opinion?

Well, I do and sitting there at that table," she pointed toward the palace, "with those insufferable men is *unbearable.*"

Cameron chuckled. "Say how you really feel."

Amani stomped her foot. "I will. Because when do I get a chance to do it? None of them want to hear the ideas I have to improve Bahara's economy to ensure we aren't dependent on other nations for imports. Nor do they want to know my thoughts on how we can improve our relationship with the Bedouin tribes."

"I'm sorry. That has to be very frustrating, given the degree you hold in business administration and economics."

She frowned. "You know about my degree?"

"I made it my business to know everything there was to know about you."

"Is that a fact?" Amani stared at Cameron with his close-cut wavy hair accentuated by his captivating face and cheekbones any male model would die for. He was much taller than her, she barely reached his shoulder. "That's a shame because I know nothing about you."

His head cocked to one side. "What would you like to know about me, Amani?"

She stared into his hazel eyes and spoke the truth. "Everything. Your past. Your family. How you ended up here being a bodyguard for Khalil?"

Cameron was silent for several moments, but then he shocked her by answering. "My father and mother are Cal and Camilla Mitchell. There's me and my older brothers, Caden and Cage."

"All names beginning with a C. How cute!"

Cameron snorted. "My family has a legacy in the military. My grandfather, Carter, my father, Cal, and my brother, Caden, all served in the United States Army."

"And Cage?"

"A Navy Seal."

"And you?"

"The Air Force."

From his tone, Amani could tell how proud he was of his family's legacy of serving their country. "Why aren't you still in the Air Force?"

"I was in a plane crash last year. Injuries didn't allow me to continue my career."

Amani walked over to Cameron and without thinking touched his arm. "I'm so sorry."

He glanced down at where her hand still remained. "Don't be. I've made my peace with the situation."

She eyed him suspiciously. "I don't believe that for a second."

"You don't know me, Amani."

"I'd like to."

"I won't be here long enough for that to happen. Once the threat to your safety and the crown is over, I'll be headed back to the States."

"You're not staying?"

He shook his head. "I'm doing Khalil a favor because we go way back. He knew he could trust me with your safety."

Amani filed the information away in her head. If Cameron wasn't staying long, it meant she didn't have to worry about any long-term effects of anything that might happen between them. And something was going to happen. She knew it low in her belly where she ached because when Cameron thought she wasn't looking, he looked at her as if he wanted to eat her up. She may not know much about the opposite sex, but she knew attraction and Cameron wanted her.

Perhaps she should test her theory?

No one was around. It was just the two of them in the gardens. This was a private spot away from peering eyes.

Without thinking, she moved away from Cameron and deeper into the gardens.

"Amani, where are you going?"

She didn't respond. She just waited for Cameron to follow her as she knew he would. Sure enough, when she stopped, he was right behind her. High on life, she spun around to face him. She breathed in his glorious male scent and time stopped and tautness filled the area.

"You can't run off like that, Amani."

"I'm not in any danger in the palace."

"Are you sure about that?" Cameron asked.

Alarmed, she sucked in a breath. "You think Khalil can't trust the palace staff?"

"I don't know. You can never be too careful. Why else do you think I keep an eye on you?" He tipped his head down and fixed her with that unwavering gaze of his that she'd come to love.

"I think it's because you can't keep your eyes off me."

"Pardon?"

"When you think I'm not looking, you look at me as if you desire me."

"You're mistaken, Amani. Listen, you're young and innocent in the ways of the world between a man and a woman. I'm sorry I didn't see it any sooner that you were becoming infatuated with me."

Her eyes flashed fire. She didn't appreciate him talking down to her as if she were a child. "I'm not naïve. I know what I saw."

"We should head back to your suite."

"Why?" Amani had already made a fool of herself. She might as well go all the way. She stood up straight and arched her back, causing her nipples to pucker in the silk of her gown. Cameron glanced down at her breasts and she watched him visibly swallow.

Did he see them puckering to life at his searing gaze?

Did he know how much she wanted him?

She stood on her tiptoes, leaned in, and softly brushed her lips against his. Once, experimentally, and it was electric. Her ears filled with a wild buzzing sound. The flame inside her intensified by the one kiss. So, she tried another, settling her lips over his and this time he responded by kissing her back. When he deepened the kiss, she found his mouth to be hot and wet.

Her heart skipped a beat. This wasn't just sexual attraction; it was sexual *hunger*. It consumed her and her hands twined around his neck of their own accord as she became dizzy with need. She arched closer to him and felt the unmistaken evidence of his arousal pressed against her. She wanted more of this, wanted him to ravish her like she read about in all those romances, with his mouth, tongue and teeth, but Cameron grasped both her forearms and held her loosely away from him.

"Amani... you forget yourself!" His breathing was ragged, just as hers was. "You're the Princess of Bahara. You must be beyond reproach. You can't be caught in a scandal with a bodyguard."

Words of protest came out of her quickly. "What about what I want?"

"It's immaterial." Cameron set her aside, his expression inscrutable. "Go inside now."

"I thought I was in danger." She gave him her best pout.

"Go, Amani! Now!"

Amani thought about arguing with Cameron, but realized it was futile. He wasn't going to give in. At least not now, but there would come a time when Cameron Mitchell would no longer be able to ignore the flame burning between them. And when his walls came crumbling down, Amani would be right there with open arms.

CAMERON HAD NOT BEEN PREPARED for that kiss with Amani in the gardens. She'd completely taken him by surprise with her sweet innocent kiss, but that hadn't meant he hadn't responded. He hadn't pushed her away after the first attempt, giving her courage to try a second time. For just a moment, every rational thought had flown out the window and he reacted on impulse to a beautiful woman pressing her lips to his. But then common sense prevailed, allowing him to push her away.

Cameron had known there was a growing attraction between them. He thought he could stay close to Amani and still maintain his distance, but that was becoming more and more difficult. How could he protect her if he was distracted by her beautiful, gleaming ebony hair? He wanted to run his fingers through it and see if it felt like silk. He wanted to touch her intimately and see if the lush curves he suspected were underneath the gowns were real or just his imagination.

It wasn't like she wore anything overtly sexual. She couldn't as Princes of Bahara, but it was the sensual way she moved that spoke to Cameron. And the way she kissed. Her lips were soft and pillowy and he'd wanted to sink his teeth into her bottom lip until she moaned. He'd wanted to invade her with his tongue and tangle and duel with her until they drank from the same well of passion.

His hands had ached to sweep over her ripe curves, to feel her supple softness cushioned against his hardness.

Damn. He had been too long without a woman.

He hadn't been with one since Monae, his former girlfriend and now sister-in-law. She and Cage had gotten married a few months ago, but Cameron didn't attend. Although, he didn't begrudge them their happiness, there was no way he could go there and stand by Cage's side as he married the woman Cameron once thought could be his own Mrs. Mitchell.

Had they been meant for each other as he'd thought? No.

Neither was he pining away for a love-lost. Cameron had moved on. He was going to find himself a woman who was meant for him and him alone. Who loved him unconditionally with everything that was in her — but that woman couldn't be Amani Naseer. She was his best friend's sister and Princess of Bahara.

He couldn't, *wouldn't* complicate his relationship with Khalil by getting involved with Amani. Khalil had given him a job to do. Protect his sister. Cameron was a man of honor and loyalty. He couldn't betray Khalil this way.

He would have to be careful of his looks and facial expressions so he didn't give Amani any false hope that anything more could develop between them. He was bound by duty. Duty to Khalil and duty to himself to do the right thing.

3

———

Amani ignored Cameron over the next few days because she was embarrassed over the way she threw herself at him only to have him rebuff her advances. He seemed to be doing his equal best to do the same. They only spoke to each other when spoken to. They didn't engage each other in conversation like they usually did so much so that Nadia asked Amani if everything was okay.

"Everything is fine," Amani stated as she read through correspondence sent to Khalil and Nadia wrote the appropriate responses. Khalil had no idea she'd taken over the task her mother used to do. Why should he? He was busy running a kingdom. It's the least she could do, and it kept Amani knowledgeable about what the people wanted.

"Are you sure?" Nadia inquired as she penned a letter. "You and Mr. Cameron have been quite frosty toward one another."

"We both know where we stand," Amani replied. She thought he was perfect while he thought she was some simpering naïve princess in need of saving. Perhaps from those who might want to harm her, but not from Cameron. How could she convince him to see her not as the princess he was guarding but as a woman?

"Very good. It wouldn't do for you to set your sights on a man that's out of bounds."

That might be what Nadia thought, but Amani didn't. Cameron was the only man to ever make her not feel *frigid*. When other boys at school tried to talk to Amani or when men danced with her at balls in the past, she'd felt nothing. She'd never wanted to break protocol and kiss them. Yet, Cameron made her want things she had never wanted before, but he was giving her the shaft.

And if Amani couldn't get the man she wanted, then she would try and talk to Khalil and explain her desire for a bigger role in the country. Amani was tired of being looked at as incompetent or incapable. She'd already helped several charities and organizations in Bahara achieve great things. Surely, he could see that?

After she finished dressing for the day, Amani headed to Khalil's offices. Unfortunately, her shadow was waiting for her when she emerged from her suite.

"Good morning." She nodded curtly at Cameron. Her mind was focused on the task at hand and that was getting her brother on her side.

"Did you sleep well?" Cameron inquired.

What do you think? she wanted to say. *You rebuffed me after I kissed you days ago.* But instead, she kept her eyes trained ahead. In finishing school, she'd been taught never to allow people to know what she was thinking or feeling or they could use it against you. She used her training now.

"Very well, thank you."

They walked in an uncomfortable silence until they reached Khalil's office which was in the west wing of the palace. Along the way, they passed by housekeeping staff, each of whom Amani acknowledged.

After her mother's death, she'd become lady of the house and ensured everything ran like a smooth ship. Amani was sure Khalil assumed the head of operations ran the household, but he was mistaken. It was time she was acknowledged for her hard work.

She kept her back ramrod straight until she reached the King's office. It was weird thinking of Khalil as King of Bahara. For so many years, she'd looked at Malik as her sovereign, especially when their father died from a stroke several years ago. She missed Malik terribly. She felt all alone even though she knew she had Khalil.

When they arrived, Khalil's assistant Omar Malouf rose from his desk. "Good afternoon, Princess. Mr. Cameron. Is there something I can help you with?"

"Yes, I'd like an audience with my brother."

"Oh, I'm sorry. He's quite busy today," Omar replied. "I could add you to his calendar for later in the week."

"That won't be necessary," Amani responded and walked past Omar. She briefly knocked on Khalil's door before barging straight in.

Khalil looked thoroughly startled when she breezed through the door. "Amani, what are you doing here?"

She could see him looking at Cameron and then Omar who'd rushed into the room behind her.

"Your highness, please forgive me," Omar looked flustered and his face was turning red. "The princess rushed in even after I advised her you were not available."

Khalil laughed. "It's fine, Omar. Don't worry. Go ahead and close the door behind you. So I can talk with my sister." His assistant quickly left the office.

"Thank you," Amani responded.

Khalil nodded. "It must be important if you managed to get by Omar. He's quite the guard dog."

Amani chuckled. "I doubt he would appreciate you speaking about him that way."

"He'll live. So, what can I do for you?" Khalil came from around his large oak desk toward her and sat on the edge.

Amani spun around to find Cameron was still in the room. "If you don't mind, I'd like a word alone with my brother."

"Of course," Cameron said and quietly left the room as Omar had done.

"Someone is in a mood today."

Amani raised a brow. "Am I?"

Khalil shrugged. "If you ask me, you're spoiling for a fight, but I'm afraid I can't give it to you. There are too many pans in the fire to put out. Did you know Malik left a lot of Bahara's business influx?"

"No, I had no idea. Malik didn't include me in Bahara business which is precisely why I'm here."

"Go on."

"I can be a resource to you, Khalil. If you allow me to be. You may not know this, but I handle the household operations as well as taking care of palace correspondence. Also, I have a business degree and studied finance. But no one here in Bahara appreciates women - that we have a mind of our own. The men here, royal council included, think we're less than men, but that's not true."

"I agree with you, Amani. I employ a great many women in my company. And I plan on bringing Bahara into the future, kicking and screaming if I have to, but it will take time to change people's opinions."

"I understand that, but surely, I can be of service to you now.

I can help with the oil deal with Sheikh Jamal and the treaty with the Bedouin people."

Khalil stared at her in surprise. "You really do know a lot."

"Of course, I do, I've practically lived here my entire life outside of my time at school. Besides which, do you have any idea how many state dinners I've attended? I listen, Khalil, and I can offer you valuable advice or at least another opinion than that of the royal council."

"Thank you, Amani. I appreciate your offer. You have no idea how hard it's been coming back here to Bahara. There's so much to do, so much is expected of me."

"Well, I'd like to lighten your load at least a little. I'm your sister, Khalil. I know we didn't grow up together. That my mother kept you apart from our father because she wanted Malik to be king."

His brows furrowed together. "You knew about that?"

Amani laughed wryly. "The palace might be big, but the walls aren't. I have ears. People gossip. I know my mother wasn't your biggest fan."

He frowned. "No, she wasn't, but I won't speak ill of the dead."

"I appreciate that, but Queen Fatma wasn't without her faults. She doted on Malik while I was left to fend for myself with nannies and my governess. She never showed me an ounce of the affection she gave Malik."

"And here I was thinking you and Malik had the perfect life while I was left out as the outsider."

"You weren't the only one." Amani reached across the distance between them and grasped her brother's hand. "I know we don't know each other well, but I'd like to change that. I'd like you to lean on me and vice versa."

Khalil smiled broadly. "If anyone had told me when this day started, I would gain a confidante, I would have thought they were misinformed. I would love your help, Amani. Matter of fact..." He rose to his feet and strode over to his desk. Amani watched Khalil rifle through several papers until he located what he was looking for. He came back with a folder. "Look this over. Let me know what you think."

Amani beamed with pride. Khalil believed in her and was willing to give her the chance to prove her worth? It was more than Malik or anyone in her family had ever done. She held the folder to her chest. She wanted to fling herself into her brother's arms, but instead she said, "Thank you, Khalil. Your trust and faith in me, means a lot."

"You're welcome. We're both navigating an entirely new world. It's strange for the both of us, but I'm willing to meet you halfway, Amani."

A broad smile crossed over her full lips. "That's all I can ask for."

Minutes later, she was walking through the double doors and into the inner office. Omar bestowed her an angry glare before rushing off into Khalil's office, but Amani didn't care. She'd gotten what she came for.

A chance.

A chance to prove to Khalil that she had the knowledge and wherewithal to help him lead this country.

"You're looking awfully smug," Cameron commented from the adjacent sofa.

Amani turned and regarded him. Her mind was whirling with all she could do to help; she'd completely forgotten Cameron had accompanied her to Khalil's office. "I do I believe I am," she responded, and without waiting for him, left the room.

CAMERON DIDN'T KNOW why he let Amani get to him. She had a way of getting under his skin that was uncanny. He hadn't known what she was up to when she informed him she was going to see Khalil, but whatever it was, she'd gotten her way.

She looked like the cat that ate the canary.

"Your talk with Khalil went well?" Cameron inquired once he caught up with her on the walk back to her quarters.

"Yes, it did. Unlike many in this country, my brother thinks I can be an asset in helping him lead our nation."

"That's wonderful."

She stopped mid-step and hazarded him a glance. "Do you really think so? Or are you telling me what I want to hear?"

Cameron frowned. "Why would I lie? I wasn't raised here, Amani. I don't hold some of the more," he was about to say *outdated,* but instead said, "traditional views some have in Bahara."

"That's good because those views need to change. Women are a lot smarter than we're given credit for."

"Agreed." He wasn't about to argue. Cameron liked seeing the fire in her chocolate brown eyes and that she wanted to change the world. It made him attracted to her all the more.

Amani was a woman destined to do great things. It was too bad he wouldn't get to see them. Once his work here was done, he'd go back home. To do what? Cameron didn't know, but he couldn't stay here indefinitely. He had family in the States.

"Is something wrong?" Amani asked.

Cameron blinked and found they'd stopped in front of her suite and he didn't remember getting there. "I'm fine."

"Well, if you'll excuse me, I have some reading to do."

He nodded. "Of course."

She closed her door, leaving Cameron on the outside. He wished he weren't. He wished they were in a different time and place where he could act on his feelings toward Amani, but he couldn't. He had to figure out if anyone harmed the Crown Prince and make sure Amani and Khalil weren't the next targets. That's what he had to focus on — not the way Amani's entire face lit up like a Christmas tree because Khalil had given her more responsibility.

4

———

Amani was overjoyed with how well the last couple of weeks were going. First, Khalil allowed her to go to a children's play one of the evenings, because he hadn't been able to break free from his meetings. It was important someone from the royal family attend so Amani had gone in his absence.

She was finally feeling like a part of the royal family and not an appendage to be trotted out on special occasions. A stylist had come to her suite with a selection of dresses followed by a makeup and hair artist. Soon, she and Nadia were whisked into a limousine for the event.

Amani was surprised to find Cameron was already inside the vehicle. She assumed he wasn't accompanying her because he hadn't personally walked her to the vehicle. He'd been giving her a wide berth lately since that amazing kiss they'd shared in the garden. Amani would have liked nothing more than to have a repeat. The sensations she felt when their lips brushed was nothing short of spectacular and she wanted more.

She glanced over at Cameron and found his hazel eyes on her. She wondered what he was thinking. Did he wish their kiss had gone a step further? She had. She dreamed of his lips plundering hers and their tongues mating just like she read in her romance novels. She licked her lips in response and Cameron's eyes glittered from across the short distance. If they were alone and Nadia weren't with them, would he act on this tangible connection sparking back and forth between them?

Blinking, she turned to stare out the window at the beautiful landscape of Bahara. She loved the old mosques alongside the modern high-rises, the souks and the trendy boutiques and shops lining the main boulevard. Eventually, their limousine stopped in front of the church. Cameron exited and held out a hand to help Amani and Nadia out of the vehicle.

"Thank you," Amani replied and smiled when she saw several photographers in attendance. She was used to having a small entourage follow her. After posing for a few photos, she walked towards the expansive church doorway. The building was spectacular inside with large stained-glass windows and golden statues.

Seats were reserved for them in the front pew. Amani smiled as the service began. Children of all ages stood singing songs as they held candles. Most of them couldn't manage a harmony, but they didn't seem to care. They were having fun and that was all that mattered. Their sweet voices echoed inside the church and by the last song, Amani was so touched, tears began to well up in her eyes.

"Are you okay, princess?" Nadia asked, offering her a handkerchief.

"They were lovely." When Amani turned, she found Cameron openly staring at her again. Did he think she was blind and didn't catch him watching her? He was always observing her like she had something between her teeth, which she knew didn't, which meant it was the chemistry between them.

Eventually, after congratulating the children, their entourage returned to the limo and rode back to the palace. Amani was contemplative. What else would she have to do to get Cameron to let go of his reservations and acknowledge their attraction? She wanted to ruffle his feathers, so she said, "I'd like to stop at Zara's for dinner."

"I haven't vetted the place," Cameron replied.

"It's the most exclusive restaurant in all of Bahara," Amani replied, "Only the elite go there and considering no one is expecting us, it shouldn't be a problem."

Cameron nodded. "Very well, princess."

Amani bristled. She hated it when he called her princess. It was a put-down and he damn well knew it. She would get him back for that.

Twenty minutes later, she was seated at the best table at Zara's and given a glass of the very best wine they had to offer by the maître d' who was immensely pleased to have royalty dining that evening. The restaurant was situated on the twentieth floor and overlooked the glittering city below.

When Cameron went to stand behind her, Amani spoke up. "Cameron, please sit down. There is no need to stand on ceremony. There are royal guards at the door." She motioned to the other burly men by the entrance.

"Very well," Cameron responded and sat across from her at the table while Nadia sat by her side. He declined wine when the waiter came back with a wineglass and said he'd stick to water.

This viewpoint allowed Amani to sit across from the most handsome man she'd ever seen in her life and sip on a marvelous vintage without being stared at obtrusively. "Isn't this lovely?"

"What is?" Cameron inquired.

"Having an evening out. Away from the palace."

"You don't like the palace?" Cameron took a sip of his water.

"Of course, I do. It's the only home I've known, but sometimes it can be a bit... smothering. The ever-watchful eyes. The constant schedules. There's very little downtime to relax when you're a royal."

"I hadn't thought about that."

"That's because everyone only sees all the glitz, glamor, and grandeur, when, quite frankly, it's a rigorous schedule, day in and day out."

"And if you could, you would change that?"

Amani shrugged. "I don't know. Just for once, I'd like to know what it's like to be normal. Average."

Cameron chuckled. "You could never be average, Amani."

"I agree," Nadia replied next to her, breaking the moment between her and Cameron. "You're beautiful, smart and funny."

"Don't stroke her ego too much, Nadia. Otherwise, we won't be able to fit her through the palace doors."

Amani couldn't resist laughing. No one had ever made fun of her, other than maybe Malik, because they were so afraid of offending her. Cameron didn't care. He spoke his mind regardless of her station.

The decadent four-course menu left Amani hoping she didn't burst out of her sheath dress. She was already self-conscious about her wide hips and full breasts, but never more so than tonight. Her stylist preferred her in sheaths because they downplayed her hips rather than finding attire or materials more suited to her curves. It was a battle she'd dealt with since her bosom started growing exponentially when she'd turned fourteen.

Her mother, in contrast, had been petite and small. She always made sure the palace chef fed Amani less to ensure she didn't become overweight. As a result, Amani was self-conscious about what she ate, but tonight, being with Cameron, she allowed herself to splurge.

"Dessert?" Cameron asked, raising a brow when the waiter returned to see if they wanted anything.

"I couldn't possibly," Amani answered.

"C'mon, princess. The candied caramel apple pastry sounds amazing," Nadia said.

"Feel free to get whatever you want," Amani said, though deep down she wanted the chocolate biscuit pastry with a cream center touched with salted caramel and coffee crunch.

Cameron looked directly at Amani. "We'll have two chocolate onyx pastries to go and the candied caramel apple."

Damn him. How did he know she really wanted it? "Thank you, but I must be careful. When we visit the Bedouin people this weekend, they're already going to try and fatten me up."

"What are you talking about?" A frown marred Cameron's attractive features.

"Khalil listened to my advice when I explained the best strategy to handle the hostile factions of tribesmen was with a meeting rather than diplomacy. Unfortunately, Khalil's schedule doesn't permit him to attend, so I offered to go in his stead."

"That isn't a good idea," Cameron stated. "I'm concerned about your safety, Amani."

Amani rolled her eyes. "Not you too. I've already gone over this with Khalil. I'm more than capable of handling myself."

"It's not you I'm worried about," Cameron replied. "The desert is an uncontrolled environment that I'm unfamiliar with."

"Well, I'm not," Amani responded. She liked being in control of her destiny and not being told what to do or how to do it. "I've been riding in the desert since I was a child. My father made sure Malik and I knew how to survive in the desert. We have an oasis about an hour's ride from here."

"A desert oasis and an unfriendly group of tribesmen is quite another," Cameron responded. "I can't predict what they might do. Not to mention we'll be outnumbered."

Without thinking, Amani leaned across the table and touched Cameron's brow line. "Stop frowning. I've got this."

"You're naïve if you think you do." Cameron rose to his feet. "It's time we left."

Amani didn't appreciate Cameron berating her on why this wasn't a good idea. She knew she could get through to the elders by going to their wives first. Men had no idea how much power women held. She would endear herself to the tribeswomen and smooth over any concerns the Bedouin leader might have about Khalil becoming the King of Bahara.

And without another word to him, she stood and strode out of the restaurant with Nadia right behind her.

What was wrong with Cameron? Didn't he see what an opportunity this was for Amani to show Khalil her worth and what having her by his side could do? Cameron didn't understand because he hadn't grown up in her world. He didn't understand the limitations.

"Perhaps Mr. Cameron is right," Nadia said, later that evening when she was brushing Amani's hair at the vanity. "Maybe you should be more cautious in this matter. And you shouldn't be so forward with him. Touching him was inappropriate."

"Nadia, I didn't ask for your opinion," Amani replied sharply, but as soon as she said the words and saw her maid's downtrodden expression in the mirror, Amani realized she'd offended Nadia. She didn't want to do that. Nadia was her only ally in the house. Had been for years when Amani felt nothing but loneliness because neither of her parents had given her much thought. It had all been about Malik, while she was an afterthought. "I'm sorry, Nadia." Amani spun around and patted her hand. "I'm not angry with you, but I need you to believe in me. Believe I can do this."

Nadia nodded. "Then I will."

"Thank you." Amani wished Cameron felt the same, but either way she was going to the desert. With or without him.

"ARE YOU OUT OF YOUR MIND?" Cameron asked, bursting into Khalil's office a short while later after they'd returned to the palace. Once he was sure Amani and Nadia were safe, he'd high-tailed it to Khalil's office. It was late. However, Cameron knew Khalil worked well into the night.

Both Khalil and Omar's heads shot up, but it was Omar who wore a horrified expression at Cameron's outburst.

"Your h-highness..." Omar began stuttering, but Khalil stopped him.

"It's fine, Omar. Cameron and I go way back," Khalil glanced in Cameron's direction. "You have something on your mind, Cam?"

Cameron inhaled deeply and forced himself to calm down, especially when Khalil used his nickname. "Sorry about that. I forget you're King now and I have to show you deference."

"No worries, we're still brothers. This title is just that. A title, nothing more. I'm still the same Khalil I've always been."

A smile curved on Cameron's lips. "That's good to hear. So perhaps you can explain why you agreed to allow Amani to go off into the desert on her own?"

Khalil snorted. "She won't be alone. She'll have you and the Bahara guard. No harm will come to her head."

"Are you sure about that?"

"The Bedouin tribesmen are old school, for sure, and I know they would prefer to speak to me, but Amani made a valid argument that she could do damage control with the women of the tribe until I can get there to personally allay their fears."

"I don't know." Cameron paced the floor. "We could easily be ambushed. I don't have a clear lay of the land to ensure Amani's safety. Twenty-four hours is not ideal."

"I understand, but I'll be sending my best guards alongside you. Men who are familiar with the terrain. If there's anyone I trust with Amani, it's you."

Khalil's trust and confidence made it untenable for Cameron to consider getting involved with his sister. He valued their long-standing friendship and brotherhood and would never want to do anything to jeopardize it, but Amani had a way of getting under his skin like no other woman had.

"Thank you, I appreciate that. I'll do my best." And he would. He would protect Amani at all costs, including from herself.

And if necessary, from him too.

5

A day later, Cameron was nervous as he and the guards triple checked the gear they would be taking into the desert. If it were up to him, they would cancel this excursion and he would keep Amani locked up at the palace where he could control the controllables, but Khalil agreed she could go in his stead to meet with the Bedouin tribe.

"Do you really think this is a good idea?" Ahmad, one of the guards asked.

"I'm not a fan, but the King decided the princess can make this journey."

The other man nodded and continued tying the duffel bags they were taking with their equipment onto the four-wheel drive jeep which was one of two they would be using.

Then it was time for Cameron to go in search of Amani, but he needn't have bothered. She came down to the courtyard dressed in snug fitting jodhpurs, a simple white cotton shirt, boots and a hat he assumed to keep her from burning in the sun.

"Amani, shouldn't you be dressed in something more suitable?" he inquired.

"You mean as befitting a princess?" Amani replied with a

chuckle. "I'm riding into the camp on my horse. Wearing a bedazzled gown won't work."

Cameron frowned. "You're riding? No one told me."

"It's the best method of transportation," Amani responded. "Those vehicles..." She motioned her hands to the jeep, "although high end, are no match for the desert sands. Plus, I want to arrive at their camp as they would, not like some pampered princess."

Cameron turned to Ahmad. "Were you aware of this?" The other man was a native Baharan.

"It is customary to ride in the desert, but these are all-terrain vehicles. They can handle the trip."

Cameron sighed. He couldn't remember the last time he'd ridden on a horse. Had to have been over a decade, but he also didn't want to set the tone by arriving like a Westerner and cause undue friction. "So, what do you propose?"

"Ditch the wheels," Amani replied. "And saddle your favorite horse." She didn't wait for Cameron's response and instead sashayed past him toward the direction of the stables. Her cute curvy bottom was so visible in those snug riding pants, that Cameron had a hard time focusing.

"Well, I guess, this is a bust," Cameron said, tossing the duffle bags out of the jeep. "We'd better saddle up."

"ARE YOU TERRIBLY UPSET WITH ME?" Nadia asked when she came down to the stables to see Amani off a short while later.

Amani's brows furrowed together. "Of course not." She secured the harness to Jewel, her favorite horse in all of the Bahara stables. She loved Jewel's deep chestnut color, white tail and mane and her refined head and muscular back. Her canter and trot were made for endurance riding, which they would need for this journey. "I know how afraid you are of horses. I would never make you get on one after your tumble last year."

"But you can't very well go off by yourself without a maid," Nadia replied, handing Amani her overnight bag.

"Why not?" Amani added the bag to the harness. "I'm perfectly capable of looking after myself." She knew everyone thought she was pampered and spoiled, but when she was at finishing school, she'd thrived. It had been so nice to be away from home and have some semblance of freedom like other girls her age.

"I know, but it's unheard for you to go unchaperoned."

"I won't be. I have my security detail."

"Which includes Cameron," Nadia replied quietly, "the man you happen to have..." But Nadia didn't get to finish her statement because Amani placed her finger over Nadia's lips.

"Loose lips sink ships." She glanced around the stables to be sure no one overheard them. "Mr. Cameron has done an excellent job of ensuring my safety."

"Perhaps I can get one of the other maids to come with you?" Nadia asked.

Amani shook her head. "Absolutely not. I'm a grown woman for Christ's sake. I don't need a chaperone. I *can* and *will* do this on my own." Rather than wait for one of the men to give her a foothold, she swung her leg over Jewel just as Cameron and the three other guards accompanying her entered the stables carrying several large duffel bags.

"Someone is eager to get moving," Cameron replied.

"It's a long ride to the encampment and we'd better get started before the sun is too high in the desert."

"Duly noted," Cameron responded.

She watched him quickly secure their belongings onto several large thoroughbreds. Once they were ready, Cameron climbed on top of one of the animals as if he were lord over the entire Bahara kingdom instead of a hired gun. A gun she so desperately wanted to get to know better but who constantly kept her at arm's length.

Going to the camp without a maid was a calculated risk because Amani wasn't sure how the tribespeople would react. She hoped it would show them that she was one of them and willing to forego the usual trappings of royal life. It was also the opportunity to be in a different environment with Cameron. One in which her every move wouldn't be scrutinized. Sure, there were elders, and she would have to carry herself as befitted a princess.

"Then we should go," Amani replied. "I hope you're up for it."

"I can ride," Cameron responded tightly.

"We'll see about that," she said, and with a shout, took off at a gallop toward the sands. She heard Cameron's surprised laughter echo from behind her, but that didn't stop him from giving chase.

Amani felt a thrill of exhilaration at being on Jewel again as the desert flashed by in a blur of sand. When she was riding, she felt free because no one could tell her what to do, how to act or how to behave. The only sound she could hear was the horses' hooves as they galloped. She thought she was ahead of Cameron until she turned and saw he was only a short length behind her and gaining fast. He was by no means a novice.

Eventually, she pointed to the oasis in the distance as the finish line. To her, it was a Garden of Eden in the midst of sand dunes. Cameron must have understood because she crossed the finish line a beat before he did. When they both finally slowed and reined the animals in, she patted Jewel's sweat-soaked neck. "Good job, girl," she said, climbing down. "That was close," she tossed over her shoulder as she led Jewel over to the oasis so the animal could drink some water.

"I almost had you." Cameron's white teeth gleamed and his hazel eyes blazed fire at her. With his headscarf protecting him from the sun and the bright light illuminating his commanding profile, Amani couldn't drag her gaze away from him.

"Almost isn't enough," Amani replied, grinning. "I bested you."

The way he looked at her sometimes made Amani swear he felt something for her, but as usual his eyes shuttered and she couldn't read them. She flushed at the memory of his lips on her mouth. Cameron set off fires within her every time she was within a few feet of him. Even though it wasn't quite noon, heat pulsed throughout her body. She might have made a move, but then the rest of the guards came bounding into the oasis.

"One day I'll get a re-match," Cameron stated and then he walked past her to help the rest of her detail.

Ignoring them, Amani walked toward the shimmering pool of water that was fed by a spring. The luxury encampment was a place she and Malik came when they wanted to get away from the pressures of palace life. As a result, there were several well-stocked tents throughout, the whole surrounded by a grove of palm trees, a variety of shrubs and plants that bloomed with the desert sun. It was also a respite for travelers should they get lost and not be able to find their way. Malik had always made sure there was a radio and satellite phone kept at the ready. He was Crown Prince, after all.

Jewel was already drinking her fill, so Amani rubbed her down and fed her before heading inside the tents for a light snack before they continued on the journey to the Bedouin tribespeople. Inside the tent, carpets overlapped every inch of the floor and there was a huge pile of cushions, inviting her to sit on them. Amani was eager to sit because although she was a capable horsewoman, she hadn't ridden in a while and her bottom was bit sore. But first, she removed her boots and allowed the caress of the finely woven silk to tickle her feet.

She found what she was looking for in the icebox in the corner and set about arranging the food on the low brass tables. She even lighted one of the sandalwood candles so the scent could waft through the air. Several seconds later, the flap of the tent was pushed aside and Cameron walked in.

"This place is amazing," he said, glancing around. "I've never seen anything like it. I feel like I'm in the movie Aladdin or something."

Amani chuckled and padded across the rugs to hand him a glass of juice. "Please take off your boots and come make yourself comfortable. I've laid out some drinks and food."

Cameron accepted the cup and when he did, their fingers brushed. The contact didn't go unnoticed because they both looked at each other, but it was Cameron who looked away first. He refused to acknowledge the chemistry between them. Instead, he settled onto one of the oversized brocade pillows.

"You're ever the hostess." Cameron watched her as she moved around the tent.

Amani frowned, stopping in her tracks. "Is there something wrong with that? I mean, I'm a princess. It's what I was born to do."

"Do you ever get tired of trying to please everyone?"

His comment was insightful because Amani did want to live her life for herself, but that wasn't possible. She was born into royalty and with it came duty and responsibility. "Of course, I do, but..."

"But what?"

She shook her head and came to sit down beside him on the pillow adjacent to his. "You wouldn't understand because your life has always been your own. You've never had to worry about how a decision you made might affect your family. Or worry about your every move being scrutinized, down to how much weight you gain or the outfit you wear or how your hair and makeup is out of place. At times, it feels like…"

"A prison?" Cameron interrupted.

Amani nodded. She reached for some meats, cheese and crackers she'd laid out and added a few to one of the small plates.

"I understand about living in a family legacy," Cameron replied, doing the same and adding some dates to his plate. "My grandfather served in the United States military as did my father," he paused after saying the word. Even now, knowing how Cal felt about him and that he was still his son, Cameron couldn't deny he wondered about the man he shared DNA with. But he continued on, "My older brother Caden is a decorated West Point graduate and lieutenant colonel and my brother Cage is a bad-ass Navy Seal. It was always assumed I would follow in their footsteps."

"But you chose the Air Force, right?" Amani remembered him telling her that.

"Yes, but a life of service, no less. It was all I knew and what was expected of me."

"So you understand, I have no choice in the matter. I'm making the best of the situation. I'm just glad Khalil sees my value and that I can be of service to him. That's why this meeting is so important."

"I hope it goes as well as you imagine," Cameron replied, munching on the mid-morning snack.

"But you don't think so?" Amani picked up on what he wasn't saying.

"I heard the Bedouin tribesmen are very traditional. I'm not sure how they will take a visit from you and not Khalil."

Her eyes narrowed. "I guess we will find out." Suddenly, her appetite left her and she rose to get up from the pillows, but

Cameron grabbed her wrist and sparks shot up her arm. He held it so firmly; it didn't seem as if he were about to let go.

"Amani, you misunderstand me," Cameron said, rising to his full height until he towered over her. He still held her wrist and was close enough for her to feel his heat. "I'm just saying it might be hard to change their long-held beliefs."

"That a woman is inferior and has no opinion or value?" Amani huffed. She had to do something to stop thinking about the feel of his fingers on her skin or the raw emotion that pulsed through her at his nearness.

"Why are you so mad at me? It's not what I think of you. I just want you to have realistic expectations on what you're facing when we get there."

"I thought you, of all people, might believe in me."

"Why me?" he asked huskily.

Her eyes narrowed. "You know why?" Because she had a connection with Cameron like she'd never felt before. She felt like he understood her, but was her thinking ability off because of the attraction she felt for him? As it was, he was already crowding her with his scent as he looked down on her with those hazel eyes that she could drown in.

"Amani..." Cameron let go of her hand only to stroke her hair, his fingers smoothed the dark strands. It made her aware of everything. The rise and fall of her breathing and the intense ache and need for him to kiss her. He didn't. Instead, he brought his other hand to her lips. He swept his thumb back and forth across her lips. Her eyes darted to his and the fire she saw burning there, caused the breath to catch in her throat. Desire, raw and fierce, gleamed in his eyes. His face was so close to hers, all it would take was one of them to lean in.

"The chemistry between us can't go anywhere," Cameron stated.

Amani didn't care. When his thumb moved again across her

lips, she acted and opened her mouth, taking it inside her mouth and instinctively began sucking it. She looked up at him and his mouth parted in shock and then his eyes darkened. Cameron's breathing ratcheted up a notch. Amani felt his desire as well as her own, felt his yearning. She sucked his thumb harder into the warm wet cavern of her mouth and felt him tense.

She might have done more, but the tent's flap swung open, and Cameron stepped away so fast, Amani might have imagined the charged moment between them. But how could she? It had been incredibly sensual. Thankfully, Cameron's back was to the tent opening, otherwise her guards might have gotten a shock.

Cameron didn't look at her as he left the tent, he merely said over his shoulder, "Saddle up, it's time we get moving."

6

***

Hours later, as they approached the Bedouin camp in the mountainous border region, Cameron was glad for the hours of riding because it kept his mind off what occurred between him and Amani in that tent. When she'd taken his thumb into her mouth and sucked him, Cameron thought he might lose it and throw her against the pillows and take what she was so freely willing to give. But he couldn't. It wasn't right, but that didn't stop him from aching for her. She wanted him. That much was obvious and although she was inexperienced, Amani was testing his resolve. It was a problem he didn't have a solution for.

Fortunate for him, the Bedouin people would keep her occupied for the next couple of days. After they dismounted, they were greeted by a group of robed men with dark eyes and haughty looks.

"Princess Amani, I presume?" the man at the front of the group asked and Amani nodded, causing him to bow. "I am Rafiq Al Tajir leader of the Bedouin tribe. It's so kind of you to grace us with your presence, but we'd hoped the new King would be visiting us to discuss matters of great importance."

"The King sends his greetings and good tidings for all," Amani said, nodding her head in deference, "unfortunately he wasn't able to make it due to a conflict, but sent me as Princess of Bahara in his stead so that the Bedouin people know *he* values you and wants to hear any concerns you might have as he takes over as leader of our nation."

Rafiq's eyes narrowed. "You are quite well spoken, princessa. I see you arrived alone without a chaperone."

"Thank you. And yes, I did. I'm quite capable of looking after myself." Amani bowed her head.

Cameron watched Rafiq motion to several black-robed and veiled women and immediately Amani was swarmed. "Allow the tribeswomen to show you to your tent." Then he turned to Cameron. "And I assume you're the Royal Guard?"

"We are," Cameron inclined his head to the four guards who'd accompanied them. "I've been hired by the King to personally protect the Princess."

Rafiq's brow rose. "Is that so? You must be very skilled if the King would put you in charge of the Princessa's safety."

"I am." Cameron stared the man directly in the eye. He wanted it to be clear *he* was looking after Amani, and he wouldn't stand for a hair of hers to be out of place. "So I'll need a tent either next to or adjacent to the Princess."

"That's usually reserved for women in the camp, but I'm sure I can make arrangements."

"My sincere thanks." Cameron nodded in deference. He tended to the horses and unpacked his belongings so by the time Rafiq returned to escort him to his quarters, the other guards were all settled at opposite ends of the camp.

"This is your tent," Rafiq said, leading him inside a large tent with a small cot and an opening that looked out onto the night sky. There was small table with water. It was nothing like the luxury oasis he and Amani had been to earlier. This was much more rudimentary and reminded him of being in the military.

"I know this isn't much in comparison to staying at the palace, but if you need anything let me or any of my people know and we'll do our best to make it happen."

"It's very generous of you," Cameron replied, sharpening his gaze on the older man. "And the princess?"

Rafiq lifted the tent flap. "Is just across from you."

"Thank you.

"Dinner will be out by the campfire at half past the hour. Everyone in the tribe is eager to meet the princess."

"I'll be there."

Cameron didn't waste time checking out his surroundings further and once he was assured of the condition, he stepped outside, crossing several feet to the adjacent tent. "Amani?"

She came to the tent opening. "Yes?"

"Everything good?" He searched her eyes for some sign of trouble, but he merely saw annoyance. He suspected she wasn't happy with him because she hadn't spoken a word to him the entire ride here. Not even when they paused for a water break.

She shrugged. "Why wouldn't I be? Everyone has treated me kindly."

"I'm glad to hear it," Cameron responded. "I'm just over there." He pointed to his tent. "If you need me."

"I won't."

"Amani... we should talk about earlier." He stepped closer toward her, but she moved backward, away from him.

"I'm fine. I will see you at dinner." Then she closed tent flap right in his face.

As he stalked back to his tent, Cameron was livid. Amani was seriously the most infuriating woman he'd ever met. Didn't she understand the position he was in? He made a promise to

Khalil, her brother, who'd stood by his side on more than one occasion. He couldn't let him down. That didn't mean he wasn't conflicted. He wanted Amani with a ferocity he wasn't sure he'd ever had. There had been other women, Monae included, but he'd never felt consumed by them like he did with Amani.

It had to be the fact he saw her day in and day out. There was no escaping the attraction threatening to erupt if they were alone together. During this trip and even after, he had to endeavor not to be alone with her. For his sanity as well as hers.

AMANI WAS DETERMINED to make this visit successful. Something had to go right after the incident with Cameron at the tent earlier. He refused to meet her halfway even though she knew he wanted her. She'd seen it in his eyes. Had felt the tension coming off him, but still he kept her at a distance. It was nerve-racking.

She wanted just this one thing for herself, but Cameron was being stubborn and she had no choice but to accept it and the make the best of this visit. Khalil had sent her to help with his relationship with the tribespeople not seduce Cameron. Amani had to do her duty. And so without Nadia, she dressed herself in the tent. Although, the tribeswomen had offered one of their daughters to assist her, Amani was determined to show them she was no better than them.

Donning a simple blue dress with minimal adornments, Amani wore her long dark hair down because she would need to wear a hijab out of respect for the culture, but she wanted to look pretty so she added some eyeliner and mascara and a swipe of lip gloss to her lips. Glancing at her reflection in the full-length mirror, she was happy. She looked demure, but still herself, a princess.

When she opened the tent, to walk out, Cameron was right beside her. "You look lovely," he stated.

She didn't look at him. Her goal tonight was to focus on getting through to Rafiq that he had nothing to fear from the monarchy or Khalil. They walked in silence until they arrived at a large fire in the middle of the camp.

As soon as she arrived, the tribe clapped and cheered.

"Thank you so much." Amani raised her hand in prayer and moved toward Rafiq who stood at the center of the fire.

"We appreciate you joining us for dinner, Princessa. Please…" He motioned to a seat beside him. "Sit here with me."

"It's my pleasure to be here," Amani replied, sitting next him. She assumed it would just be her, but Cameron sat down as well. She gave him a quizzical glance, which he ignored. Clearly, he'd told Rafiq, he wasn't leaving her side because the man didn't protest. She turned to the tribal leader. "Is there anything I can do to help?"

"We wouldn't dream of you soiling your hands, but I'm afraid it's a humble meal, the women made a stew of lamb and vegetables." He motioned to the women who were separate from the men on the other side of the fire.

"I'm sure it will be delicious because it was made with love and care." Amani ignored Rafiq's comment about soiling her hands.

Shortly after, a bowl of something rich, spicy and delicious was presented to her along with a carved spoon. "Thank you." She inclined her head to the small child who'd brought her the bowl. Another one brought her a goblet which Amani assumed was fruit juice.

Rafiq held up his goblet. "To our honored guest, Princess Amani of Bahara."

The rest of the camp held up their cups and only then did

Amani take a drink. "It's refreshing," she commented, setting the cup down.

"It's guava juice made locally by tribe."

"That's only one of many things that you make here in the desert. You make clothing, shoes, purses and more that are sold in town," Amani said, tucking into her bowl. She hadn't eaten since they left the oasis and Amani found she was ravenous.

If she had her choice, she would devour the man at her side like she'd done at the tent when she'd sucked his thumb into her mouth. It had been incredibly erotic, but he seemed unbothered as he sat beside her as if women threw themselves at him every day. And maybe they did. Amani's relationship experience was nil, but she was trying to change that. One day, she might be forced to marry for her country in an arranged marriage, but before that day came she intended to choose her first lover.

And she wanted Cameron.

But she had no idea what else she could do to entice him to act on his desire.

"You're very up-to-date, Princess," Rafiq responded to her earlier statement, stopping her musing about her bodyguard.

"Does that surprise you, Rafiq? The King is very aware of the contribution the tribespeople have on our nation. Often, when travelers and tourists come here, they want something authentic and local. The pieces made here are beautifully crafted."

"That's kind of you to say, but we know the monarchy wishes to change our way of life. Make it more modern like the rest of the country."

"Would we like to see your daughters and wives educated," Amani replied, "that's true, but it is a choice. The King is not looking to usurp your authority here."

"The Crown Prince threatened to take our land."

Amani sighed. This had been a bone of contention between

her and her brother. "You're correct, Rafiq. I won't deny it. But that was the Crown Prince. The King is of a different mindset. He believes in protecting the history and culture of the Bedouin tribe."

Rafiq turned to her. "If that's true. He should have come here himself."

"Agreed. And he would have if state matters didn't require him elsewhere. I can assure you on the King's behalf that the sanctity of your traditions will be protected."

Rafiq eyed her suspiciously. "That remains to be seen."

"The King would like your support as he heads into the coronation."

"I'm sure he will, but I'm not sold yet," Rafiq said. "If you will excuse me. Please enjoy your supper." The tribal leader stood to his feet and with no further comment, walked away.

"Damn!" Amani said underneath her breath.

"Tough sell?" Cameron replied, from her side.

Amani turned in his direction for a moment. "Malik made an enemy of the tribe before he died. It's going to take time to fix the rift he caused."

"And you'll do that. It's why you're here, taking the time to get to know the people. Show you care and they will respond."

"How do you know that?"

"Intuition," Cameron responded. "Like right now." He inclined his head to the women huddled in a circle admiring her from afar. "Didn't you tell Khalil the key were the women? Go over, talk to them. Ask them to show you how they made dinner and what they are working on..."

"All right! I will." Amani put down her bowl and strode over to do just that. She wouldn't let Rafiq's skepticism stop her from her mission which was to prove to Khalil she could be useful.

∼

CAMERON WATCHED AMANI. She'd taken his advice and approached the tribeswomen. She was fearless. Although she spoke Arabic, she didn't completely understand their dialect, but she was doing her best, and from the looks of it, she was making inroads because the women had carted her off to their tents. He was outside, but close enough should Amani need him.

"Care to join the menfolk instead of watching the Princessa?" Rafiq asked, coming to stand by Cameron.

"It's my job to protect her."

"The Princess is safe here. No harm will come to her."

"So you say, but am I supposed to take your word on that?" Cameron inquired. Because he'd learned the hard way that people lied. His own mother had lied to him his entire life.

"You can," Rafiq stated definitely. "Please, follow me." He motioned Cameron forward.

Cameron didn't want to offend the man and chose to walk with him. If anyone stormed to the camp, the royal guard was camped out at every entrance.

Along the way, Rafiq pointed out different points of interest, such as where they prayed, the school and the makeshift hospital. It was a simple operation but the man was clearly proud of it. Eventually, they stopped in front of a tent and Rafiq motioned him to precede him. Inside, several men were smoking shisha and drinking what Cameron assumed was some form of liquor.

Rafiq sat down on one of the cushions splattered across the floor so Cameron did the same thing. When he was offered a drink, Cameron accepted and took a sip. He didn't know what was in it, but the beverage was strong and burned as it went down his throat.

"So what brings an American man like you all the way out to the desert?" Rafiq inquired.

"I'm protecting the princess."

Rafiq chuckled. "You know that wasn't what I meant. You're a long way from home, soldier."

"What makes you think I'm one?"

Rafiq shrugged and reached for the shisha and took a long drag. "Your manner, the haircut and the tattoo."

Cameron had an American flag tattoo on his right arm, "That obvious, huh?"

"To me. I served in the Baharan Army."

"You did?"

Rafiq nodded. "Every man is required to serve two years, but as my duty was over, I came back to my people. After my father died, they needed someone to lead. Someone who would still honor the traditions we have."

"And that's important to you?"

"Isn't it to everyone?"

Cameron thought about Rafiq's comment. It was definitely true for his family. A tradition of service and one he could no longer participate in.

"Something troubles you," Rafiq wisely surmised, eyeing him. "Is that why you've left your land and came here to Bahara?" When Cameron didn't answer, Rafiq continued speaking. "You're running from something."

Cameron turned and glared at him. "I don't want to talk about my life."

"I'm sorry if I struck a nerve, but if you're looking to find yourself, I have found the desert gives me a certain peace I can't find elsewhere."

"That's good to know," Cameron said, "Thank you for the drink." He rose to his feet. "I really have to get back and check on the Princess."

"Of course." Rafiq inclined his head.

Cameron left the tent as quick as he could. He didn't like that somehow Rafiq sensed he was on the run. Because he was. He was running from his life, from the past and from a future that would never be.

7
———

Amani was getting to know the women of the tribe. There were a couple of daughters who knew a bit of English so she was able to converse with them and they were able to help with the other women. After two days, she felt as if she were making inroads. She had helped bake bread and they'd taught her how to help sew a quilt.

She'd even got Rafiq's wife Maryam to open up and found that many of the women were happy and content. They didn't want the Western ways to come and change their way of life. All this time, Amani assumed they wanted change and access to education and other opportunities, but that wasn't the case. They wanted to protect and preserve their culture.

Amani vowed she would go back to Khalil with this information. The King was new to the Bedouin people and their customs and his goal wasn't to make sweeping changes, but rather understand them. That seemed to go over well with the tribeswomen and they understood what she was trying to achieve. If only Maryam could get Rafiq to see Khalil wasn't trying to obliterate them off the map. Maryam promised to speak with her husband and that was all Amani could hope for.

On their last night in camp, she was going to help the women make a big dinner for the entire tribe. The women were surprised Amani would even consider getting her hands dirty, but it was important they knew she wasn't above them. She was headed back to her tent when she ran across Cameron. He'd been nearby the last couple of days but always from a discreet distance.

Was he struggling to deal with this insane attraction between them? If so, he was doing a good job at acting as if he was unaffected while she couldn't forget the flash of heat in his eyes when she'd had his thumb in her mouth. It had sent arrows of desire straight to her core. She didn't know she could feel something like that from such an innocent action.

"How did it go?" he asked, falling into step with her on the short walk.

"Good. The women were receptive to hearing what I had to say. Hopefully, word will get to Rafiq."

"He's a hard nut to crack."

"Yes, he is, but you and he have been quite cozy," Amani responded. A handful of times, she'd seen him with Rafiq and wondered what he was up to.

Cameron turned to look at her. "What's that supposed to mean?"

"Nothing." She shrugged and kept walking to her tent. "Just that your heads have been together during this visit." When they made it, Amani stopped short and folded her arms across her chest and faced him.

"I've been trying to get to know the man. Understand his motives."

"Would you care to enlighten me?"

"That depends on if you can behave," Cameron retorted.

Amani's eyes narrowed. "I'm not a child, Cameron."

"No, but you and I both know that you do things without thinking of the consequences."

Her face flushed with embarrassment. "I hoped you would have been gentleman enough not to mention that."

"I haven't forgotten."

Amani's eyes flew up and widened in surprise at the intensity in Cameron's expression. She swallowed hard. "Come inside," she opened the flap of her tent, "and we can talk."

Cameron shook his head. "Not a chance."

"You're not going to tell me you're scared of little ole' me?"

"It's you who should be frightened, Amani, because you're playing with fire."

"Maybe I want to get burned."

Her words must have been like spraying a bucket of ice water over Cameron because he didn't hesitate to turn on his heel and walk toward his tent. Amani wanted to run after him and force him to confront what was happening between them, but it was useless. She didn't know what it would take to get him to break, but she wouldn't stop trying. She knew what she wanted and she wanted Cameron Mitchell to be her lover.

CAMERON WATCHED Amani from across the campfire. She and other tribeswomen were making dinner for the entire camp. She was so youthful and vibrant that he noticed everyone in the tribe was as entranced by her as he was. Amani had changed clothes and was wearing one of the traditional outfits the Bedouin women wore, a black robe and veil. She was covered pretty much from head to foot, but that didn't stop Cameron's imagination from reliving what she felt like underneath all those clothes.

Her lush curves and those soft pouty lips. He was completely ensnared by her as if she were a siren summoning him to his fate. All he wanted to do was dive in and surrender. He would give anything to drown himself in her and forget about everything, but he didn't have that luxury. He made promises and he kept his promises.

"The Princessa is amazing, yes?" Rafiq said suddenly from Cameron's side.

Cameron's head swung around. He hadn't realized the older man had joined him on the rock where he was perched. "Excuse me?" He raised a brow.

Rafiq chuckled. "Ah, I am not blind. I see how you look at her."

Cameron shook his head. "You're mistaken."

"I think not. You look at her like a man looks at a woman, not like a guard looks after his charge."

Cameron glared at him. Was it really that obvious how much he wanted Amani?

"She's a beautiful woman," Rafiq continued, "but I imagine your situation would make it difficult to act on those impulses."

"I have no impulses."

"You can try fooling yourself, but not me. I think the princess shares your sentiment. However, royalty is expected to marry other royalty, typically in an arranged marriage."

"I'm aware." It was what made Cameron afraid to touch her. He knew the custom. They preferred their women to come to the marital bed untouched. Unspoiled. If he had his way, he would ruin Amani for any other man but him.

"If you were here in our tribe, you could go after what you wanted and make her yours, but alas, that's not the case."

Cameron turned to Rafiq. "What's your point?"

"Be careful, my friend. You're walking a dangerous tight rope. One wrong move and you can find yourself in unchartered territory."

Didn't he know it!

Rafiq stood and walked over to join several of his tribesmen around the fire, leaving Cameron to think about his advice. For the rest of the evening, he made sure to keep Amani within view, but not within reach. She was right. He was afraid. He was afraid if he touched her again, he might not be able to stop.

BY THE FOLLOWING EVENING, they were back in Bahara after a punishing eight hours on horseback earlier that day. Amani was thankful to be sitting in a soaking tub to relieve her aching muscles.

"Was it a good visit?" Nadia inquired, coming into the bath with Amani's favorite fluffy robe.

Amani nodded. "Yes, it was. I think the Bedouin leader, Rafiq, concluded Khalil means them no harm and is rather an ally than an enemy."

"That's wonderful news." Nadia held out a towel so Amani could step out of the tub. "I know the King will be quite pleased."

"I hope so," Amani said, stepping out of the tub and into the towel Nadia had opened. Once she was dry, she slid her arms into the fluffy robe and belted it around her middle. She was just about to lotion herself when her suite phone rang.

"I'll get it," Nadia said.

Amani heard Nadia say, 'she'll be right down' before she returned to the bathroom. "What's going on?"

"The King has requested your presence."

"Of course." Amani was excited to share the details of her visit with Khalil. She was eager for him to see her as a resource and possible partner in his duties. She wasted no time getting dressed and with Nadia's help her hair was placed in a sophisticated updo. She dressed in a simple sheath, dark pumps and a string of pearls and headed to meet Khalil.

Opening the door, she was greeted by Cameron. "Princess." He gave her a nod which she returned before striding ahead down the corridor.

They walked in companionable silence until they reached Khalil's office. Cameron knocked twice and after hearing his voice, Amani entered her brother's private chambers. Before closing the door, her eyes found Cameron's and he held her gaze for a second longer than necessary. He might be back to body-guard mode, but things were far from finished between them.

"Amani, glad to have you back." Khalil's tall form came striding toward her and he enveloped her in a quick hug.

"I'm glad to be back." Amani wasn't used to displays of affec-tion. Her parents, including Malik, rarely showed it so when Khalil did it the first time he saw her after nearly fifteen years, she'd been surprised, but it wasn't unwanted. She found she liked it and didn't realize how starved she'd been for affection—*for love.*

When they finally parted, Khalil grasped her hand and brought her over to the brocade sofa in his living room, "So, tell me how it went with Rafiq, was he receptive to your visit?"

"Initially, no." And at Khalil's crestfallen expression, she patted his thigh. "But he warmed up to me, Khalil. I think I even earned a little bit of admiration from him by my willingness to spend time with the tribeswomen. I made bread, sewed and cooked with them."

"You? Cooked?"

Amani chuckled. "Okay, maybe not cooked exactly, but I was their assistant, chopping up vegetables and spices."

A broad grin spread across Khalil's cheeks. Her brother was a fine-looking man with his black-as-night hair cut short and cropped to his skull, intense moss-green eyes and a high-bridged nose. He was the epitome in fashion in dark trousers and jacket along with a snowy white shirt that emphasized the gold tone of his skin. He would make a great husband one day. "That's wonderful news, I'm happy to hear things went well."

"Yes, they did," Amani replied. "And you should know the Bedouin people are happy with their way of life, Khalil. They are not looking for us to come in with our Western ways and modernize their society. They want to be left alone to keep the traditions they hold dear. That's what they want to hear from you. That you won't come in and bulldoze their village and build skyscrapers."

Khalil frowned. "Is that what Malik was going to do?"

Amani lowered her head. She didn't want to speak ill of her brother. She loved him even though she didn't always agree with him.

Khalil nodded at her unspoken answer. "I see. Well, thank you, Amani. I appreciate you making this visit when I was unable to. You're a great asset."

Amani beamed with pride. Never had anyone told her that. "Thank you, Khalil. If there's anything else you need, please let me know."

"Not at the moment. Besides, don't you have a wedding to attend?" Khalil asked.

"Omigod!" Amani's hand flew to her mouth. How could she have forgotten her dear friend, Soraya, was getting hitched in a few days? Between wanting to help Khalil and this raging chemistry she had with Cameron, she completely lost sight of the wedding. "Yes, of course. I need to leave the day after tomorrow."

Khalil smiled. "Then I suggest you get packing." Amani stood and started for the door, but Khalil's words stopped her. "Thank you, Amani. I appreciate you."

Amani swung around with a smile across her face. "You're absolutely welcome."

She rushed out of the room and right into Cameron's broad chest. All the air in her lungs whooshed out of her chest because she got a tantalizing whiff of Cameron's male scent and was rendered speechless.

"Where's the fire?" Cameron asked, grasping her by the shoulders and setting her away from him.

"We have a wedding to go to."

A wedding that was the perfect occasion with lots of distractions for Amani to put Cameron's resolve to the test.

8

Cameron sat across from Amani and Nadia in a small luxury plane with the Bahara logo that was headed to Faharat. You could cut the sexual tension in the small cabin with a knife. He knew what Amani wanted, but he couldn't take her up on her offer in the desert.

It wasn't like he could have ravished her at the oasis with the royal guard outside or gone into her tent in the Bedouin camp and made love to her all night long. Did she have any idea how hard it was for Cameron to not only be around her with the sweet scent of her wildflowers perfume surrounding him? Worse yet, he was on a plane again. He'd only flown once in the last year and that was to get to Bahara.

Once, he'd loved to fly. Lived for it. Growing up, he always had toy airplanes and as soon as it was legal enough for him to do so, Cameron started taking flying lessons. It came to him as naturally as breathing and he'd never wanted to do anything else.

Not being permitted to fly was like a death sentence for Cameron. What was he supposed to do with a life he'd spent dedicating to serving his country? All the hard effort and flying hours he'd put in was gone. Poof! In the blink of an eye, his dreams went up in the fumes of smoke that covered the aircraft as they pulled him out of wreckage. That's why he accepted this short-term position with Khalil, to help him out. Because right now, Cameron wasn't ready to face a world in which flying wasn't a part of his life.

"Sir, we will need you to buckle up as we are getting ready for takeoff."

Cameron glanced up to see a smiling flight attendant standing in front of him. "Of course." He buckled the seatbelt and tried not to stare at Amani in her smart skirt and matching blazer with high-heeled pumps. Her curtain of jet-black hair was in a side swept ponytail. She looked thoroughly put together and every bit the Princess of Bahara that she was. Her olive skin gleamed, her dark chocolate eyes mesmerized and he would love nothing better than to brush his lips across her pink-tinted lips and mess her up just a little bit.

Instead, Cameron looked out the window and had to force himself not to clutch the arm rail of the luxury recliner when the aircraft began taxing down the runway. This was usually his favorite part, but now all Cameron could think about was fear. Fear of being in the jet when he knew it was going to crash.

Cameron remembered the interminable seconds as the jet went on a downward spiral. How he tried to take control and failed. He'd thought he was going to die along with his buddy, Max, who'd been in the jump seat. Cameron saw the tree tops just before they struck one and plummeted down to the earth. The sound of metal fracturing his leg, breaking his arm in multiple places and then the explosion with shrapnel flying everywhere before he blacked out.

"Cameron, Cameron?" He could hear Amani's soft voice

calling out to him, but he was too far gone in his memories. "Cameron, are you okay?" She spoke again, this time a little louder. She touched his hand, clutched it and he slowly started blinking Amani into view.

He was breathing hard and realized he had her hand in a death grip. He instantly released it as if he'd been burned and there was no denying the hurt expression on her face. She moved back into her seat across the aisle.

"I was just checking on you," she replied with a huff. "You scared us. You were white as a ghost when we took off, but we're in the air now."

Cameron glanced through the window and indeed they were ascending high into the clouds and leaving Bahara in their rearview. He exhaled deeply. "I'm sorry about that. I haven't flown much since the accident."

Amani nodded in understanding, but didn't say more.

The rest of the plane ride continued as it started with Cameron and Amani on opposing sides of a very small cabin. There were times of a ceasefire when the flight attendant came through with light snacks for the short flight to Faharat.

Soon they were touching down and Cameron was glad to be back on solid ground. He did his job and checked in with Sheikh Jamal's team whom he'd talked to yesterday before their arrival. Everything was in order. Additional guards were already on the tarmac and in the nearby private airport terminal. Once Cameron was sure the airfield and surrounding area was safe, he allowed Amani to exit. She headed straight for the limousine waiting for them.

Once Amani and the bags were safely inside, he closed the door and sat up front with the driver. Cameron couldn't take another moment of tension between them. Amani didn't know the ways of the world and he was certain she'd never been with a man. She was infatuated with him which would soon pass. However, he had to stop sending her mixed signals that he was interested in anything else except protecting her. Because the sooner she accepted that, the better they both would be.

As they drove to Sheikh's Jamal's palace, Amani wondered about the accident that caused Cameron to lose his career in the Air Force. Whatever it was, had traumatized him because he'd been petrified on the plane.

Amani wanted to ask Cameron more about what happened, but his eyes shuttered and he'd shut down, which told her he wasn't interested in discussing his fears, at least not with her. And that stung. She was trying to be his friend, but apparently, they couldn't even manage that.

But Amani wasn't done with her offensive. Although the kiss by the fountain might have been ages ago, she was certain Cameron wanted her and would act with the right motivation. For now, however, she had to put her feelings about her body-guard aside. She was here for Soraya, her best friend's wedding. She would put on a happy face even if it killed her.

When the limo stopped, Cameron was right there opening the door and ushering her and Nadia into the foyer of the Sheikh's palace. Amani was no stranger to wealth and loved the marble floors, three story columns and mosaics in a variety of colors with gold inlays surrounding them. She saw Cameron speaking into his earpiece. Just then an olive-skinned man came walking toward them, dressed in traditional clothing.

"Princess Amani, welcome," he said and bowed. "My name is Farooq and I'm the house manager here at the palace. Please allow me to show to your suite of rooms."

"I would love that, thank you," Amani replied and followed

him down an intricate series of hallways and up a flight of stairs before he finally opened two double doors into a suite. However, before they could walk in, Cameron held Amani back with one hand. He swept the room before allowing her and Nadia to enter. She could see Farooq was offended by the gesture, as if she weren't safe in the palace, but she knew Cameron was merely doing his job.

There was a magnificent four-poster bed covered with silk bedding, a sitting room, kitchenette, ensuite bath fit for a queen and another bedroom and small bathroom for Nadia.

"If you need anything at all, please let," he turned to a woman who suddenly appeared at his side, "Farah know. She will be at your service while you are here and can assist you with anything you might need."

"Thank you." Amani inclined her head to the elderly man who turned to Cameron. "We have several rooms for you and your security team on this floor."

"Much obliged."

Then the door was closed and it was just Amani, Nadia and Farah.

"Is there anything you need, princess, before dinner this evening?" Farah inquired. "I could make you a warm bath or have some light snacks brought in."

Amani could see Nadia was about to speak and patted her hand. "Thank you, Farah, but I have Nadia and she's been with me for years so I don't need another maid, but I would love it if you can find Soraya and let her know I'm here. I would love to see her."

"My pleasure, princess." Farah bowed again and left them alone in the room.

"Amani, there is an itinerary for the wedding," Nadia stated, holding up a piece of paper she commandeered from the bed.

Amani scanned the document. The nearly weeklong event

would give her plenty of time to test her feminine wiles on Cameron. He may have thought he had her exactly where he wanted, but he was mistaken. Between the picnic, the horse race, the Muslim ceremony, the American ceremony and the public reception afterward, there would be plenty of opportunities for Amani to find time alone with Cameron.

She intended to use every weapon in her arsenal to attract him. Because try to deny it as he might, Amani was certain Cameron wanted her. She just had to get him to act on his feelings.

"CAMERON MITCHELL," Sheikh Jamal Syed stood when Cameron walked into his office. The Sheikh equaled Cameron's six-foot height and then some. His olive skin and dark eyes were shrewd like a hawk while his jet-black hair was tied into a pony tail. "I'm so glad you could make it to the wedding festivities. I've heard a lot about you from Khalil."

"I hope all good things?" Cameron replied.

"For certain," Jamal responded. "He told me how you saved his life when his plane went down during a mission and that, against orders, you went out to find him and brought him back to safety."

Cameron nodded. "I did, and I caught a lot of slack with the higher ups. Was on grunt duty for months for my insubordination."

"We need more men like you who aren't afraid to think on their own when convention tells them otherwise."

"You're too kind. I really appreciate you allowing me to work with your security team to ensure the Princess's safety."

"Of course. She's here on my watch and I will do everything

in my power to protect her. I appreciate Khalil allowing Princess Amani to come for the ceremony. She and my fiancée have been friends for ages and it would have broken Soraya's heart if her maid of honor wasn't able to attend. So, anything, anything you need at all, it will be at your disposal."

"Thank you." Cameron nodded. "I'm going to go check out the rooms for tonight's event."

"Thorough too. Khalil is a lucky man. Otherwise, I'd be trying to steal you for myself."

Cameron chuckled as he left the Sheikh's office and headed to the banquet room that would be used for this evening's welcome dinner. After reviewing the layout, exits and a private corridor which they could exit through in the event of an emergency, Cameron felt satisfied with the security, but rather than go back to his room and shower or rest before the meal, something brought him to Amani's door. He knocked a beat or two, but rather than Nadia opening the door, it was Amani.

"Yes?" She looked at him earnestly.

"You shouldn't be answering your own door."

"I'm not in Bahara, Cameron, so I can do as I wish." Amani started to close the door, but he stopped her with his foot and with very little effort stepped into the room.

"Do we have a problem?" he inquired, keeping a discreet distance between them. He needed them to be on the same page because her safety was of utmost importance.

She shrugged. "Do we?"

He frowned at her parroting his words back. He scanned her chambers and found it empty. "Where's Nadia?"

"If you must know, she's resting." Amani indicated the closed door. "Poor dear, isn't feeling well."

Cameron walked around the room and checked the balcony. They were on the third floor and it was some ways down to the main entrance. It would take a skilled assassin to climb to this height. He walked back inside and halted several paces away. Amani had removed the rubber band holding her hair in place so it cascaded down her back like a ripple of luxurious silk. To make matters worse, she'd hung her jacket on the back of the sofa and wore only a thin camisole. Cameron tried not to look, but his eyes couldn't help but skim her hour-glass figure.

"I want you to be careful here, Amani. No taking chances. This isn't the Bahara. We don't know these people. And while I will do my best, you don't know what criminals are capable of. You must be on your guard."

"But I have you here," Amani said, stepping closer to him with come-hither eyes until she was a foot away from him. Her scent, like wildflowers, teased his nostrils. "You'll protect me, right?"

Cameron swallowed because the thin camisole showed the swell of her bountiful breasts. Desire scorched through him, making him yearn for something he couldn't have. "Of course."

"Good." She moved away from him and Cameron had to force himself to drag air into his lungs. This woman overloaded his body with heat, making him want to back her up to the bed and introduce her into the ways of the world.

"I'll see you tonight," he rasped and turned toward the door.

She laughed as if she knew she had him tied up in knots. "I can't wait."

As soon as the door closed, Cameron fell back against it. His heart was pumping faster than it ever had. He wasn't some novice, wet behind the ears and getting his first taste of passion. He'd had his share of women before Monae, and even a couple after her, because he needed an outlet after realizing his dreams had gone up in flames. But Amani. She was different.

He hadn't felt this way ever and it was unnerving. He wanted her from the front, from behind, on top, riding him, and every which way in between. He had carefully constructed his world and was used to no one penetrating him, but Amani was proving bolder, stubborn, and more determined than he could have imagined. Just how long would he be able to keep his defense mechanism up without giving in?

9

"Amani! I'm so glad you're here," Soraya said, an hour later when she stopped by Amani's suite and they sat together on the couch to catch up like they did in the old days when they were at school together. "I don't think I could do this without you."

"Of course, you could," Amani replied. "You're head over heels for Jamal."

Soraya grinned broadly and it lit up her entire round face. It was no wonder Jamal was wild for her bestie. She had dark, sleek hair with a hint of auburn, almond-shaped eyes and a slender, tiny waist encased in a beautiful emerald gown. Amani had always envied her figure.

"Jamal is everything I didn't know I wanted. He can be quite commanding and might come off as domineering to some, but when he's with me," she sighed, "he's a pussycat."

"I'm so happy for you, Soraya." Amani grabbed both her friend's hands and squeezed.

Soraya cocked her head to one side. "Thank you, and I just know your person is going to come one day soon."

"How will I know?"

"For me and Jamal, it was just meeting his eyes across the crowded ballroom. I had no idea he was the Sheikh my parents arranged for me to marry. I just knew he was the most intriguing and handsome man with raven hair and striking features that I had ever met."

"You do realize you sound like a hopeless romantic."

"I know." Soraya blushed. "And I didn't think it was possible to feel this way, but later when Jamal found me in the courtyard. We talked and then talking led to an explosive kiss. He fulfills all my desires and then some."

"Soraya..." Amani was shocked and then lowered her voice so no one could hear them. "Have you and the Sheikh made love?"

Soraya shook her head. "No. He wanted to save the actual act for our wedding night, but we have explored, how shall I say this delicately..." she paused for several beats, "our attraction to one another and it's off the charts."

"Wow! I can't wait to experience that kind of passion one day."

"And you will when the right man comes along."

"I think I've found the one, Soraya. He just doesn't know it yet."

"Cameron? But Amani, he's your bodyguard."

"I know, but he speaks to my soul and I can tell when he looks at me so intently with his smoldering hazel irises that he feels something too."

Soraya shook her head. "I dunno, Amani. Getting involved with your bodyguard is very complicated."

"No more so than you signing a marriage contract to a Sheikh you'd never met."

"But we've fallen for each other."

"And we will too," Amani said without hesitation. She felt it deep in her blood. "Watch Cameron tonight and you'll see what

I mean."

"I will."

Soraya left her alone with the promise she would see Amani later that evening while Amani thought about her game plan and what she would do and say to ensure she and Cameron shared another kiss. The trick was to make it seem like it was his idea entirely. She had little doubt, in time, she would have him eating out of the palm of her hand.

RATHER THAN STAND by the sidelines like he usually did at such events, Cameron was asked by the Sheikh to sit at the dinner table *with them*. When he tried to decline, Jamal had insisted and now Cameron found himself seated at Amani's side. A place he shouldn't be.

The conversation was lively about what would happen over the next week. Cameron found it rather dull and uninteresting. He wouldn't be getting married *ever*. He'd soured on the entire institution. He'd thought he might propose to Monae at some point once he went further in his career in the Air Force, but then she'd met Cage at Caden's wedding and his fate had been sealed. She'd fallen for Cage.

Then there were his parents, whom Cameron looked up to for having a forty-year marriage, but then he'd learned his mother had cheated on his father with another man and begat him. So, no, he wanted no part of the institution of marriage.

"It sounds rather a lot to do," Cameron stated after everyone gushed over the itinerary, "isn't it enough to just say the vows?"

"You think it's over the top?" Jamal asked with a broad smile. "I suppose in the American culture you might think so, but we are Faharian. We like to enjoy life's pleasures, not wrap them up in one day and go on to the next. It's an honor and a privilege to marry this woman and I want the entire world to know it." Jamal looked across at Soraya sitting adjacent to him and it was clear how besotted he was.

Cameron's look must have begged to differ because Jamal responded, "I take it you don't believe in matrimony?"

"I think it's highly overrated."

"Then you have not known a great love, my friend, and I wish one day you will know a love like I do. When it hits, you will find yourself moving heaven and earth to have it."

Cameron knew that kind of love was possible. Had seen Caden forgive Savannah after she kept his nephew Liam away from Caden for over a decade. Had seen with his own eyes exactly how far Cage would go to be with the woman he loved, Monae. But Cameron doubted he ever would.

Eventually, the conversation continued about royal duties and Cameron listened. It wasn't much different from his own family gatherings. The Mitchell clan were composed at times, but they also could be loud and boisterous. Cameron missed his brothers and vowed to call them after dinner.

"Is everything all right?" Amani asked.

Cameron didn't know how, but she was as attuned to his mood shifts as he was to hers. "I'm fine."

He had to be because it wasn't like he was going home anytime soon. He had a job to do. Khalil needed him to protect Amani, but she certainly wasn't making it easy. Just sitting beside her tonight and hearing her husky laughs made his belly tighten. She was a contradiction.

In one moment, she was all spirit and fire and in the next, she was sweet, innocent and guileless. Like tonight, she was dressed in a Grecian-style one-shoulder gown with a shimmer finish. The material clung to her ripe curves as if she were made for the dress and not the other way around. Her raven silk tresses which were usually coiffed into an elaborate updo, but tonight, her hair hung in soft waves down her back. Cameron didn't recall ever seeing her look so beautiful.

She drove him mad. He needed to get away from the web she had him in. He rose to his feet and looked at Jamal. "If you'll excuse me, I have some rounds to make."

Jamal nodded. "Of course. Thank you for joining us this evening."

Cameron didn't bother turning around and seeing the look of regret that passed over Amani's face.

After completing a sweep of the perimeter, Cameron eventually found a quiet corner and called the US. There was a nine-hour time difference to Washington, D.C., but he couldn't avoid calling his family any longer.

He decided talking to Caden was his best bet and video called his brother. Caden was always the most sensible of the Mitchell brothers and it was why he was governor of Maryland, while Cage was the hothead and Cameron the peacemaker.

Caden answered almost immediately. "Cameron? Is that you?"

"Yeah, it's me."

"It's so great to hear from you, Cam. We've all been so worried about you. You took that job in Bahara so suddenly without much notice to any of us."

"I'm a grown man. Should I have checked in with you first?"

Caden sighed. "You know, I didn't mean it like that, Cam. I'm glad you called. How are you doing? How's it going protecting the royal family?"

Cameron wasn't going to lie to his brother and sugarcoat the facts. "I came here because I needed distance, Caden. After everything that happened..." His voice trailed off.

"I get it. You experienced a lot of blows in a short time, but that doesn't change the fact that I'm your big brother and I will always be there for you."

Cameron smiled. That was Caden. He'd always been a standup guy and loyal. Someone Cameron could lean on. Rely on. "Thanks, bro. I appreciate that. And as for the royal family, there's been some challenges."

"How so?"

"The evidence on the helicopter crash of the Crown Prince was inconclusive. We still have no idea if it was an accident or sabotage. As a result, Khalil is keeping a close eye on the family."

"That's understandable, but I don't like that you're in harm's way."

"I'm doing nothing different than what I did as fighter pilot for the Air Force."

"I know that, but it doesn't mean I, *we*, the entire family isn't worried about you."

"I appreciate that and that's why I called. I want you to know I'm all right. I'm taking this time for myself and hopefully figure out the next step in my life."

"And is something else bothering you?" Caden inquired. "I know how you look when you have something on your mind."

Cameron laughed. "Yeah, I do find myself in a quandary of sorts."

"Oh, yeah, what's going on?"

Cameron sighed. "I have an inconvenient attraction to Khalil's younger sister, Amani."

"Damn!"

"Exactly. And I've tried my best to ignore it, but it isn't working, especially because the feeling is mutual."

"But you haven't acted on it?"

Cameron shook his head. "Not exactly, other than one kiss. I just feel guilty thinking about Amani in this way. Like it's a betrayal of Khalil's trust, but I can't ignore the feelings either. They're there, just underneath the surface."

"Given this attraction, are you sure staying in Bahara is the right thing to do? Are you certain you won't give into temptation?"

"I'm not sure, Caden, and therein lies the problem."

"Perhaps you should speak with Khalil. Let him know of your interest in his sister. If your friendship is as strong and solid as you think, he may appreciate having a man like you with her."

Cameron never thought about it like that. He and Khalil did have a decades long friendship. However, friendship is one thing, being with Amani could be quite another. "And if he doesn't approve? What then?"

Caden shrugged. "I guess you would have to decide what's more important. Your friendship or what you could have with Amani. Keep me posted on what you decide."

"I will." Cameron ended the call. Although he was happy to speak with Caden and it gave him the sense of family he was craving, it hadn't given him clarity on the Amani situation. Instead, Caden presented him with options. None of which were very appealing to him. He wasn't sure how Khalil would react if Cameron told him he had the hots for his sister. It's why he needed to tamp down any attraction he felt toward Amani and lock it away like Pandora's box. Never to be opened.

10

───────────

Amani was saddened when Cameron mentioned he didn't believe in love and marriage. He crushed all her romantic fantasies and notions with his words. She wanted to get married one day. Have a husband and a slew of babies.

"Are you all right, Amani?" Nadia inquired once they were in the sitting room and listening to Soraya play on the piano for Jamal. It was so clear the love they both had for one another. It shone in their eyes.

"No." Amani shook her head. She was anything but. The first man she'd ever been interested in was jaded about the institution. Even though she was required to make a dynastic marriage, most likely arranged by Khalil, she wanted to be in love with her partner. She supposed that was naïve of her, given her situation, but the heart wanted what the heart wanted.

"Come, let's go back to our suite," Nadia said.

"I think you're right," Amani said. As much as she loved Soraya, she couldn't bear being witness to their unabashed love, not when she was so alone. "Soraya, Sheikh Jamal," Amani bowed her head. "It's been a long day. We're going to retire for the night."

Soraya immediately rushed to her feet. "Of course, you must be exhausted from your journey. If you both need anything, we can have Farah bring it to you."

"Thank you," Amani said, patting her friend's hand. "I'll see you in the morning." After a quick hug, she and Nadia left the sitting room.

Amani wanted a moment of peace, but when she opened the door, Cameron was standing outside. When had he returned? He hadn't bothered re-joining them after dinner. Amani didn't speak to him. Instead, she faced forward and started heading to their suite. He had no choice but to fall into step behind her.

She wanted to turn around and ask him why he was closed off to love and marriage, but she wasn't sure she wanted to know the answer. There could be some past hurt or even love he was still holding on to. Is that why he wasn't open to seeing where this attraction between them could go? Was there another woman involved?

When they made it to her suite, Nadia went in first, but Amani stayed behind in the corridor. "Thank you for walking with us, Cameron, but your duties for the night are done."

"As if," Cameron snorted and without preamble, brushed past her into their suite. Nadia was nowhere to be found and Amani could only assume she was making her bath as she often liked to do.

Amani couldn't believe his nerve or impertinence. She watched as he walked from room to room, checking the suite. "It's all clear in here," Cameron said, after his perusal.

Amani folded her arms across her chest. "Great. If you're done..." Her words trailed off.

His eyes narrowed. "Are you dismissing me?"

She glared right back at him. "Yes."

"Why do I get the feeling you're angry with me? Have I done something to offend you tonight?"

Even though she knew she shouldn't ask, her curiosity got the better of her and Amani blurted out, "Why don't you believe in love?"

AMANI's dark brown eyes peered into Cameron's hazel ones and he could tell she really wanted to the know the answer. "It's a long story, Amani. One I'm not about to get into."

"So, it's another woman?" Amani inquired, peering up at him with her big brown eyes. "Who is she? Did you love her?"

When he didn't answer, she kept pushing. "Are you in love with her still?"

That was an easy enough answer. "No, I'm not."

"What happened?"

He sucked in a deep breath and reminded himself Amani was just a young woman with no experience when it came to men. He was a novelty to her. An infatuation at best. This attraction would fade in time.

"I told you. I don't want to talk about it," Cameron stated perhaps a little too abruptly. "It's in the past."

She began walking toward him, her dress and hips swaying as she did. She glanced up at him underneath mascara-coated lashes. "That's not exactly true, is it? Because whatever happened between you is still here." Amani planted her palm on his chest. Her warmth heated him from the inside out.

He had to get away. "Sleep well, Amani. I'm right next door if you need me." Cameron spun on his heel and walked out of the suite to his, adjacent to theirs. Once inside, he leaned against the door and sucked in a deep breath. Amani didn't have to do anything but exist in that soft sweet way of hers to have Cameron tied in knots.

He was doing his best to protect her. Keep her safe, but this thing between them was a living, breathing thing he didn't know how to turn off. She made him want to throw caution and common sense out the window and take her in his arms, but it was wrong. She didn't understand the risk or chaos that would stem from them becoming sexually involved.

He would have to be the stronger person because he knew a liaison could lead nowhere except turn into an international disaster.

CAMERON SAW the trees coming toward him as he lost control of the jet. He tried half a dozen maneuvers but none of them worked. They were going to crash and he was going to die. Seconds later, the deafening sound of metal hitting trees as the jet nosedived. He was paralyzed. Unable to move. Unable to get himself free.

Flames were rising from the wing and smoke was engulfing him inside the cockpit. There was nowhere for him to turn. There was no way out.

"NO!" He thrashed around in the bed, but then suddenly, he felt soft hands comforting him, whispering soft words.

"It's going to be all right."

Was that Amani's voice? What was she doing in his dream? She wasn't there when he crashed the jet.

Immediately, Cameron's eyes bolted open. Amani was sitting on his bed and from the moonlight cascading through the window, she was wearing a nightgown. Her large, puckered areolas were clearly visible through the sheer fabric and the more he stared, the more pronounced they became. Would they harden beneath his tongue?

He had to stop this way of thinking and forced himself upright. "Amani, what are you doing in here?"

"I was having trouble sleeping and then I heard you cry out," Amani responded. "I came in to see if I could help."

"In the middle of the night?" he asked incongruously.

She didn't respond. Instead, she touched his bare thigh which was partially on display thanks to him tearing up the bed and tossing off the covers. Electricity arced between them at her touch. He glanced into her chocolate brown eyes and saw she felt it too. Instead of moving her hand, Amani kept it right where it was. Her touch scorched him.

"You feel it too," she whispered. "I know you do." She never ceased to surprise him with her willingness to speak exactly what was on her mind. "There's something between us. Why deny it, Cameron?"

"Because it isn't right," he spoke quietly even though it was just the two of them in the room.

She smiled. "Well, that's the first time you've not shied away the chemistry between us."

He shook his head. "It might exist, but nothing is going to happen." One of them had to do the right thing. He supposed it was going to have to be him because Amani was impetuous and often leaped before she looked.

"You don't think so?" she asked and to his utter surprise, her hand slid downward dangerously close to his manhood.

He glared at Amani, giving her a 'don't you dare' stare, but she didn't heed it. Instead, she caressed *him*, slowly as if to get acquainted with him. Cameron sucked in a deep breath and tried to act as if nothing was going on underneath the covers, but he was lying. Her soft sure strokes were causing him to swell.

"Stop it, Amani!" Cameron grasped her hand to fling her

away, but before he could, she launched herself forward on the bed, capturing his mouth with her own and pressing a hot, hungry kiss onto his stunned lips.

Cameron stiffened and his muscles tightened, but then the damn minx wrapped her arms around his neck and pressed her nubile body against his. He had no choice but to let himself fall into her web. His mouth softened against hers and he gathered her close, returning her kiss for kiss.

AMANI COULDN'T BELIEVE it was finally happening. After all these weeks of buildup. She was in Cameron's arms, in his bed, on top of him and his lips were on hers. And not just his lips. His hands were lacing into her hair and cupping her head so he could hold her exactly where he wanted her and deepen the kiss. The brief kiss they shared previously had been nothing like this.

Cameron was a force of nature and flipped her backward onto the pillows and kissed her again, harder this time. Amani was breathless and she desperately needed oxygen, but Cameron didn't give her any room to breathe. Each time his lips touched hers, she wanted it to go on forever. Her whole body was on fire and burning up with need for Cameron and the feelings he evoked.

She pressed her body tight against the hard wall of his chest and felt the warmth of him surround her. She breathed in his clean male scent and it drove her wild. Cameron's mouth was no longer gentle, but demanding as he stroked his tongue inside her mouth. Amani moaned as his tongue tangled with hers and explored the innermost caverns of her mouth. She mirrored his actions and let the intimate dance they were doing take over. She didn't know kissing could be *this good, this intense.* She reveled in the fact she could make a man like Cameron want her.

And he did want her. She felt the heated evidence of his arousal pressing against her stomach. To her surprise, Amani wanted to touch him, to feel his skin next to hers. Even though she'd never been with a man before, she knew, *knew* making love with Cameron would live up to her wildest dreams and imagination.

Cameron's hands began roaming over her body and Amani felt her nipples swell in the gown she wore and heat pool low between her legs. *What was happening to her*? She clung to him, desperate for purchase. She'd read books, but surely this was something altogether different. This was carnal and dark and totally wicked, but she wanted it.

His hands slid down her sides and Amani shuddered when he fit his palms to her breasts. She had never thought about her breasts, other than to think she was too large up top, and not small like the Caucasian women in her finishing school.

Unable to help herself, she moaned. Cameron made her feel beautiful, sexy and desired like she was a woman and not a girl. Then he was pushing one leg between hers and her hot center was flush against the rock-hard steel of his thigh. When he pressed his open mouth to her neck and began nuzzling and suckling her most sensitive spot, she moaned aloud.

Amani felt more alive, wilder and hotter than she'd ever been in her life. She gave herself over to the moment. She had no idea she was rocking herself against his hard thigh until sensations began to assault her. And when Cameron pushed down her nightgown to reveal one of her engorged nipples, Amani was stunned, even more so when he took the taut peak in the warm cavern of his mouth and he sucked her nipple deep and hard.

Her thoughts crashed and flew apart. She wanted nothing

more than to be with *him,* to be have *all* of him. Shamelessly, she moved harder and faster against him and when she reached the pinnacle and shattered, Cameron covered her scream with his mouth and once again proved his prowess by angling his head and feasting on her lips.

WHEN AMANI'S shudders had finally calmed, Cameron pulled his mouth from Amani's and she let out a groan. He suspected she was disoriented, but no more than he was.

"Don't stop!" she moaned.

"I have to while I still can," Cameron said, falling backward against the pillows. His breathing was labored. He was angry at himself for what he allowed to happen here. His erection was painful and he was frustrated, but he'd already taken a risk by how far he'd let things go between them. "What have you done to me, Amani?"

The burst of flame between them had been unexpected, but all consuming, so much Cameron forgot time and place. He'd wanted her and consequently forgotten that not only was he here to protect her, but she was Khalil's sister, an innocent, who knew nothing about men. Or at least she hadn't until he'd just given Amani an orgasm. He was certain it was her first because the astonished look on her face spoke volumes.

"Apparently, I haven't done enough to you," she murmured, looking over at him with passion-glazed eyes. "We're still clothed."

Cameron took Amani's rounded chin in his hand and held her gaze. She shivered at his touch and he could see the swirling emotions and longing he felt shining back in her eyes. He could smell the sweet fragrance of her soft skin that he'd touched. *Tasted.* "This was a mistake, Amani."

A deep frown etched her features and she sat upright wrenching her chin from his grasp. "How can you say that after what we just shared?"

"I should never have touched you. You're Khalil's sister."

"But I'm a woman first," she replied. "A woman that's attracted to you and vice versa. I felt," she looked down, unable to meet his eyes, "the way you responded to me. You weren't indifferent."

"Any male would have that reaction when kissing a beautiful woman."

She grinned and realized he'd made a fatal error. "You think I'm beautiful?"

"You know you are, Amani," Cameron replied, frustrated he'd spoken his real feelings aloud, "and any man will be lucky to have you."

"Just not you?"

Her question was bold, but should he be surprised? From the moment they'd met, Cameron had quickly realized Amani wasn't the naïve princess, the media played her out to be. There was a lot more underneath those layers. Layers he would like to explore if they were in different circumstances—but not now. As it was, he'd already compromised her safety. If someone had wanted to strike at her a few moments ago, they would have caught him with his pants down and possible harm could have come to her. He couldn't allow it.

"That's right," Cameron answered sternly. "You and I," he pointed between them, "aren't going to happen. Do you have any idea of the danger you were just in? Anyone could have come upon us and not only would you have been compromised, but, worse, you could have been attacked."

She rolled her eyes and quickly rushed to her feet and righted her nightgown to cover the breast he'd just had in his mouth. "Stop being so melodramatic. I have you here, and the royal guard. I'm safe. What I'm not safe from is the way you keep oscillating back and forth as if you don't want me. But now, I know otherwise. And know this, Cameron."

"What's that?"

She kept her gaze trained on him and folded her arms across her chest. "I won't stop trying to break down the barriers you keep putting between us."

"Meaning?"

"You and I are inevitable."

11

———

The next morning after Amani had bathed and Nadia did her hair in an intricate pattern of braids, she left her suite to head to the morning room for breakfast with Soraya and Jamal. Amani had taken an extraordinary amount of time getting ready this morning. Why? Because she hadn't wanted to get out of bed.

All night, she kept replaying the intimacy she'd shared with Cameron in his bedroom last night. The way he kissed her. The more he took, the more she gave, arching into his impossibly hard chest. His mouth on her breast and the way he tasted and tugged on her nipples. She'd wantonly writhed against him because she'd been completely lost. Swept away by Cameron and the sensations coursing through her veins.

Eventually, Nadia came to her bedside to ask if she was ill. Amani quickly recovered from her daydream, and said she was lounging. As close as she and Nadia were, there were some things she wanted to keep for herself. Plus, Nadia was her maid and wouldn't approve of Amani's scandalous behavior.

So she got dressed and marched into the morning room to face Cameron, but he wasn't there.

"I hope you're feeling better this morning and are well rest-ed," Soraya said from her seat, "because there's much to do, we need to get your dress fitted and make sure there are no last-minute adjustments."

"Of course," Amani smiled brightly. Her measurements had been sent to Faharat's seamstress months ago, but she'd yet to try the dress on and she knew Soraya was a perfectionist. "I'm here for you, whatever you need."

"Excellent."

"And where is his Majesty?" Amani asked, glancing around the empty room for Jamal.

"He and Cameron took off to discuss security for the wedding and all the celebrations. Your Cameron is quite intense."

Amani chuckled. "My Cameron?"

"Oh, c'mon, Amani," she glanced around to make sure no servants were around, "it's just me and you here."

"And?"

"And I saw how Cameron looked at you last night. If you recall, you told me to watch him. And I did. I can see that he fancies you, though he's trying his best to act as if you're nothing more than a client."

Amani released a long-held sigh. "So I'm not imagining it?"

Soraya shook her head. "But even though I acknowledge there's sexual tension between you, you must know it can't go anywhere."

"Why can't it?"

"You're royal, Amani. A princess," Soraya replied. "You know as well as I do that you will have an arranged or dynastic marriage. We don't get to choose."

Amani frowned. She didn't want to be reminded of the posi-tion she was in.

Soraya moved from her seat and sat in the empty chair

beside Amani. "I'm not saying this to upset you. Only to remind you of your position. Cameron understands it. It's probably why he's struggling with his feelings."

"It's not fair, Soraya. I should be able to choose the man *I* want."

"And maybe you can. Have you ever spoken to Khalil about this?"

Amani shook her head. When Malik had been alive, he'd often talked of her marrying a prince from another kingdom to stabilize Bahara, but she and Khalil had never discussed it. He'd been thrown into ascending the throne with very little preparation, given he was the forgotten heir. "No, I haven't, but maybe I should feel him out? I mean, I know he'll have to marry to continue the legacy, but why should I have to?"

"You should talk to him, but do so delicately," Soraya responded, "you don't want to raise any antennas and have him wondering why you're asking."

"Yes, of course." Amani rose to her feet. "Now, it's time we focus on you. I did come here to be your support system, not the other way around."

Soraya smiled and stood. Then she looped her arm through Amani's and they left the morning room, but as they focused on the dresses later that day, Amani didn't forget their conversation. She was determined to forge her own path when it came to marriage and she refused to be dictated to by anyone, not even her brother, the King.

"Everything seems to be in order," Cameron stated after Jamal generously agreed to walk him through the different venues where the various wedding activities would take place.

"You didn't have to come with me today. I could have walked with your security company."

"True, but I thought it prudent we speak," Jamal replied. "Man-to-man."

Cameron stopped walking and turned to him. "Yes?"

"Is there something going on between you and Princess Amani?"

Cameron shook his head and rather than lie to Jamal, whom he respected, he answered honestly. "No, but I think she would like there to be."

"Then I warn you to be on your guard. I have known the princess for many years and although she has a reputation for being kind and sweet, there is steel underneath that spine of hers and when she wants something, she goes after it."

"How so?"

"Amani wanted to go to a finishing school versus staying nearby. She convinced her parents, the King and Queen at the time, to allow her to go. She's always been good at convincing people to see things her way."

"I can handle her."

Jamal chuckled. "That's what I thought about Soraya and I'm about to be married this week."

"Amani's brother is a good friend of mine. I can't betray him by getting involved with her."

"If you say so," Jamal replied, "but lust is a powerful thing and if what I felt between you last night was any indication, you're in pretty deep."

Jamal's words echoed with Cameron long after he departed and Cameron went over instructions with the security team on the ground. Once the wedding festivities were in full bloom, there would be men positioned inside each room as well as along the perimeter and beyond. Cameron wasn't taking any chances. If the perpetrators were able to get close enough to the

Crown Prince's helicopter to cause it to crash, they could get to a wayward princess.

Once he was certain everything was in order, he set about finding Amani. Instead of guarding her himself today, he'd sent one of other Baharan royal guards. After last night's debacle when Amani had been in his bed, Cameron realized he'd underestimated her.

Yes, he found her attractive and when he touched her there was a certain physical chemistry between them, but he'd never thought it would be as combustible as it had been last night. The kisses had been potent and beyond anything he expected.

She'd opened her mouth to the demanding pressure of his and traded him kiss for kiss until the passion grew so hot, he could have made love to her. Thank God, common sense had prevailed, but that meant Cameron had to be more on his guard. By dallying with Amani, he'd given her the ammunition she needed to be more assertive and he didn't doubt she would use it to her advantage.

It was a serious situation he'd put himself in and he would have to take better care. Getting this gig on the heels of losing his Air Force career had been a lifesaver. Not to mention, giving him space and distance from his family. He was still grappling with not being Cal Mitchell's son and not knowing his biological father.

But Cal was the only father he'd ever known. Cameron modeled himself to be like him and to live up to the legacy he and his grandfather Carter started. And he'd always fit in—until now. Now, he felt adrift. With no anchor to keep him in place. This position was supposed to be drama free, but instead it brought its own set of hurdles.

Cameron needed to finish this assignment and hopefully, in that time, Khalil and his military would find out who was behind his brother's assassination so Cameron could move on with his life before he did something foolish he couldn't come back from. Because Cameron wasn't sure how long he could keep saying no to Amani.

AMANI MADE it through the fitting and did her best to show the right amount of enthusiasm. She oohed and aahed when Soraya tried on both wedding dresses. The American dress was a stunning beaded tulle gown. Meanwhile, the traditional Muslim dress was embellished with cap sleeves and a full skirt covered in high-shine appliques along with a traditional cathedral-length bridal veil with lace and a scalloped hem.

Amani was happy to be there for her best friend, she really was, but she couldn't stop thinking about Cameron and, of course, his absence throughout the day. He had another of the Baharan bodyguards with her instead of himself. It was as if he wanted to sweep what happened between them under the rug and it angered her. It was like he was punishing her as if she were some disobedient child. She hadn't been the only one in his bed. He could have pushed her away, but he kissed her back, indicating he wanted her as much as she wanted him.

The way he was ignoring her made Amani feel hollow and how she felt as a child. Amani suspected her desire for validation and appreciation was a character flaw because as the female child in the family, everyone doted on her brothers. The only thing she was supposed to do was save herself for her husband, but Amani cared about none of that. She wanted to pick the man she wanted to be intimate with and she had. Cameron, but he was now acting as if he didn't want her.

By the time dinner time came, Amani's anger had been seething for hours, so when Cameron knocked on the door of her suite, she was fit to be tied.

"Enter," Amani announced.

She watched Cameron walk in wearing a dark navy suit with a crisp white shirt. He looked every bit as handsome as he had the night before. "Amani" Cameron inclined his head toward her but kept a discreet distance. "How was your day?"

His aloofness made her launch into a verbal tirade. "Really? Is that all you have to say to me after last night?"

Cameron's eyes sent her a warning glance when he saw Nadia reading on the sofa in the sitting area nearby.

"Do you mind giving us some privacy, Nadia?" Amani asked.

"Of course, my lady." Nadia bowed on her way out of the room and closed the double doors to her adjoining room.

Cameron glared at her. "That was reckless, Amani."

"Don't scold me like I'm some errant child. I'm an adult and I handled the situation."

"I assume you have something to say?" Cameron folded his arms across his chest and regarded her warily.

"Yes, I do." Amani replied and rather than stay where she was by the doors of the terrace. She walked toward him and he instinctively took a step backwards. "Why are you acting this way as if I've done something wrong?"

"You haven't. I have. I was charged with looking after your safety and I can't do that if I'm romantically entangled with you."

"So, you can just turn your feelings on and off?" She snapped her fingers.

"My will is strong."

"Ha! I think I proved you wrong last night."

He ignored her response and said, "My behavior was completely unprofessional and unethical and I'm sorry. It won't happen again."

He was apologizing for kissing her and making her feel like a woman? Was she so abhorrent that he wanted to take it all back?

"I'm sorry you feel that way."

She didn't believe it for a second, but she wasn't going to push the issue. She would allow nature to take its course because she was certain Cameron thought he could control what was happening between them, but he was wrong. The sexual tension between them had a life force of its own and it wouldn't be denied.

12

The following morning Cameron was already downstairs with the rest of the wedding party and security crew by the time Amani and Nadia came downstairs. After a light breakfast, the entire wedding entourage set off for a day at the horse races. Sheikh Jamal had several horses competing.

The event was going to be chock-full of celebrities, starlets and politicians all jockeying for a moment alone with the Sheikh. That meant Cameron was going to have to be on his guard. There was too great a risk of a rogue assassin sneaking past the Sheikh's defenses to get at Amani. It was his job to ensure nothing happened, but Cameron was certain after the other night, Amani wasn't going to make his life easy.

Instead, when she came down the stairs in a strapless custom navy dress with intricate gold embroidery, stacked bracelets and a vintage diamond necklace; she looked incredibly beautiful and every bit the princess. Amani took his breath away. Her icy gaze was the only acknowledgment Amani gave him in terms of communication. He understood. He felt the tug of desire between them, but it wasn't going to happen. In time, she would get over this infatuation and find someone suitable.

"Good morning, Amani." He opened the door of the limousine and offered her his hand which, to his surprise, she took. His breath caught when she took it and he sensed she felt the echoing thrill at the touch of their hands because a soft blush rose under her skin. But just as quickly, it was over and she was taking her seat. This time, he slid inside across from her.

Cameron wanted Amani to know he wasn't afraid of the attraction he felt towards her and could control it. So, he purposely joined them in the rear. When he glanced across at her, he didn't get her usual smile inviting him to smile back. Instead, Amani stiffened and resolutely stared out of the window. It took everything in him to stay rooted where he was and not cross the distance between them to touch her despite Nadia's presence in the car.

He hadn't forgotten their kiss and his blood stayed hot with the memory. She'd been so responsive when he touched her that he could easily have seduced her and taken her virginity, but it would have been the wrong thing to do. He did have some ethics. He'd chided Cage about his when he chose to sleep with his ex, Monae, so soon after their break up. Cameron held himself to a higher standard, but he was tempted like a bee was to honey. He had to remain indifferent.

They arrived at the horse track and immediately Cameron exited, hurrying Amani inside and away from the paparazzi who were eager to catch a glimpse of the Sheikh, his soon-to-be bride and the princess of Bahara. "This way," Cameron stated.

Once they were inside and away from the throng of onlookers, they followed Jamal's entourage to the top floor and the penthouse overlooking the track. The Sheikh spared no expense for the event. There were rows and rows of finger foods laid out, along with a full bar.

Amani, it seemed, had intentions because she immediately asked for a glass of champagne. Cameron would have to keep his eye on her because she was usually more emotional. It was like she'd taken a page out of his book and was practicing ambivalence and Cameron found he didn't like it. He had gotten used to Amani showing her every emotion that he was unnerved when she gave nothing away and kept her lashes lowered. Damn it, he told himself he wouldn't get caught up with thoughts of her and once again he was falling down the rabbit hole.

"Ahmad," Cameron called the other guard over. "You take over watching the princess. I'm going to do a perimeter sweep."

Cameron had to do something to protect himself from getting too close. He'd already lost the battle once when she came into his room after his nightmare about the crash. Instead of pushing her away, he pulled her to him and kissed her like his life depended on it. He refused to admit defeat again. He had to exercise the control he'd used to get him through the Air Force Academy and keep Amani at distance.

Amani sipped on her second glass of champagne. She needed something to ease the pain of having Cameron avoid her like she was the plague. She understood it was his way of proving he could control the lust between them, but it was still there and ever present. On the drive over in the limo, it pulsed between them so much so, Amani had been forced to stare out the window other than gaze at Cameron's delicious full and sensuous lips which she'd had the pleasure of kissing.

Now she was looking out at the horses as the jockeys were getting ready for the race. Spectators were already taking pictures with their cellphones.

"Are you all right, Amani?" Soraya asked, from her side. Her friend looked at her. "You've been very quiet today."

"I'm fine."

"Doesn't sound like it," Soraya responded. "Is this about Cameron? I noticed you two seem different today."

Amani eyed her sideways. "How so?"

"If I'm honest? Cold. It's like the heat I felt between you the night before is completely gone."

"That's because Cameron is not interested in pursuing the attraction he has for me."

"I'm sorry, Amani, but maybe it's for the best."

Amani gulped down the champagne in her hand and placed it on the tray a nearby waiter was carrying. "I'm sorry, but I need some air."

"Of course. I'll be here when you need me."

Amani left the penthouse and when Nadia started to follow her, she held up her hand. "I need time alone, please, Nadia. Thank you."

Amani was tired of having her feelings unrequited. She knew she had to stop carrying a torch for Cameron, but it was hard to do. She swiped another glass of champagne and headed downstairs towards the VIP area on the lower level where she could see the horses up close. She didn't have to look behind her to know Ahmad was on her heels. Cameron handed her off to him after the limo drive because he couldn't stand to be around her.

As one of the jockey's and his horse came close to the fence, Amani reached out and patted the horse's mane. "What's his name?" Amani inquired.

"Spirit," the jockey told her.

Amani smiled. She sensed the animal had a lot of it, he pranced about, eager to get started.

"He's beautiful."

"Thank you," the jockey responded.

"What are you doing down here?" The deep male voice she'd come to know very well asked from behind her.

Amani spun around a little too fast and her feet tangled and she stumbled, but Cameron was right there to catch her before she fell into the person beside her.

"How much have you had to drink?" he inquired, steadying her as he took the empty champagne flute from her hand.

"What's it to you? I don't need your permission to go anywhere. I do as I please."

"Not out here you don't." He glanced around. "It's too out in the open. I can't protect you if someone wanted to take a shot at you. Let's go." He grasped her arm and pulled her towards the exit.

His touch sent a shock of electricity coursing through her like it always did.

She jolted and snatched her arm out of his. "You're not the boss of me," she replied and stomped away. Amani didn't know where she was going; she just knew she was tired of the sick feeling in the pit of her gut. She didn't realize she was heading towards the stables until she arrived and found them deserted because everyone was out in the field. That meant they were alone.

"Stop acting like a spoilt child who can't get her way," Cameron stated from behind her.

Amani turned and faced him. "And why don't you stop acting as if you're impervious."

Cameron drew a hand down over his face and released a harsh breath. "I can't do this with you, Amani. In this situation, I have to train myself to not care, to not react, to control my desires. Your brother is depending on me to protect you."

"And what about what I want?" she asked, looking up at him. Her mouth trembled as she spoke. "Don't I matter?"

"Of course, you do."

"Then why do you keep pushing me away when I know you don't want to?" She knew her voice sounded choked, strained even, but she was at her breaking point. "Don't shut me out, Cameron."

For several seconds, he looked tortured. "I would give anything to touch you right now."

"Then do it," Amani said, and glancing around, saw an empty stall. She stepped backwards toward it and to her surprise, Cameron moved forward toward her.

"Damn you, Amani!" He made a growling, primal noise and the next thing she knew, Cameron was encircling her with his hard arms and kissing her. He kissed her like a starving man, greedy and without hesitation. His lips demanded while his tongue took and gave. She'd never felt so energized than she did in this moment.

She needed this. Needed Cameron. She didn't know she'd spoken the words aloud until she felt Cameron tumbling her backward against a bale of hay.

CAMERON KNEW HE SHOULDN'T, but he had to have her. He was drawn to her like a magnet. He was no longer the bodyguard, but a man whose senses were invaded by the urgent need to mate with this woman.

It was visceral and all-consuming and he had no choice but to give in. His tongue laced with hers and Amani moaned softly and pressed herself harder against his chest. One of his hands left the tangle of her hair to explore her peaking breasts in her dress, his thumb circled over the pebbled nipple which made her squirm. He liked that so he cupped his palms over her buttocks until his body was imprinted on hers and deepened the kiss.

Amani began circling her hips against his as if she knew what to do. He was just a man, after all, and slipped his hand beneath her dress. Amani opened her legs inviting him to touch her freely and Cameron did just that. When his hands found the lace covering her mound, she jumped.

He lifted his mouth from hers to try and end this madness.

"Don't stop!" She moaned and hooked her arm around his neck and brought him back down to her waiting lips.

Cameron's hand returned and pushed aside the lace fabric of her panties which were shockingly wet and skated his fingers across her damp folds. Amani gave a little cry, but she didn't stop him so he continued his quest and gently slid a finger inside her. She was tight and Cameron felt himself swell in his pants.

"Oh!" Amani moaned and closed her eyes, but he didn't stop touching her. Cameron caressed her sensitive nub and then began to move in a slow rhythm in and out of her sex. He made love to her with his fingers.

"It feels..."

"How does it feel, princess?" he asked against her lips as he increased the friction. Cameron didn't know if it was for her or him because his entire body was on fire.

"So good..." she panted as she writhed in pleasure underneath him. Cameron wished he could do more, but as it was, he'd already taken things too far, but he could give her this moment. He pressed his mouth over hers and tweaked her nub and her entire body shuddered as a climax rolled through her in waves. He kissed her through it, taking the kiss deeper until eventually, she sagged underneath him.

Only then, did Cameron ease her dress back over her hips to her knees and sat forward on the bale of hay. Amani looked thoroughly sexy laying there with her hair mussed and her lipstick smeared.

"I hope that eased the ache you felt."

Amani bolted upright at his words and her eyes narrowed as she glared at him. "And you're an asshole, Cameron Mitchell!" She began straightening her clothes and used her fingers to comb her hair. "I don't need you to give me an orgasm. I'm perfectly capable of giving myself one."

And with that, she rushed out of the stall and away from him. This time Cameron didn't chase after her. He couldn't because he had to calm down his raging erection. At least, he'd made sure she was fulfilled, but he doubted that would alleviate the problem he found himself in. Because he'd just made his bed and now he was going to have to lie in it, but he wouldn't be alone. He was tired of fighting it. He was going to sleep with Amani. It was just a matter of when.

13

———

Twice.

Twice she'd orgasmed with Cameron and both times she'd been fully clothed. How was it possible in a few uncontrolled, thrilling heartbeats, she could be so lost in passion in his arms? It didn't seem to matter the time or the place. His bedroom. A horse stable. Whenever she and Cameron were together, it felt like she couldn't breathe and had run a marathon. They were combustible.

But he was right about one thing. The climax had eased the ache she felt, but what now? Since she'd been introduced to his lovemaking, did she need regular doses of it? And would they ever get to the point of actually being naked? She couldn't wait to touch him and feel his skin against hers. What would it be like to have him buried deep inside her body?

"Amani? Are you sure don't want anything to eat?" Nadia asked after she returned from the stables. She'd had to make a pit stop at the bathroom and touch up her hair and makeup as best she could with no assistance. "You haven't eaten much today. I can make you a plate."

"That sounds lovely." Amani realized she'd been terribly

rude to Nadia earlier when she asked for space. It wasn't her fault she'd become addicted to Cameron's kisses. Nadia was always there for her when she needed it and when she returned with a plate and a bottle of sparkling water, Amani thanked her.

"This looks delicious." She placed the napkin on her lap. "I'm sorry for being short with you earlier."

"It's all right," Nadia said. "I know you are struggling."

Amani frowned. "Pardon?"

Nadia leaned in closer so no one would hear them. "About you and Mr. Cameron. You are completely taken with him, are you not?"

How observant Nadia was and it showed what a terrible actor Amani apparently was. Did everyone know she carried a torch for him?

She nodded. "I am."

"But you know you must marry someone royal," Nadia stated.

"I know tradition," Amani replied, "however, I want to be able to choose the man *I* want. Not someone the King or the royal council selects for me that's advantageous to the country. And that's not to say I don't love my country, I do, but this is *my life* we're talking about."

"I just worry about you, Amani. You're setting yourself up for heartbreak and you risk shame coming to the crown if anyone found out about this."

Amani took a bite of crostini with prosciutto and nibbled on it. "Thank you for your counsel, Nadia. I appreciate you looking out for me."

Nadia smiled. "Always, princess."

Amani was afraid, however, that there might be no turning back from the path she'd set herself on. It was Cameron or there was no one.

"How is everything going in Faharat?" Khalil asked Cameron later that evening when he checked in to see how the wedding events were progressing.

"All is well," Cameron replied. "The Sheikh has been very accommodating of the security detail. He even walked all the venues with me to ensure everything was up to par."

"I would be surprised of anything less. Jamal is a good man. Soraya is lucky indeed to be marrying him," Khalil replied. "And Amani?"

"Is the same spitfire she was when I arrived," Cameron responded.

"I'm sorry she's being a handful, Cameron. My sister has spent too much time abroad and is still swayed by their customs."

"I can handle her."

"Good. She needs a strong hand. I have no idea who I'll convince to marry Amani, especially with her ideas about women's equality and the like. Baharanian's are still very traditional in many respects and although over time, my family convinced them to allow their daughters to get educated; there are some that still hold on to the old ways like the Bedouins whom I will accommodate. As it is, there are some who don't think I'm good enough, but I've done my best to dissuade them. However, if Amani were to marry a royal with a secure and stable kingdom it would work wonders for Bahara."

"Does she have to marry soon?" Cameron was curious. He and Khalil had never discussed marriage before because the Crown Prince had been alive and was heir to the throne. He would have been required to produce an heir, but now that he was gone...

"Not at this second," Khalil replied. "Everyone will be

looking to me, as their king, to find a queen. There is still time for Amani. Perhaps even to make a love match, but she has to at least be open to the idea of marrying someone royal."

"I understand."

And that wasn't Cameron. He was an American through and through. He couldn't offer Amani any of the things Khalil wanted for her. All he could give her was an incredible night of passion. And then what? She'd be a disgraced princess no one would want.

"I'll leave you to the festivities, so I'll see you tomorrow at the wedding." Khalil planned on flying in later that evening after he had concluded his business.

"See you then." Cameron ended the call and fell back in bed.

He was flirting with danger by the interludes he was sharing with Amani.On the way back to the castle, she'd been somber and quiet as she sat across from him. Every so often, he would catch Amani looking at him underneath her lashes when she didn't think he was watching.

He was.

He noticed everything about her— including the way she shifted uncomfortably in her seat throughout the limo ride. He knew women and although he'd given her a taste of pleasure she wasn't fully satisfied and wanted the whole meal.

Chivalry could only take him so far and the rampant desire he felt for Amani wasn't abating. Why did she feel so wonderful in his arms? What was it about her that made her so irresistible? He wished he knew so he could turn it off. Instead, he went to bed dreaming of long, flowing dark hair, chocolate brown eyes, and lips that begged to be kissed.

THE NEXT MORNING, Amani woke up feeling damp and aroused. She hadn't gotten much sleep because inexorably her mind moved to the man who always seemed to be in her thoughts. Cameron, with his smoldering hazel irises, full lips, a five o'clock shadow on his sexy vanilla complexion, and zero buzz cut. She felt as if she could still taste him in her mouth. It made her want more.

Throwing back the covers, she reached for her robe and slid her arms inside, and without belting it, opened the terrace doors. The sun was already overhead and palace staff were bustling about preparing for the wedding.

Amani sighed deeply. Today, two things needed to happen. One, she had to get Soraya down the aisle to the Sheikh, the man she adored. Second, she and Cameron needed to be alone so the inevitable could happen and they could become lovers. She was tired of the seesaw of emotions, one of them had to act. If it had to be her, so be it.

Are you prepared for the consequences?

She was. It was her body. Her choice. She didn't have to lie down and do what was expected of her. Give herself to a man she not only didn't love, but didn't desire. What was the harm in having one day, one night for herself? Tomorrow, she would return to reality. Back to the world where her brother the King or the Royal Council would map out her life and arrange her marriage to someone they found suitable or some sort of political alliance. She would be as useless as a Christmas tree ornament and equally ineffective.

It bothered her. She knew it shouldn't when this was what she'd been bred to do, but Amani also wanted to carve out an identity for herself, one that wasn't just about being a showpiece or a breeder to have an heir.

"Amani, there you are," Nadia said, "Princess Soraya's maid

was looking for you. The princess is very nervous and I suspect in need of a friend to calm her nerves."

Amani spun around. "Of course." Today wasn't solely about her and the independence and freedom she craved to make her own decisions. It was about her best friend finally finding love and happiness. "Let's go."

AMANI HAD NEVER LOOKED LOVELIER, Cameron thought as he watched her move across the reception hall after the American wedding ceremony of Princess Soraya and Sheikh Jamal. She wore a stunning gold sequined long-sleeved dress that on some might look dowdy but not Amani. The V neckline showed a bit more décolletage than he would have liked, but then the dress nipped in at the waist and showed off her great curves before flowing out to her feet.

Cameron remained nearby but not close enough to touch. Amani didn't seem to mind. She appeared to be having the time of her life. Her dance card was never empty at the reception because she'd caught the eye of several princes and a Sheikh, all of whom were anxious to have her acquaintance.

Those were the kind of men Amani was expected to be with, not a bodyguard and a disgraced former Air Force pilot who couldn't even fly a plane. He had nothing to offer her other than a great night in bed and while it would assuage the heat between them, it wouldn't change the fact that Khalil said more was expected of Amani. She had duties to fulfill, as did he, but that didn't mean he didn't hate having to watch other men hold her. Or like the way each of them looked like hungry wolves ready to devour Little Red Riding Hood.

"Cameron!" He heard his name called and turned to see Khalil striding toward him in a black tuxedo just as he had on.

"Khalil. Glad you were able to make it."

"Just," Khalil responded. "I missed the ceremony, but was able to get here for the reception and of course there's the traditional ceremony tomorrow."

"I'm sure the Sheikh will be pleased."

"And Amani?" Khalil asked, peering over the large crowd. "Where is she?"

"Dancing. The princess has been quite popular this evening."

"Has she?" Khalil's brow rose in query. "Perhaps that isn't a bad thing. I will see what she thinks about some of her admirers. Who knows, one of them could be her husband?"

Khalil's words lodged in Cameron's gut and made his stomach churn. He didn't want Amani with another man. Even though he knew he didn't have any right to feel this way, it felt like she was his and he had a prior claim. "Could Amani ever marry someone who wasn't royal?"

Khalil glanced sideways at him. "I suppose it's possible, but it would certainly break with tradition and that's not what we need. Bahara is in a tenuous position. It would be helpful if she could marry a prince or Sheikh from one of the neighboring islands to help secure our alliances."

"And how does she feel about that?"

Khalil was silent for a few beats and Cameron wondered if he was going to answer him, but then Khalil spoke. "I'm ashamed to say I've never asked her. I assumed she knows her duties, Cameron. Unlike me, who was an outcast to my father. Amani was raised in the palace and with that upbringing comes certain obligations and expectations."

"Like you coming back to take up the mantle?" Cameron asked.

Khalil nodded. "It wasn't easy returning to this place that held so many bad memories, but I did so because, at the end of the day, even though I wasn't raised here, I'm still of royal blood and was the only logical choice to lead the nation."

Cameron nodded. "I understand. If you'll excuse me, I'm going to make my rounds." He needed some air because he was tired of thinking and hearing about duty and obligation because all of those held him back from having Amani and finding a moment of happiness in her arms.

That was how he found himself walking along the length of the outside pool. Once he reached the edge, he walked down a sweeping path. The wedding celebrations were going on in full blast and it gave Cameron time to clear his head. Nothing would or could ever happen with Amani. She was forbidden fruit, but he wanted her all the same. Why did this have to happen? He didn't need any more complications in his life. He'd come here to help Khalil and instead found himself in an untenable situation.

He heard the snap of leaves on the ground and without thinking, Cameron pulled the handgun out of his pocket and pointed.

"Don't shoot." Amani held her hands up as she came forward to stand in the light. "It's just me."

"Amani, for Chrissakes!" Cameron put his weapon back in the holster. "I could have shot you."

"But — but you didn't." She gave a half-hearted smile, but he could tell he'd frightened her.

Cameron frowned. "What the hell are you doing out here anyway? Shouldn't you be inside dancing the night away with one of your many admirers?"

She surprised him by chuckling softly. "Are you jealous, Cameron?"

"Of course, not."

She huffed. "There you go again, refusing to admit what we both know."

"Which is?"

"That you want me!" she hissed. "And I want you."

Fuck! Why did she have to say shit she couldn't take back. "Go back inside," Cameron bellowed. "Now!"

"And if I won't?" She asked haughtily folding her arms across her chest. The action made his eyes drop to curve of her breasts in the V of the dress. Her dress might be gold but it shimmered in the moonlight. "Because if you don't, I won't be responsible for what happens next."

Her eyes glittered with something like determination and then she said, "Good." It was a dare. An invitation for Cameron to take what he wanted, but should he? Could he?

He didn't get to think further because Amani lifted a hand, pressing her fingers to his chest. Her touch was like a match to tinder because Cameron couldn't hold back any longer. He'd never felt this way in his life, so he gave in to temptation. He dropped his mouth to hers and claimed her lips with all the desire threatening to erupt inside him.

14

She'd won.

A surge of triumphant elation flooded Amani's veins as she wound her arms around Cameron's neck. He took the kiss from zero to one hundred within seconds. His tongue slid inside her mouth, exploring the moist cavern and causing shivers of delight to race up her spine. This was how he'd kissed her that night in his room and again at the stables, but each time he'd stopped.

She didn't want him to stop tonight, but they couldn't stay here. What if they were caught?

Reluctantly, she pulled away and grabbed his hand, linking her fingers through his and pulling him along. "Come with me. I know a place."

Amani expected Cameron to fight back like he'd done all these weeks, but instead he allowed her to lead him through the garden maze to a secret door. She pulled a key from her bosom and heard Cameron's shocked gasp as she unlocked the door and held it open. "Are you coming in?"

Cameron stood in the doorway and at first she thought he might deny her, but instead, he pushed her inside, into the darkness. It took several seconds for her eyes to acclimate and she fumbled for a moment until she found the switch and illuminated the room in a soft light.

"What is this place?" Cameron asked.

"The Sheikh's harem."

At Cameron's surprised expression, Amani clarified. "Jamal's father used this place for his former's wives and mistresses, but it's not in use anymore. Or, at least, it wasn't until today when they prepared Soraya for Jamal."

"What if someone comes back?"

"They won't. As you can see," she spread her arms wide, "the place is spotless. No one is here but us, Cameron. We can finally be alone together."

She noticed he didn't take a step toward her and she wanted his hands on her as they'd been in his bed and in the stables.

"Tonight, I want to forget about everything, but you." She came closer to him and pressed her body against his. "I want you, Cameron."

A jagged breath came from his lips. "Amani—"

"Don't, Cameron," she whispered. "Don't say no to me, not again."

"Do you have any idea what you're asking of me?" he demanded.

"Yes, I do. I want you to make love to me. *With me.*"

Cameron scrubbed his jaw with his hands. "Are you sure, Amani? Because once we do, there's no going back. And if I'm not mistaken, you're a virgin."

Amani flushed. "So, what does that matter? I brought you here and it's my choice." She grasped his hand. "One night. Why can't we have this?"

"I— I didn't bring anything."

"Protection? Well, I've got that covered."

Her cheeks turned fiery when Cameron laughed. "You do?"

Amani reached into the bosom of her dress and produced a three-pack of condoms and tossed it on the divan.

"How in the hell…"

"I'm resourceful," Amani responded.

"Yes, you are, but that doesn't make this, right. This can have emotional ramifications for you besides physical ones. I don't want to hurt you, Amani."

"You won't. You think I'm going to fall in love with you?" Amani asked. "Well, I won't."

"You don't know that; you've never done this before."

"I'm making a conscious decision to choose something for me. Someone I want. Not someone chosen for me. And I want my first lover to be you."

And without further ado, she reached behind her and unzipped the golden gown she'd put on earlier. She heard Cameron's husky groan and looked up to find him watching her undress. She stared at him as the dress dropped to the floor and she stepped out of it in her heels and wearing the flimsy white lace bra and panty set she'd decided on earlier.

Even though she'd never stood in front of a man in her lingerie, the hungry way Cameron was looking at her didn't make her nervous. "Well?" Amani asked. "What's it going to be?"

CAMERON SWORE UNDER HIS BREATH. "Fuck it!"

Then he began dispensing with his clothes, stripping out of them as quickly as he could, but not without taking his eyes off Amani. He was afraid she might change her mind and if she did, he would stop, but she didn't. Instead, her eyes widened with each article of clothing he removed until he was in his black boxer shorts.

This was utter madness, a whim of desire and pleasure, a

whim Cameron knew he should deny himself, but wouldn't be able to, not this time. Slowly, he stepped toward her.

"Please" she hissed.

The single word was his undoing. He groaned and then pulled her toward him, slamming her into his chest and then he began kissing her once more. Their tongues clashed as he pillaged her mouth, but Amani gave as good as she got and sucked on his tongue shamelessly.

Cameron was delighted that, although a novice, Amani wasn't inhibited. Instead, she pulled away long enough to reach behind her and unclasp her bra, revealing full orbs with dark engorged nipples that he couldn't wait to feast on. Then she was reaching for the elastic of the scrap of material that was supposed to be panties, but he shook his head.

"Let me."

Her eyes widened and she dropped her hands to her side. Instead of removing them, he sunk to his knees, bringing his head level with her breasts and then he licked one nipple. Amani's eyes fluttered shut as he continued his ministrations. He lathed the peak with his tongue and then took it in his mouth and began sucking.

Amani grasped his broad shoulders and he captured her hips to hold her steady as he tormented her. When he was finished with one breast, he played with the other nipple and captured it between his lips and teeth. Her body bowed backward as he blazed a trail of wet kisses over both breasts.

When she began to pant and was unable to stand, Cameron rose, lifted her into his arms and carried her over to the low divan in the harem. He looked down at Amani. With her dark hair spread across the colorful pillows, she looked like a goddess.

She stared at him with passion-glazed eyes, taking in every inch of his body from his pectoral muscles to his abs and finally to his boxers which could not disguise his burgeoning erection. Swiftly, he removed them and saw her stunned expression.

"Oh, my," Amani whispered.

Desire surged through Cameron as he came down beside her. "You want to touch me?"

She glanced up nervously at him and nodded. Reaching out, she traced her hands up and down his length at first as if she was scared. When Cameron released a low groan, it must have given her confidence because she wrapped her fingers around him and began pumping him up and down. His muscles tensed and his breathing accelerated. Amani had no idea how her inexperienced touch was driving him mad.

A bead of moisture appeared at the tip and to his stunned fascination, Amani bent down and flicked her tongue across the head. Cameron made a guttural sound and grasped her hands, pulling her away.

"Enough," he murmured. "There can be time for that later."

She smiled. "Really?"

He laughed. "Yes, and two can play that game." He slid the lacy fabric of her panties down her hips and legs and tossed them aside. Cameron didn't give her time to be embarrassed that no one had ever seen those dark curls. Instead, he grasped both her hips and pulled her toward his face.

"Cameron, no!" She squirmed but Cameron was determined to make Amani's first time the most sensual of her life.

He glanced up to see her vivid chocolate gaze. "Don't you worry, baby, I'm going to feast on you." Then Cameron lowered his head and licked across her flesh. Her hips began to buck involuntary, but Cameron held her firmly as he probed and swirled with his tongue. When he found the heart of her, he ruthlessly exploited the nub with his tongue first and then his fingers until she sobbed aloud.

Did he stop? No. He'd been dreaming about tasting her and

now that he had, he would drown in her. He pushed one finger into her depths and used his thumb to stroke her, she groaned so he added another into her warm feminine core. Her body responded instantly and it showed Cameron how perfectly they were suited. He added his tongue, along with his fingers, until she was a bundle of raw nerves and sensations and writhing on the divan. He captured the nub at her throbbing center and suckled hard until an orgasm slammed into her and her legs shook with the force of it.

"Please no more..." She moaned as he licked her through the orgasm.

Cameron reached for the condom packet she'd tossed on the divan and tore off a small foil. He rolled it on his thick length that was so distended it was painful.

"Are you sure, Amani?" he asked, glancing down at her. "Do you want me to stop?"

"Of course, I'm sure." She parted her legs, making room for him.

Cameron's breath came out in ragged pants as he brought his body over hers. She felt so soft and so right. It was as though this was meant to be. He positioned himself and braced on his forearms and then he entered her slowly. She was tight. Very tight.

"You okay?" he hissed through clenched teeth.

"Yes, yes. *Please.*"

His every instinct made him want to thrust harder and possess her, but he went deeper inch by delicious inch. She wrapped her legs around his waist, pulling him further inside her soft body. It was heaven and hell, but he reined in his desire for her. Amani deserved a great first introduction to sex. He would do that for her because all they would have was this one night.

~

AMANI HAD no idea the joining of their bodies would feel like Cameron was taking up space in an empty place that was desperate to be filled. When he probed her entrance and pressed forward, she'd gasped, gripping his shoulders at the immense fullness of having him inside her. She needed to get adjusted to his size, but she didn't want him to stop. Didn't want him to withdraw and change his mind.

The entire experience was overwhelming, from the earth-shattering orgasms he'd already wrung from her body, and now this. She glided her fingers over his shoulders. "More..."

Cameron understood because he eased out, then pressed back in again, and Amani moaned. He rolled his hips, stretching her to accommodate him and slowly, Amani felt pleasure began to ripple from her center.

"Good?" he asked. His back was slick with sweat and the effort to keep himself at bay.

"Y-yes, so good." She could only stammer because he was buried so deep inside her. If this was heaven, she wanted more. Cameron gave it to her because when he started to move, the friction of his body inside hers increased an ache of pleasure within her. When he pulled out and thrust back in again at a different angle, rubbing a spot she didn't know existed, Amani cried out from the ecstasy of it all. Cameron's movements began to get more forceful as he demanded all of her. Amani tried to find purchase by wrapping her arms around his sweat-slicked shoulders as she braced for what was to come.

Each thrust took her higher and she was aware of nothing but his body. Growing accustomed to his rhythm, she rose to meet him, moving with him and intrinsically working her hips.

"Yes, like that!" He groaned and cupped her buttocks, holding her steady. His pace was so fast she gasped with surprise.

"Oh, yes...yes." She clung to him and heard her wails and the sound of his guttural groans as they both reached the precipice and fell over the cliff, dissolving into pleasure.

SLOWLY, Cameron moved off Amani to dispose of the protection and then he returned to lie on his back and stare at the ceiling. Neither of them spoke for several long minutes.

He was shaken.

It was the most amazing sexual experience of his life.

Was it because it was Amani? Was it because he'd been her first? Was it because she was a princess and they had no future together? But yet, he couldn't deny the feeling of rightness of being with her, *inside* her. However, he'd been very demanding. He turned onto his side. "Are you, all right? I didn't hurt you?"

Amani softly caressed his cheek. "Why would you think that?"

"I was rather demanding."

She rose on her elbow and gave him a lazy smile. "I enjoyed that part. You didn't treat me like I was fragile flower or was going to break. You treated me like a woman."

He stroked her hair. This was temporary. Only tonight. At least he would have the memory. He started to rise, but then Amani grabbed his arm and pulled him back down. "Cameron...where are you going?"

"We should get back to the party before it's noticed that you're missing."

"But we still have the two of these." She grinned mischievously and held up the other two foil packets.

He stared at her for an endless moment. "Amani, I was pretty rough earlier. You might be sore."

"I'm fine," she murmured. "Besides, if all I get to have is one night with you, then I want it all." She sat upward and her bare breasts teased his back, causing him to swell to life.

Amani must have noticed because the little minx pushed him backward against the pillows and, to his surprise, lowered her head and closed her mouth over him.

Sweet heavens.

She tasted him, taking him deeper into her moist, silky warmth. She lifted her head long enough to ask, "Does this feel good?"

"You can't tell?" he asked hoarsely.

She shook her head.

"I love it, Amani."

A sexy smile spread across her lips and she returned her attention back to him. She stroked his length, up and down and then took the silky tip of him back into her mouth and Cameron couldn't help it, he began thrusting. Amani grasped his thighs as he made love to her mouth. She didn't back away and took all of him, but when he was close, Cameron pulled out. He wasn't about to come in her mouth. She wasn't ready for that.

She frowned. "Did I do something wrong?"

"No, but unless you are ready to suck me off, you were going to be in a for a rude awakening."

Amani blushed and he loved that she still could. Although he'd taken her virginity. She was still inexperienced. "I want to come inside you," he added.

Her smile returned. "Then how about we take care of that." She reached for one of the foil packets and opened it with her teeth. Then she removed the protection and tried to ease it on his straining dick. Cameron placed his hand over hers and helped her slide the condom on.

"Would you like to try a different position?" he asked.

"Yes."

"Lie on your stomach."

She looked suspicious at first, but then did as he asked. The sight of her plump ass facing him made Cameron even harder. He leaned over and pressed his chest against her back and reached down to her stomach to lift her onto all fours.

"Cameron?" His name was a question on her lips, but not for long because he kissed and suckled her neck while his hands moved lower to her wet center. He fingered her to make sure she was ready for him and she was dripping.

Jesus. He was going to lose it if he wasn't inside her fast. He placed his hand over her head and pushed her head down and lifted her ass, long enough for him to position himself at her entrance and then he slowly surged inside her.

"Oh!" Amani cried out, grasping the divan as he began thrusting in and out. Her tight pussy clenched around him and Cameron wasn't sure how long he would last. He wanted to make it good for her because this was all he would ever be able to offer her.

Reaching underneath Amani, Cameron slid a finger inside her as he thrust and Amani began to jerk uncontrollably as a climax began to overtake her. "That's it, Amani. Just let go."

She sobbed and fell forward onto the bed. The position gave Cameron greater access and he used it to his advantage to pound into her relentlessly. When he was near the edge, he leaned over and whispered in her ear, "You're beautiful, Amani." Then he gave one final thrust and collapsed on top of her.

15

———————

Amani slowly opened her eyes, and, at first, she wasn't sure where she was. Then she remembered last night. She and Cameron had made love three times until they'd used the packet of condoms she brought with her. Her first time had been a spectacular display of slow exploration and sensuality as Cameron introduced her to lovemaking. The second time had been fast and furious. The way he'd taken her from behind and played her body like a fiddle had made Amani exhausted and she'd passed out immediately afterward.

However, there had been one condom left and she'd awoken to find Cameron had slipped her legs over his shoulders, opening her completely to him. She'd been surprised, but not scared. She trusted him fully and had closed her eyes, letting her entire world shrink to the just the two of them and Cameron's skillful tongue. When the storm finally broke, she'd cried out as wave after wave of pleasure flooded her entire being. Then Cameron had entered her once again. He moved slowly and possessed her in the most sensual way possible. He'd cupped her face in his hands and kissed her deeply, tangling her tongue with his before plunging into the dark recesses of her mouth. All the while, the lower half of him moved deeper, inhabiting her completely.

She'd been greedy for him, thrusting her pelvis to meet his and grinding hungrily against him. She'd begged him to take her and dug her fingers into his back, driving him, encouraging him to take pleasure in her body. Cameron had steadily thrust inside her, bringing her over and over to the cusp of pleasure, before easing back and going slow.

"I want to feel every part of you." Amani had urged him on until he was bucking against her and she was thrashing help-lessly beneath him. Then he'd stunned her by flipping her over to be astride him.

"Ride me!" he commanded, and she had. She ground against him, nursing and stroking him into a frenzy of desire until he was her slave. He'd thrust upwards to meet her movements. Neither of them had held back and when the last wave of climax had washed over them, she'd bucked convulsively against him and he'd savagely clung to her as he roared out his own release.

She'd taken as much pleasure as she could from her sexual awakening because she knew when the morning came, it would be over and all she would have were the memories.

And she did. Because Cameron had ruined her. Wrecked her for any man that might come after him. She was thoroughly satisfied. And as she glanced around the room, she saw him getting dressed. He was pulling his shirt over his broad back which showed markings of her fingernails when she'd clung to him as he made love to her. His body was honed to perfection and he was all muscle and strength.

"Cameron," she called out, "come back to bed." He turned to stare at her for an endless moment. Was that regret lurking in those hazel depths?

"We have to get back, Amani. We shouldn't have fallen asleep. The palace is awakening. I'm not sure how I'm going to get you back to your room unnoticed."

He was right, of course, but she refused to be ashamed of the intimacy they'd shared last night. She'd done this for herself. She refused to allow the one thing she had control over to be dictated by her brother, the Royal Council, or even Bahara. She hadn't known what her body was capable of feeling until Cameron had taught her. Cameron leaned over and stroked her hair. "Are you okay?"

Amani understood what he was asking and although she was sore in places she never imagined she could be. She was thankful for the fantasy of the single night they'd shared.

She nodded. "I'm fine."

Then she rose and began picking up the articles of clothing strewn across the floor. She slipped her bra into place and was glancing about for her panties, when Cameron, fully dressed, held them out to her with a smile on his face. Her belly flopped. She was in danger from this handsome sexy man who'd opened her eyes to what mutual desire meant.

"Thank you." She slid on her undies and stepped into her gown. Once she was in her in dress, she looked at him over her shoulder. "Can you zip me up?"

He didn't answer and merely moved over to reach down and do as she'd bid him. Amani walked over to one of the mirrors in the harem and fixed her face and hair as best she could. She still looked like a wanton woman with her glazed eyes, flushed cheeks and swollen mouth.

"Ready?" Cameron asked and held out his hand.

Amani nodded and took his hand. "Lead the way."

Although it was still early, the palace was starting to buzz to life. Luckily no one was in the secret corridor and she and

Cameron were able to walk by unnoticed until they arrived on the second floor.

Amani's heart literally stopped when she saw the royal guard who protected her brother, the King, standing in front of her door. She glanced at Cameron.

His eyes were shuttered.

Did he have any idea what they were up against? If he did, he didn't show an outward sign of fear. Instead, he started toward the door. The scowl on several of the men's faces were evident as they passed and then one of them opened the door to her suite.

Amani sucked in a deep breath and prepared herself for what was to come. Once she and Cameron were inside, the men closed the door after them, sealing their fate.

Khalil was pacing the floor of her suite like a caged lion and when he saw her, he rushed toward her, pulling her into a quick hug. Once the preliminary greeting was over, and Khalil saw that she was safe, there was no denying the stony set of Khalil's features and the implacable line of his unsmiling mouth before he yelled, "And where the hell have you been, Amani? Or, more importantly, should I ask who have you been with?"

Khalil's furious gaze turned to Cameron.

CAMERON HAD KNOWN there would a price to pay for the night he'd spent with Amani and as he looked into Khalil's stormy dark gaze, he realized, it might be the cost of the friendship he held dear.

"Well, are either of you going to answer me?" Khalil's voice boomed across the room. "Or shall I assume?"

Cameron cleared his throat and then spoke calmly. "Khalil, I would do Amani a disservice if I..."

"Stop!" Khalil held up a hand. "Are you saying that you and my sister..."

He was no coward, so Cameron didn't lower his head. He merely stood silent and looked his friend dead in the eye. Khalil was a smart man and could put two and two together.

"Damn you, Cameron." Khalil spun away and shook his head furiously. "If you were any other man..."

"You'd do what?" Amani asked, jumping in, coming to stand in front of him. "It was my choice, Khalil. Cameron didn't coerce me."

"Amani, please!" Cameron interrupted her.

"What?" She looked at Cameron and then at her brother. "Khalil you're acting as if I did something wrong. I didn't. I'm a grown woman capable of making my own decisions."

"Enough!" Khalil roared, turning around to face them. "You were an innocent, Amani and Cameron knew that. Hell, I wanted him to protect you. Make sure you stayed safe and instead... he used you for his own selfish desires."

Cameron took the abuse because he deserved Khalil's fury. He'd behaved dishonorably in giving in to his attraction to Amani, but in the moment, it had felt right. He'd felt a connection with her that he hadn't found with anyone else. The circumstances, however, were not ideal.

"So men can go off and have lovers, but I can't?" Amani asked. "That's a double standard, Khalil, and you damn well know it."

Khalil pointed a finger at her. "Amani, I've heard enough from you. Leave us."

"No!" Amani cried. "This isn't fair."

When Khalil turned to glare at her, Cameron could see Amani realized the enormity of the situation they were in and to his surprise, did as Khalil asked and stalked out of the suite. The guards opened the door letting her through and leaving Cameron alone with Khalil.

Cameron was so busy watching Amani's exit, that he didn't see Khalil coming toward him until it was too late and Khalil's fist connected with his jaw, sending him sprawling to the floor.

"You fucking deserve that and a whole lot more," Khalil said, standing above him as Cameron held his face.

Cameron sucked in a breath. "Yeah, I do." He nodded from the floor. "And you can beat me to a bloody pulp if it will make you feel better, but it won't change things."

"Really, Cam?" Khalil asked, glowering at him. "My sister? How could you do this to me?"

Slowly, Cameron placed one foot down and then the other until he could stand upright and face Khalil again. "I'm sorry, Khalil. I — I didn't plan this."

"You just happened to fall into bed with my sister, a virgin?" Khalil inquired. "Is that what you're trying to say?"

Cameron snorted. "Of course, not. I just..."

"You just what?"

"I lost my head."

"Clearly. You weren't thinking with the right one," Khalil replied. His brow furrowed as his face turned into an angry mask. "Of all the people I thought would betray me, I never imagined you would. I thought I could trust you. You saved my life for Chrissakes!"

"I know." Cameron scrubbed his hand across his face. "And I'm truly sorry." He knew what it was like to feel betrayed. When he discovered Cage was seeing Monae behind his back, he'd been livid. He couldn't believe his own brother would stab him in the back and date his ex-girlfriend when the ink was barely dry on their breakup.

"Your apologies mean nothing, Cameron," Khalil responded and Cameron noted his voice had changed from one of friend to that of a King, a man with authority to probably throw Cameron's ass in prison.

"What can I do to regain your trust and faith in me?" Cameron asked, moving toward Khalil. "Tell me and I'll do it." Khalil might deck him again and if he did, Cameron would take it because he done an injustice to their friendship.

"I'll tell you what you can do. You can marry my sister."

16

———

"Marry?" Cameron asked incredulously.

"You heard me," Khalil responded. "You've dishonored me and my sister. The least you can do is marry her and make an honest woman of her."

"C'mon, Khalil, is that really necessary? Doesn't that seem old-fashioned to you?" Cameron asked. Besides, he didn't intend to marry *ever*. He was over the institution and intended to stay a bachelor. Love no longer factored into the equation. Where had it ever got him? Nowhere. Except watching his brother marry the woman who he thought he might marry someday. Except seeing his mother lie to his father year after year.

"This isn't about me, Cameron. Bahara is still a very traditional country and once word gets out about Amani's scandalous behavior here in Faharat, she will be scorned. No man will want her, least of all, a royal."

"Khalil..."

"Do you dare to challenge me, Cameron? You shouldn't forget who I am. I am King of Bahara."

Cameron rubbed the back of his neck with his hand. He could feel tension forming. "I haven't forgotten, Khalil."

"And yet you helped yourself to my sister."

Cameron scowled. "That's not what happened." What he and Amani shared was more than that and Khalil was reducing it to something dirty.

Khalil stormed toward him, but Cameron didn't back down. He'd never backed down a day in his life. Cal had taught him it was a sign of weakness and Khalil certainly would think so.

"I don't give a fuck," Khalil responded. "Look what you've done, you've reduced me to cursing, which is beneath me. Beneath you."

"Then stop this foolish talk," Cameron replied. "I should have come to you first and expressed my interest in Amani." It's what Caden advised him to do and he hadn't done it. He'd been afraid to admit his feelings for Amani and now look where they were?

"To what, date her?" Khalil chuckled. "Amani is the Princess of Bahara, Cameron. She's not the average woman you can take to bed with no thought about the consequences."

"We were safe."

Khalil rolled his eyes. "I don't mean those kind of consequences, but that's beside the fact. You will do the right thing and marry her."

"Or what?" Cameron's eyes blazed right back at Khalil. "You'll make me?"

Khalil stared at him for several beats. Neither one of them blinking. "I'm hoping it doesn't come to that, Cameron. I'm hoping you will be the standup man I've always thought you to be and do the right thing by Amani."

"And make an honest woman of her?"

"Yes!" Khalil roared.

Cameron turned away from Khalil and walked out onto the terrace. The sun had already risen and was shining bright all around the palace. Staffers were out milling about the grounds, oblivious to what was going on inside. Khalil was threatening to turn his whole world upside down if Cameron didn't marry Amani of his own free will.

He hung his head low. How the hell had he allowed himself to get into this position? Because somehow Amani had entranced him and he'd been unable to stop himself from going down the rabbit hole. Oh, what an experience it had been!

But was he supposed to pay for it for the rest of his life? He didn't love Amani. Marriage wasn't on his agenda. And if he married her, there would be risks emotionally for Amani. Although he cared for her and found her desirable, she would want more than he was willing to give.

"What's it going to be?" Cameron heard Khalil's voice behind him and knew it was a losing battle. He would have to accept his fate.

He would have to marry Amani whether he liked it or not.

Amani didn't appreciate being summoned back into her room as if she were some errant child in need of disciplining, but that's exactly how Khalil was treating her. She thought, or at least, hoped he would be different. More open-minded to the fact that she was a grown woman and capable of deciding for herself who she became intimate with.

Instead, he was acting superior. *Acting like a King, an inner voice said.*

She straightened her back and when the royal guard opened the suite doors, she swept into the room. She hadn't been sure what she was going to see. Cameron in handcuffs? Cameron bloody and bruised on the floor after a scuffle with a Khalil? What she didn't expect was to see both men sitting down as if they were waiting for her arrival.

Khalil was looking straight at her while Cameron's gaze was fixed across the room as if he would rather be anywhere except near her. And she understood. They'd taken a moment in time for themselves, but surely it wasn't as dire as both men's somber expressions.

"So, is everything settled between you?" Amani asked, folding her arms across her chest.

"You could say that," Khalil replied. "Cameron has agreed to marry you and the wedding will be held as soon as we can arrange it back in Bahara."

"What!" Amani shrieked and her eyes grew wide with fear. "Have you gone mad?"

Khalil rose to his feet, buttoning his suit jacket as he came toward her. "There are consequences for your actions, little sister, and this is one of them."

"But marriage? Khalil, that's crazy. Just because we spent the night together?"

"Not another word!" Khalil said, raising his voice, and Amani immediately shut up. Since he'd returned to Bahara, she'd never seen her brother have a temper until today. "You have brought shame to yourself and the crown. You *will* marry Cameron and make this right."

"But Khalil…"

"I will not hear another word of this, Amani. My word is law."

Amani heard the authoritative tone in his voice. Khalil was pulling rank as King. He was no longer her brother in this moment, but her sovereign. She had no choice, but to do as she was told. "Yes, Your Highness." In defiance, she curtsied in front of him, something she'd never done.

Khalil caught the action and rolled his eyes. "You both will meet me on the royal jet in an hour. Until then, govern yourselves accordingly." And without another word, he stalked out of the room.

Amani was still frozen to the spot and staring at Cameron in disbelief. "Have you nothing to say?"

Cameron looked up and regarded her. The aloofness in his eyes turned the blood in her veins cold. "What do you expect me to say, Amani? Khalil is right. I dishonored our friendship and betrayed his trust. All we can do is make the best of the situation."

"Make the best of it?" Amani asked incredulously. "You don't even want to get married. You said so yourself, you don't believe in the institution."

"I don't."

"Then why are you doing this?"

"Did it look like we could stop your brother?" Cameron asked, pointing toward the door. "His mind was made up before we even walked in here."

"So? You couldn't change his mind? You've known him for years."

Cameron shrugged. "Yeah, I did, and I just blew up a fifteen-year friendship…"

"Go ahead, finish that sentence," Amani replied. "You blew it up by sleeping with me. There, I said it for you. You regret being with me, don't you?" Despite herself, tears started falling down her cheeks.

"Amani…"

She shook her head and angrily swiped the tears away. "Please don't lie. It's beneath you." He regretted what was the most beautiful night of her life and it killed her.

"I won't." Cameron jumped up and strode toward her and grasped both of her hands. "I enjoyed every moment of our night together. You know that, but I would be lying to you if I said I wanted this marriage."

"Then don't do it. You can just leave and go away." Though it would break her heart to never see him again.

Cameron shook his head. "Khalil has made it very clear he will accept nothing less than our marriage. He said it's the only way to prevent further shame and embarrassment from coming to you or the crown. I don't want that for you or him, not when he's trying to stabilize the country. I did this. I can make it right."

Amani tilted her chin up to look at him. "You weren't in that harem, alone. I know you both think I'm a naïve, but I knew what I was doing, and I didn't care. I wanted you."

Cameron's eyes darkened at her words and Amani was thankful because although he didn't love her and he never wanted to get married, he desired her. She could work with that. Standing on her tippy toes, she brushed her lips against his. Once, and then twice, before Cameron grasped her and slanted his lips across hers and plundered her.

AMANI PARTED her lips as Cameron thrust his probing tongue inside her mouth. Their tongues twined and meshed together in mutual hunger. She tipped her head back, allowing him to lean in and take what he wanted. The softness of her mouth, the slight quiver of her body, the sweetness of her tongue had desire leaping throughout every cell of Cameron's body.

He wanted her, and that's why he grasped both of Amani's shoulders and set her away from him. Both of their breathing was coming in rapid bursts as they stared at one another.

Damn it! This is how they'd gotten here to begin with, and now they were being forced to marry. "I'm going to my room to pack," Cameron said. "You should do the same."

"But…"

"For once, don't argue, Amani!" Cameron said. "Khalil gave

us an hour. I suggest we're both ready by then." He didn't hazard a second glance at her. Otherwise, he was afraid of what he might see. What he might do, like take her over to that bed and bury himself in her and hope this morning was a nightmare he would wake up from, but it wasn't.

He'd selfishly taken something he wanted, which should have been reserved for the man Amani was going to marry, a man who would love her. Now he would have to pay the ultimate price and give up his bachelorhood.

He walked past Amani's stunned face and headed to his quarters. He needed time alone to gather himself and figure out what came next.

A marriage ceremony, according to Khalil. How could he marry Amani when he didn't even have his own shit together? He was still figuring out what to do with himself now that the Air Force was no longer an option. And now, the one job he had, he'd fucked up by sleeping with the woman he was supposed to be protecting.

Could he be any more of a screwup?

He was used to having his life in order. He had a plan and he'd followed it to the letter, but now the direction he had set for his life had gone completely off the rails and Cameron didn't know what to do next.

Khalil might force this arranged marriage, but Cameron had nothing to offer Amani. Not love. Not companionship. Not even stability. He and Amani would need to have a long talk about the future and what he was and was not capable of. He didn't want her getting any false illusions that he would ever be able to offer her love and affection. All he could offer her was good sex because they had chemistry in spades, and better she understand that now than hope for anything more because he wasn't capable of giving her anything else.

"Amani, are you all right?" Nadia inquired, coming into the suite after Cameron had gone. "The King's aide, Omar, informed me that you and Cameron are to be married and that I needed to pack our things and have you on the plane within the hour."

Amani sat shell-shocked on the couch, reliving the past half hour. She couldn't believe that Khalil, of all people, was enforcing some medieval law to make Cameron marry her. It was downright archaic. So what if she gave her virginity to Cameron? It was hers to give. She'd wanted him from the first moment he'd walked into the palace and she'd enjoyed the heaven she'd found in his arms.

But now?

She had no clue what was going to happen next.

Nadia rushed to her side. "Amani, did you hear a word I've said?"

Amani blinked Nadia into focus and saw her maid's stricken expression. "Y-yes, I did. I'm just trying to wrap my head around the fact that I'm going to be Cameron's wife."

"It's what you wanted, yes? Or you wouldn't have spent the night with him?" Nadia replied.

"I— I didn't want this. I wanted a break from being a princess for one night. I wanted to enjoy life on my own terms. I guess that was too much to ask because my brother is laying down the law and forcing Cameron to marry me all because he dared to sleep with me. It's so humiliating."

"Amani, I warned you that the path you were taking wasn't going to end well."

Amani laughed wryly. "Yeah, and I didn't listen. Now, I'm about to be shackled to a man who hates the idea of marriage. How long before he hates me because I'm the reason he was forced into this?"

Nadia shrugged. "I wish I knew, Amani, but alas, I must get you ready for the plane. We don't want to keep the King waiting."

"No, of course, we don't," Amani responded and sat despondently on the couch while Nadia fluttered around the room gathering all her belongings. A half hour later, Cameron knocked on her door to fetch her.

"Are you ready?" he inquired. His face was stony and his eyes were devoid of emotion.

Amani nodded and walked by his side as they went down the corridor. It wasn't until she heard Soraya's voice that she spun around. She'd completely forgotten about the wedding and her best friend because she'd been so caught up in a nightmare of her own making.

Soraya rushed toward Amani with Sheikh Jamal right behind her. She grasped both of Amani's hands. "Is it true? Are you and Cameron to be married?" Soraya glanced back and forth between them.

"I'm afraid so," Amani replied. She noticed Jamal walk over to Cameron and the two men moved several feet away. She couldn't hear what they were saying.

"Oh, Amani!" Soraya wrapped her arms around her shoulders and Amani forced herself to remain calm and not give into the histrionics threatening to bubble up inside her. "Are you sure about this?" Soraya whispered. "If you need my or Jamal's help to extricate you from this, we'll do whatever we can."

Amani shook her head feverishly. "No. I have to do this. If I don't, it will bring shame to my kingdom and my family. It's hard enough already with rumblings that Khalil isn't fit to rule. I can't upset the apple cart anymore than I already have."

"What were you thinking?"

Tears welled in Amani's eyes and she fought them back by

biting her lip until she tasted blood. "I wasn't thinking. I was *feeling.*"

"I know this marriage isn't ideal for you both, but perhaps in time, love might grow between you?" Soraya offered.

Amani gave a half-hearted smile. Her friend was a hopeless romantic because she'd found her great love. It wouldn't be that way with Cameron. Amani was a noose being put around his neck, shackling him into marriage. "I have to go. The King is waiting."

Soraya squeezed her hand. "Please call me if you need me."

Amani glanced at Sheikh Jamal who had a somber expression. "I wouldn't dream of it. Enjoy your honeymoon. I'm so happy for you both. My apologies for having caused you any trouble."

Jamal placed his arm around Soraya. "We wish you both well."

Minutes later, Cameron was tucking Amani into the limousine parked at the palace entrance and climbing in beside her while Nadia sat across from them. Gone was the formality of Cameron sitting upfront with the royal guard. He was to be her husband, but what did that mean?

She had no idea. It wasn't like they actually had a moment to talk about it. Khalil delivered his edict and they had no choice but to follow. Amani folded her arms in her lap and tried to remain calm, but it was hard to do. She was filled with anxiety about what came next.

Cameron, however, seemed as calm as a cucumber. He sat beside her stoically as if it were every day he was asked to marry his virgin lover. She wanted to mess up his calm demeanor, but didn't want an audience when she did. She would have to bide her time. When they were alone, she would come out swinging and find out exactly where her fiancé stood on this new marriage.

17

―――――

Cameron was quiet and reflective on the plane ride back to Bahara. Multiple times he'd had to stop himself from clenching his fists. True to his word, Khalil had waited for them at the plane and even now, Cameron sensed his censure from across the jet even though Khalil acted as if he were deep in his work. Or maybe he was putting his guilt onto his friend? Although he wasn't the injured party, Cameron was the one being forced to give up his freedom to appease Khalil's sense of duty.

As much as he enjoyed the sex with Amani, and their chemistry was explosive, he didn't *want* to marry her or anyone else, for that matter. Amani was beautiful, enchanting, and alluring, but she was also headstrong and willful. Their *marriage* wouldn't be an easy one. Amani would push him at every turn, which is why he needed to lay some ground rules so there were no misunderstandings, but they weren't alone on the plane. Cameron wondered if Khalil had purposely ensured that.

Why? Did he think Cameron incapable of keeping his hands to himself?

Maybe.

Earlier, when Amani talked about how much she wanted him, he'd been unable to stop himself from kissing her. But he had halted the intimacy when common sense prevailed. Is that what should have happened last night? Should he have walked away when Amani grasped his hand and led him to the harem?

He hadn't. Instead, he'd let the incendiary chemistry between them close around him, and he'd taken her three times last night. He spared her a cursory glance and found Amani reading her tablet. However, as if sensing his gaze, she glanced up at him and smiled. It was an innocent smile. The smile of a woman who had no idea of the sacrifice they would be required to make after she'd requested he make love to her, *with her*.

Cameron looked away and when he did, he found Khalil scowling at him. He knew his friend was upset with him and disappointed in the way he'd behaved. Cameron had no recourse but to accept his disdain because he'd made his bed and now he would have to lie in it.

IN JUST UNDER TWO HOURS, they landed back in Bahara and everything moved at breakneck speed. Too swiftly for Amani. Khalil was barking out orders which they were expected to obey without question. She and Cameron were summoned to his office where he'd given them their instructions. They would be married tomorrow with a press release going out later today announcing Princess Amani's marriage to Cameron. The union should look like a love match and that Amani had fallen head over heels for a foreigner.

A photographer and journalist would be allowed to attend the ceremony to document the wedding and assure its legitimacy. Khalil would stand in as best man and Nadia would stand in as the second witness. After the ceremony, there would be a small reception.

Khalil went on tell Amani that a selection of dresses would be brought to her suite later this afternoon for her to choose from. He also told them that her suite would be moved to a different side of the palace as benefitting a married woman, giving her and Cameron privacy.

"And what of my position here?" Cameron inquired.

"Naturally, it's terminated," Khalil responded. "As Amani's husband, you will be given title of Prince consort and be expected to carry on royal functions and duties like any other member of the royal family."

"And if I choose not to?" Cameron asked, and Amani couldn't resist the gasp that escaped her lips.

Her brother's eyes narrowed. "That isn't up for discussion, Cameron. Perhaps if you'd thought of the consequences of your actions, we wouldn't be in this position."

Amani felt the tension emanating from Cameron by her side and from the angry expression on Khalil's face, she worried they might come to blows.

"Is there anything else, your Royal Highness?" Amani replied, hoping to stop the interaction. "Or can we both leave?"

"There's nothing further."

"Excellent." Amani turned to Cameron. "Can I speak to you alone?"

"I don't think that's a wise idea," Khalil responded.

"She didn't ask you," Cameron replied, glaring at Khali. "And, yes, I think we should speak privately."

Amani spun on her heel and Cameron followed her out. They walked in silence to her old suite which would soon be changing. She suspected Cameron was about to explode. She doubted Cameron was used to being told what to do, especially regarding his life.

Once they were in the safety of her suite, Cameron let loose. "Of all the high-handed…" He started to speak, but then noticed Nadia was standing in front of two large racks which held wedding dresses of all shapes, sizes and materials. "Oh, I'm sorry, Nadia."

"It's no problem." Nadia bowed, backing away toward her room. "I will leave you both."

Seconds later, the door to her adjoining room closed and it was just Amani and Cameron who paced the floor. Tension ebbed off his broad shoulders and Amani wasn't sure what to do about it. She was already nervous about the prospect of marrying Cameron and what that might mean.

On the plane ride, Cameron had sat silent and brooding for most of the journey. His gaze was fixed on the view outside the windows as if the land below were the most beautiful thing he'd ever seen when Amani knew that wasn't true. He hated flying, but their predicament must have been foremost in his mind.

After Nadia had gone, Amani walked over to the sofa and sat, folding her hands in her lap. "Cameron, can we talk?"

He stopped pacing long enough to see her and said, "Of course. I think that's wise."

She motioned to the chair across from her and he took a seat. "I know all of this is my fault because I kept coming on to you, kept pushing you…" she began.

"It's not your fault, Amani. I'm a grown man. I knew what I was doing."

Well, that was a relief, but it didn't make her feel any better. "I know marriage isn't something you wanted, but I'm hoping we can make the best of it."

"And how do you suppose we do that?" Cameron asked.

"Well, for starters I can help you with transitioning to royal life. You weren't born here so I know there will be a lot of changes and challenges for you, but I will be here to help. We can get you some protocol training and..."

"Amani, stop it!" Cameron snapped. "That's not why you wanted to talk to me and we both know it. You want to know if this marriage will be a real one."

Amani lowered her head. How did he manage to read her so easily? She did want to know what their union might look like. She glared up at him. "Yes, I do. Is that so wrong? You didn't speak to me at all on the plane."

"How could I with Khalil glaring at me?"

"He's not now."

Cameron let out a long sigh. "No, he isn't." He rose from the chair and came over to sit beside Amani on the couch. "As you know, marriage was never in the cards for me. It's not something I've ever wanted, not anymore."

Meaning, he once did? What changed his mind? Amani wondered, but she was too afraid to ask.

"I didn't know what I was going to do with my life after I stopped being your guard, but it appears as if my destiny is to become a royal of Bahara. So I guess that gives me some direction."

"And us?" Amani asked. "What about us?"

"What are you asking me, Amani?"

"What will our marriage look like? Do you just see it as one of duty to the crown? Or will there be more?" She hated that she sounded so whiny and needy. Instead of the strong woman she knew she was. The woman who chose to decide what to do with her own body instead of letting others dictate who she would wed.

"Amani." Cameron took her hand in his, and just as it always did previously, her breath caught in her chest. "The chemistry between us is insane. Clearly, I've been unable to control it, despite my best efforts. So, to answer your question about more,

I intend this marriage to be a real one. Meaning, we will share a bed."

Amani searched his eyes and realized he was holding back. "But?" She asked the word lingering in the air around them.

"But if you're looking for love, I'm unable to offer you that." He glanced up into her eyes and his eyes held remorse, but it didn't make Amani feel any better that he was crushing her dreams and hopes for the future.

"Perhaps in time, you could come to—" she began, but Cameron placed his finger on her lips.

"Don't say it, Amani. Listen, I'm not capable of much more than the physical side of our relationship."

"I see." Her lips thinned into a line and she snatched her hand out of his. "You will stand beside me and fulfill your duty in public and in the bedroom, but I don't get your heart?"

"You make it sound callous!"

"Isn't it?" Amani asked. "It's like I'm getting half a husband."

"I never asked for any of this, Amani," Cameron responded tightly. "I'm doing the best I can under the circumstances. Khalil is furious with me and demanded I put a ring on your finger. I will because it's the right thing to do."

"Everyone gets what they want, but me!" Amani cried, jumping to her feet. "Khalil gets to clean up the mess I made by marrying me off and wrapping this up like some perfect bow around a gift. You, get a warm body in your bed every night. But I, I get to be in a loveless marriage!"

"As if that wouldn't have happened," Cameron responded and it was like he'd sent an arrow through her chest. "You were always going to be in an arranged marriage, Amani. At least you know me."

"Do I?" She couldn't stop the hysteria coming into her voice. "Do I really know you, Cameron? You refuse to let me in or tell me anything about yourself other than the bare facts. I have no idea what happened or who hurt you to make you feel this way."

Cameron threw his hands up in air. "And I don't have to tell you. I get to have a past, Amani, that has nothing to do with you."

"Clearly." She rolled her eyes as angry tears spilled down her cheeks. "Just go, Cameron. So I can find a dress and get on with this charade."

"Amani..." He came toward her and placed his hands around her shoulders.

"Don't." She shrugged him off and turned away. "You've said your peace and told me what to expect and where you stand. I'll see you at the altar."

Amani could feel Cameron behind her, willing her to turn around and face him, but she couldn't. She was embarrassed at pleading and begging him to at least consider loving her in the future. Sure, he would keep her satisfied in the bedroom, but that was all. Was she always destined to be unloved? Although she wasn't in love with Cameron, she was nearly there and had strong feelings for him, but he was intent on keeping himself at a distance.

He was unwilling to share himself with her, leaving her out in the cold and alone just as she'd always been her entire life. Why wasn't anyone capable of returning her love and affection?

WELL, that went terrible, Cameron thought to himself. Surely, he could have been more tactful and gentler with Amani? He was her first lover, after all, and she had no experience in heartbreak, not like he did. But she kept pushing him for *more* and he couldn't give her that.

He certainly wasn't about to lay his heart bare. Instead, he had to absorb what he was about to undertake. Khalil fully expected him to take the title of prince consort. Him? A prince? What the natural fuck? He was a pilot. Being behind a plane was the only thing he knew. As for being Amani's bodyguard, he'd done so out of loyalty to Khalil, but becoming part of the royal family of Bahara was quite another.

Yes, he'd been looking to find his way, but not like this. He was being handed a new career, a new life because he made the mistake of sleeping with a princess. Though, damn it, despite the hot water he found himself in, Cameron couldn't bear to think of the night he and Amani shared as a mistake.

It had been magical. Otherworldly, and he couldn't think of any other way to describe it.

Yet, as they'd driven back in the limo and finally reached the Bahara palace, Cameron had looked at the palace through different eyes, as if seeing the stunning structure with domes, minarets and towers and jeweled mosaics for the first time. This would no longer be a passing phase. He was expected to live here and call this place of palm trees and exotic flowers surrounded by fountains and waterways his home.

A line of staff had been assembled to greet Khalil and Amani. They dropped into low bows, some of them even kneeling, except this time, Cameron wasn't on the periphery checking for danger, he was part of the family. He saw the shocked gazes of the staff as he walked beside Amani not behind her. How did he, a servant, one of them, get to be with the King and Princess? It was strange to him too.

It wasn't that he thought Khalil or Amani were above him, because, quite frankly, he'd never looked at Khalil as King until today when he'd demanded or should he say, commanded Cameron marry his sister. Cameron understood the tenuous position he'd put his friend in and that he had to save face. He was trying to figure out how long he and Amani would need to stay married. Couldn't they quietly divorce or even annul the marriage in a year once the dust had settled?

He wanted to bring the idea up to Khalil, but the plane ride hadn't been right time. Maybe it was now. They'd always shared an easy rapport. Cameron hoped now that he was calm, common sense would prevail.

When he arrived at Khalil's office, however, Omar stopped him. "His Highness is busy with other matters."

"Surely not too busy for me." Cameron started toward the door, but Omar blocked his path. "Step aside."

"The King made it very clear he didn't wish to be disturbed. He's had a lot to deal with after what occurred between you and the princess last night." The censure in Omar's tone was evident.

He knew? Did everyone? Is that why there were all looking at him because he wasn't royalty and had sullied Amani's good name? Well, that was too damn bad. He was here to stay, *at least for a while,* and they were all going to have to get used to it.

"I'm aware and that's why I need to speak with him," Cameron said. He could easily push past the man but was trying to be reasonable. "If you could spare fifteen minutes on his calendar, I would appreciate it."

Omar huffed, but then strode to his desk to ring Khalil. Cameron couldn't hear what was said on the other side, but he was granted an audience.

Cameron knocked on the door and upon hearing Khalil's booming voice, walked in.

"Cameron. I would think you would be getting ready for your wedding and moving your things into the East Wing."

"Khalil." Cameron walked toward the desk Khalil was residing behind. "C'mon, can't we talk like friends?"

Khalil cocked his head to one side. "You mean the friend whose sister you slept with behind his back? Do you mean that friend?"

Cameron took that barb on the chin. He deserved it. Khalil had every right to be upset. "I've come to talk to you about this marriage."

"It's happening, Cameron. You're not changing my mind on that score."

"I didn't think I was. However, I wanted to discuss the duration of said union. How soon before we could divorce or annul?"

"Divorce? Annul?" Khalil parroted the words back at him. "Neither of those have happened in the royal family."

"Doesn't mean it can't happen."

"Not on my watch." Khalil's eyes were shrewd as they surveyed him. "This marriage is for real, Cameron, and lasting. I recognize you have an aversion to the institution but that changes nothing. Once you and Amani are married, you'll be expected to have children, heirs for the throne."

"C-children? No one said anything about children." Cameron could feel his chest constricting and he was having trouble breathing.

"What did you expect was going to happen, when you chose to lie down with my sister?"

I wasn't thinking, Cameron thought, but that wouldn't settle well with Khalil. He would only think he'd used Amani which wasn't true.

Khalil rose to his feet and came toward him, settling a large hand on his shoulder. "You're embarking on a new life, Cameron. I need you to accept it for your own and Amani's sake."

Cameron jerked away. "How dare you say that when you're the one enforcing this— this arrangement? You know what I've been dealing with the last year."

"I do. You've been adrift for months. Perhaps now having a course set for you will help you get on with life, move forward."

"Don't condescend to me, Khalil."

"I'm not, but you shouldn't forget I'm not just Amani's brother, I'm King of Bahara. I decreed marriage as the lesser of two evils. In some parts of this country, they might have ordered your execution."

"You're being overly dramatic."

"Think what you wish, but in," Khalil glanced down at his watch, "in twenty-four hours' time, you will be married to my sister and you'd damn well better keep your end of the bargain."

Cameron nodded. "Since I'm no longer speaking to my friend, but the King, I'll take my leave. However, I have two requests. The first, is I need a jeweler here so I can select Amani's ring, which I will pay for."

Khalil nodded. "It will be done. And the second?"

"I'd like some time alone with Amani, a honeymoon if you will. We have some things to hash out without prying eyes."

"I can have Omar arrange for you both to go to our summer house for a week. It's quite private. When you return, I'll need you to be ready to face your fate."

"I'll take that under advisement." Cameron turned to go, but then he heard Khalil's parting words.

"Don't hurt her, Cameron."

Cameron wasn't sure he could keep that promise. He would marry her as expected, but as for the rest, they were in for a bumpy road.

18

The morning of her wedding, Amani's anxiety was at an all-time high. She had no time to adjust to the reality of her situation, let alone speak with Khalil about an alternative. When she'd called later yesterday and encountered Omar, he'd told her Cameron had already left after speaking with Khalil, which meant any hope of changing her brother's mind on this farce of a marriage had been met with a brick wall.

She and Cameron would be wed.

A ring box was delivered to her which would house the wedding band she'd place on his finger. It was a simple platinum ring, but Cameron was anything but. Amani was afraid of what lie ahead, but that didn't stop the process.

The palace was already hard at work moving them to the East Wing where they would have more privacy. She no longer needed Nadia as a maid, but Amani refused to let her go. Nadia was the one constant she had in her life, so she would be housed down the hall from their suite.

"Are you all right, Amani?" Nadia asked as she put the finishing touches on Amani's sophisticated updo. Nadia had completed Amani's makeup and added mascara and kohl eyeliner to emphasize her brown eyes, blush to her cheekbones and several swipes of dark red lipstick to her full lips.

"I'm fine," Amani replied, but she didn't recognize the woman staring back at her. She looked different. Mature. Maybe she was. She'd made a decision that impacted her entire life and tied her to the one man she would give anything to see her as a woman and not the obligation he was tied to.

"Are you ready to get into your dress?"

Amani nodded and slid the silk robe from her shoulders. As an ode to her wedding, she'd put on some sexy lingerie she purchased on a trip with Soraya months ago. Soraya had been looking for her trousseau while Amani was hoping to get Cameron to notice her.

She had.

But it hadn't turned out the way Amani envisioned.

Stepping into the white silk confection, she eased the sleeves up her shoulders and Nadia zipped her up. She couldn't fault the designer who'd sent over the dress. It was absolutely lovely. It was demure at ankle-length, yet hugged all her curves and showed a slight swell of cleavage. She was pleased with her appearance, but how would Cameron feel? Khalil was foisting her on him like she was a piece of chattel to move about.

Nadia informed her there were already whispers around the palace of possible inappropriate behavior between her and Cameron. How else to explain his elevated status from body-guard to fiancé of a princess? No one knew for sure because her rebellion occurred in Faharat. The wedding would hopefully curtail any speculation the Royal Council and the rest of the court might have about their fast union.

A knock sounded on her door.

"Come in," Amani said.

Khalil walked through the door and Amani was stunned. She didn't think she would see him until she was at the altar. "I thought you might have some stage fright, so I came to collect you."

"To ensure I go through with the wedding?"

Khalil shook his head. "I've no doubt you will do your duty and obey your King, Amani. Rather, I thought you might have some nerves which I was hoping to allay."

"Unless you're a magician, Khalil, I don't see that happening."

A frown marred his golden features. "You know this is the right thing to do, Amani."

"Do I? You haven't exactly given me a chance to catch my breath before you shoved an unwilling husband down my throat."

Khalil sighed. "I'm sorry you feel that way, but your reckless actions required I move swiftly."

"Was it so bad to want something for myself before I tied myself down to a dynastic marriage? Of course, that's a moot point now."

"Cameron is a good man. He'll do right by you."

"Exactly what a girl wants to hear on her wedding day."

Khalil glanced down at his watch. "I'm sorry, but it's time. We must go."

Amani spun around and glanced at the room that had been her home since childhood. In less than an hour, her life would be altered drastically and she doubted it was for the better. "Very well." She took Khalil's proffered arm and together they walked out of her room and toward her uncertain future.

CAMERON WATCHED Amani walk down the aisle toward him in the rotary room of the palace. His heart constricted in his chest and his breath hitched in his throat. She'd never looked lovelier.

She was dressed in an elegant white dress which hit her ankles, but he was more interested in how it clung to her curvaceous body in a seductive embrace that begged a man to do the same. Her hair was caught up in curls atop her head in an intricate updo. Simple pearls adorned her ears and her makeup was simple yet tasteful.

All he could do was stare. The desire to possess her and make her his in the most primal way possible as he'd done in the harem raged through him. However, it was her face he noticed as she came closer. Her features were distant and untouchable and he could tell the smile on her face was forced. He knew how Amani looked when she was happy.

Amani was concerned about what their marriage would be like and Cameron wished he could have assured her that all would be fine, but he wasn't certain. After Monae and his mother's deception and betrayal, he'd decided that matrimony was the last thing he wanted and that he would remain single. Fate, however, had other plans and now he stood watching the most beautiful woman he'd ever laid his eyes on walk toward him. Toward their destiny.

When she reached him and the officiant who'd been brought in to preside over the proceedings, Amani offered him a weak smile. Surprising himself, Cameron reached for her hand and enfolded it in his as a way to comfort her. Amani looked up at him with those big brown eyes that still held hope for the future. He hoped the light wouldn't go out in them once they were wed.

Her hands were soft and trembling, but Amani didn't pull away from him. Instead, they held hands during the course of the short ceremony. Cameron spoke his vows as clear as he could, but Amani's voice wavered and he wondered if she would finish, but she continued allowing them to exchange rings. Cameron had precious little time to find the perfect ring for his new wife, but he'd been determined to pay for it himself.

When the jeweler arrived at his suite a couple of hours ago, Cameron had been impressed with the selection of baubles. He'd eventually settled on a cushioned diamond floating on a double halo which he placed on Amani's finger. She, in turn, placed a simple platinum band on his hand which Cameron had sent over to Amani's suite earlier. Then the officiant declared them husband and wife.

Cameron curved his arm around Amani's waist and drew her to him. He captured her satiny soft lips in his, a demonstration of how good it would be between them — at least he could give her this. When he lifted his head, her pupils were dilated and filled with desire. Later, he would fulfill the promise lurking in those depths.

AMANI WAS STILL SHAKEN after Cameron pulled away from their kiss and shook the officiant's hand, and Khalil's. She'd done her duty for her country and to protect her brother's reign and consequently shackled herself to a man who would never love her.

"There will be official photos now," Khalil said with a smile that she was certain was more for the journalist and photographer present than for her. "And then there will be a wedding lunch with a few friends, family and members of the Royal Council. I'm sorry I wasn't able to get your family here on such short notice, Cameron."

"It's fine," Cameron responded tightly.

Amani wondered what their wedding might have looked like if he'd been marrying her for love and his family were present, but it didn't matter now. Cameron offered her his arm and she had no choice but to accept it. She doubted many people would be at the lunch, at least from her side, since both her mother and Malik were killed in the helicopter crash. Perhaps there were some distant cousins curious to see who the Princess of Bahara had rushed into marriage with.

The photo session took over an hour and Amani found her head was throbbing at having to smile and force a bright happiness she didn't feel. When it was over, the journalist and photographer withdrew until the reception, leaving them a few minutes to gather their wits.

Once Cameron had finally moved away, Nadia produced some aspirin from her purse and Amani quickly downed them with a bottle of water. It had been agony standing beside him because she knew Cameron felt nothing for her.

Sure, he desired her. That was evident in the way he looked at her when she walked toward him in the rotary room, but he didn't *feel* anything for her, while she certainly had developed strong feelings. Amani didn't think those feelings were love, but they were still quite real and frightening. She would endeavor to keep them to herself so Cameron didn't feel as if she were expecting something he was incapable or unwilling to give. She had her pride, after all.

Suddenly, Cameron left Khalil's side and came toward her with a frown his face. "Are you feeling okay?"

Had he been watching her? "Pardon?"

"I saw Nadia give you some pills."

"How very observant of you," Amani quipped and saw his brow furrow in consternation.

"I was worried."

"I'm fine, just a headache," Amani responded. "Can we continue on with this charade?"

"Amani, what's done is done. You and Cameron are wed," Khalil stated, from behind him, "I suggest you accept that fact."

Amani tried not to glare at him since they had an audience watching their every move. "You don't get to control how I feel, Khalil. I've done as you demanded. We," she glanced at Cameron, "we both have."

Khalil turned on his heel and strode out of the room with Omar close on his heels. Nadia looked at Amani and she gave a slight nod, so her maid departed and they were alone. Amani started toward the door, but Cameron grasped her hand.

"I know this isn't what you wanted, Amani, but surely we can make the best of it and get through today?"

"That's exactly what I'm doing, Cameron. Let's go." And without further ado, she exited the room. She didn't check to see if Cameron was following her.

The remainder of the afternoon was filled with Amani playing princess, something she'd been bred to do her entire life. She knew how to play that role and when to speak and smile when needed. What she didn't know was her role as a wife and what that would look like other than Cameron wanting an available body in his bed. And since she'd been eager for him to take her virginity, she was certain he was gung-ho.

And while she wanted him, *desired* him, Amani also wanted more. However, Cameron had been right when he said she would have married a stranger, been intimate with one. Her heart quivered in her chest at the very thought. She'd wanted to choose and she had. She just never thought, she'd end up here, married to a man she lusted after, had feelings for, who only wanted her for her body.

After hours of keeping an adoring-wife smile plastered on her face, she stiffened when Cameron came over to her and murmured in her ear. "Are you ready to go?"

Amani nodded. "Yes."

"Great. Let's head out."

They paid their respects to Khalil as King, said goodbye to

several members of the Royal Council who all held suspicious looks. She was certain they were worried about the political ramifications of her union, given she wasn't marrying a man with a royal title and had married an American.

When they were in the hall, Amani assumed they were headed to their new suite in the East Wing, but Cameron led her outside instead. She tugged on his hand because all day, he'd made a habit of holding her hand. Why? It wasn't like she could run.

Amani stopped walking in the middle of the courtyard. The very same one where they'd shared their first kiss which seemed so long ago. "Where are we going?"

"Away from here," Cameron stated.

She frowned. "What do you mean?"

Cameron laughed. "We're going on a honeymoon. It's time you and I were alone and had some privacy to figure a few things out."

"And Khalil was all right with this?"

"I didn't give him an option." He held out his hand and reluctantly Amani took it. She wanted to know where they were going, but she wasn't in the mood to fight. Today had taken every ounce of her energy and strength to get through the day.

Several minutes later, they were seated in the royal helicopter and given headphones before they soared into the air. Fifteen minutes into the ride, Amani realized they were going to the summer villa by the old town. She hadn't been there in years because Malik didn't have the time once he'd ascended to the throne. She loved this place, it held so many great memories, but now?

She would be alone with her husband. For how long? She doubted Nadia would have been allowed to come over earlier so she would have to keep her wits about her. She refused to allow herself to get carried away by the fact Cameron wanted to be alone with her even though her pulse ticked at an elevated rate sitting next to him and smelling his heady cologne.

Minutes later, the helicopter touched down on a helipad in front of the house near the water. It was dreamy and gorgeous just like she remembered. The villa's décor was crisp and stylish. It was completely done in white with pops of color throughout. A few elegant sculptures and abstract artwork decorated the walls. As Cameron glanced up at the house, she hoped Cameron would love it as much as she always had.

He turned to her, looking impressed. "This place is beautiful."

She smiled genuinely for the first time all day. "C'mon, let me show you the house." This time, it was she who held out her hand to him, and he took it without hesitation.

She gave him a tour of the house, starting with the lower level which housed a spacious open aired and relaxed living room, a grand room, a dining room to seat at least twenty guests, and a massive state-of-the-art kitchen. Then she led him to a separate building connected to the main house via a shaded walkthrough.

"The suites are this way," she said.

She started with the guest rooms, each with ensuite and then she finally headed to the master bedroom. The polished wooden floors gleamed, then there were vast windows making the space light and airy. Light, neutral drapes created a soothing effect as well as giving privacy if they didn't want to view the pristine beach and beautiful azure water on the endless horizon off the terrace.

Usually Malik stayed in this room and Amani would be relegated to one of the guest rooms, except today it had been prepared for her and Cameron with dreamy and luxurious linens.

Rose petals were sprinkled in the shape of a heart on the

enormous bed. A bucket of champagne was cooling by a side table which was filled with a charcuterie board offering a variety of meats, cheese and fruits.

Amani ignored the bed and showed Cameron the ensuite bathroom and the spacious closet which, much to her shock, was already filled with several of her favorite outfits, along with some new ones she'd never seen.

She spun on her heel to face Cameron and found him watching her from the middle room. He'd taken off his suit jacket and tie and unbuttoned a few buttons on the crisp white shirt underneath. Her treacherous body reacted instantly and her nipples hardened underneath in the wedding dress. "You've been quite the tour guide. Thank you."

"I aim to please," she offered weakly. "If you don't mind, I'd love a shower and to change. It's been a long day."

A flare of desire sparked in his hazel eyes before he looked away. "Of course. I'll go and explore." Within seconds she heard the click of the door as it closed.

Amani didn't know what was going to happen next. Despite her annoyance with Cameron on his aloofness the last couple of days, would he be ready to consummate their marriage tonight?

And if he was, was she ready and willing?

19

Cameron stared out at the Mediterranean Sea from the terrace. It overlooked a garden and infinity pool that appeared to flow over the cliff's edge into the sea.

He was married. He had a wife. A beautiful, gorgeous woman who, at this very moment, was in the shower. He would have loved to join her there, but given how their marriage had started, Cameron wasn't about to start making demands. Khalil had done enough of that for the both of them from the wedding to the reception, neither of which his family had been able to attend.

He needed to share his new status with them before the news reached them in the States. How would they react? He expected shock and disappointment because they weren't present. His father, Cal, would want to know specifics on how this came about. What could he tell them? That he'd been bullied into marrying a princess whose virginity he took without any regard for the circumstances? She was supposed to marry someone with title and rank who came from royalty. Instead, she had him as a reluctant groom and husband.

Despite his antipathy toward marriage, his wife, Amani, deserved a partner she could trust, and not just with her body. He had to get out of his head. No, this wasn't the life he had wanted or expected for himself, but there was no getting around it. He was now Prince Consort of Bahara.

Pulling his phone from his pocket, he looked at the time. It was six p.m. which meant it was nine a.m. in Washington, D.C. since Bahara was nine hours ahead. He didn't particularly want to speak with his mother, but he only wanted to make this call once.

He pressed his father's cellphone for FaceTime and waited for him to pick up. Cameron was hoping he wouldn't and he could put this call off for as long as possible. Unfortunately, he didn't get his wish because Cal answered on the third ring.

"Cameron!" His father's face lit up when he saw him. "It's so good to see your face. How are you, son?"

"Is that Cameron?" He heard his mother's excited voice before he saw her standing behind his father. "Cameron, oh, my goodness."

He ignored her and continued on with the task at hand. "Listen, there's something I have to tell you before the news breaks in D.C."

"Oh, Lord," Cal sighed. "You're not in any kind of trouble over there are you? I thought you and Khalil were tight?"

"We are..." Cameron hedged.

"But there's a 'but'," his father wisely picked up on what he wasn't saying.

"Yes." Cameron inhaled deeply and glanced up. Amani was above him in the master suite and she needed him to be a husband she could look up to, maybe even lean on. "I'm married."

"Say what?" Cal asked.

"Did you say married?" his mother, Camilla, inquired.

"I did. I married Amani, Princess of Bahara."

"What?!" His father's expression was one of bewilderment. "When? How did this happen? I thought you were protecting her?"

"I was, and well, one thing led to another and well, I won't sully my wife's reputation by saying anything more."

"So this is real, son?" Cal asked.

"How could you get married, without us?" his mother, began crying in the background. "I know you hate me, but without your father? Your brothers?" Her face disappeared from the screen.

"Dad?"

"Yes, son?"

"Is she gone?"

His father nodded. "Your mother is overwhelmed and walked out of the room. So if you have more to share I'd love to hear it. I'd like to understand why you would do something so drastic without your family."

"I didn't have much of a choice. Khalil found out that Amani and I had been, um, intimate, and, well, given their culture and her innocence, he pretty much demanded that I make an honest woman out of her."

"I see. As much as I don't like his bullying tactics, I'm glad to see you did the honorable thing like I raised you."

"Of course. Amani is a wonderful woman, Dad, it's just...I didn't want to marry anyone."

"Well, that's water under the bridge now, Cameron. You have a wife. And Khalil? How's your relationship with your friend?"

"Strained," Cameron responded. "I'm hoping to repair the damage I've caused, but it won't be easy. However, he has given me a title: Prince Consort. He expects me to fulfill my duties as a member of the royal family."

"Wow, my son is a prince?"

Cameron snorted. "No, I married a princess, Dad. I'm no prince."

"Semantics," his father replied. "And Amani, how do you feel about her?"

"I'm attracted to her."

"Clearly, or you wouldn't be in the situation you're in, but that's not what I'm asking and you know it."

"If you're asking if I'm in love with her? I'm not. I care for her and I will do my best to be a good husband as much as I'm capable of."

Cal sighed. "Cameron, you can't hold on to the past. You have to move on with your life. You have a wife now that deserves your love."

"I don't think I can give it to her."

"That's what you say now, but the more you spend time with her, things could change."

"I don't think so."

"That's because you're cynical and you've hardened your heart, but the right woman can melt that ice block, but you have to be willing to allow it."

"I hear you."

"When we can we meet Amani?"

"Soon, we're on a honeymoon right now to figure out how to make this marriage work."

"I have faith in you, Cameron. There's never been anything you can't do when you set your mind to it."

"Thanks, Dad. I appreciate that. Can you tell Caden and Cage for me? I know they'll have questions, but I need to focus on Amani right now."

"Of course. I love you, Cameron."

"Love you too." He ended the call.

Was his father right? Was it possible he could fall in love

with Amani? If ever there was a woman capable of breaching the wall he erected around his heart, it might be her. He just wasn't sure he was ready to be that vulnerable again. It hurt too much.

God, how in the hell was he supposed to make this work?

AMANI HEARD every word from the second-floor balcony above Cameron. She was happy he'd told his parents, but then he shared with his father, the real reason they'd married. And when his dad had asked how he felt about her, Cameron hadn't even tried to lie or act as if he cared an ounce about her. All she was to him was duty and honor. It was a bitter pill to swallow.

When she'd been in the shower, she'd tried to look on the bright side. Tonight, they would consummate their marriage. Perhaps, she could reach him in the bedroom and get him to let her in. She'd taken the pins out of her hair and ran her fingers through it, leaving it down. Then she'd put on a beautiful red silk baby doll with matching panties. The nightie came to the tops of her thighs, while the top had her generous breasts spilling out.

But after hearing Cameron talk to his father, she was feeling anything but romantic. Instead, she'd taken off the contraption and placed it in the back of the closet out of view and instead put on a loungewear set of soft cotton. She needed the armor because right now she felt vulnerable. Cameron had all the experience whereas she had none. She was sitting on one of the sofas and starting to nibble on the charcuterie board when Cameron returned.

He was carrying two wine glasses, a bottle of white wine and a wine opener. "Care for some wine?"

Amani nodded. "That would be lovely, thank you."

Cameron joined her on the sofa and, after uncorking the bottle, poured them each a glass. He handed her one. "Cheers!" He tapped his glass against hers.

"Cheers!" Amani gave him one of her practiced smiles.

Cameron frowned. "Don't do that."

"Do what?"

"Give me the fake smile you give to everyone else when you don't want them to know what you're really thinking. I've seen you do it before. Today, it was in full force."

How did he know she did that? She always used it as a shield. She'd been taught at a young age not to trust the public because they might use anything against the royal family. She'd had to insulate herself to ensure she didn't get hurt. She never suspected anyone knew her secret.

She went on the attack. "You don't know what you're talking about."

Cameron put down the wineglass he'd been sipping, leaving it on the table. "Yes, I do. While I've been watching everyone else around you, Amani, for the last three months, I've also been watching you, too. What don't you want me to know?"

"I'm telling you, what I told Khalil. You don't get to control me or know my innermost thoughts."

"That's not what I'm trying to do. You're deliberately picking a fight with me when I was merely being observant. I thought you would appreciate that."

"What I would appreciate is a husband who *wanted* to be with me."

Cameron sucked in a deep breath. "So we're back to this!" He jumped to his feet and stared down at her. "I'm here, aren't I? What more do you want from me, Amani?"

Amani jumped up as well. "Nothing, I want nothing that is

not freely given, which I'm obviously not going to get. Because you're not even willing to soften your heart and let me in."

Amani knew she'd said the wrong thing because Cameron's eyes narrowed. "Were you listening to my conversation with my father? That was private!"

"I— I wasn't trying to. I came out for some fresh air and heard voices."

"So you decided to listen to our conversation?"

"Don't put this back on me," Amani replied, narrowing her eyes. "You're the one who said you didn't want this marriage. You don't want me."

"Don't want you?" Cameron charged toward her. "Wanting you is what got us in this predicament. And since we were together, I can't stop thinking about *wanting you.*"

Amani sucked in a deep breath and she could feel the peaks of her breasts turning hard at his words. As if he had some sort of radar, his gaze settled on the rapid fall of her chest. Before she knew it, she was in Cameron's arms and he was covering her mouth with his in an explosive kiss. He pushed his tongue between her lips as if he'd forgotten the taste of her.

Then his hands were reaching for the bottom of her tunic and pushing it up and over her head until his fingertips could connect to her naked flesh. The air felt cool against her exposed breasts. She wasn't wearing a bra because she'd wanted to be comfortable.

Cameron's hazel eyes turned nuclear and then he was bending to take one hard peak into the heat of his mouth and sucking her deep into his mouth.

A low moan escaped her lips, especially when he gently nipped at the flesh and then gave it wet lashes with his tongue, sending liquid heat pooling straight to her core. He didn't stop with one breast. Instead, he switched his attention to its engorged chocolate twin and administered the same sweet torture.

"You're always *so* responsive," he growled.

Abandoning her breasts, Cameron kissed his way down her abdomen until he came to her pants. He swiftly pulled them and her panties down her legs in one movement until she was naked and could step out of them. Then he was pushing her backward to the low sofa.

Amani glanced up to watch Cameron stripping out of his clothes, and all the while, his impatient and greedy eyes ate up her naked body lying on the couch. When his glorious body was finally revealed, she opened her arms to him and he dropped down to join her on the couch, covering her body with his. Then he was kissing her fiercely and his hand was spreading her legs wider apart so he could cup her hot, aching flesh in the most intimate of caresses.

She gasped when she felt Cameron parting her slick folds and filling her with one of his long fingers. She could feel her own wetness as her muscles quickly clenched around him. He withdrew his fingers and she gave a sob of disappointment, but then he was right back, filling her again and starting a rhythm that had her hips chasing his hand. And when he added another digit and then a third, his thick and powerful fingers stretching her, Amani was a goner.

Her insides tightened as he worked her, pushing her closer to the edge. She was nearly there when he found her clitoris and moved erotically over it, arousing her to a fever pitch, but then he slowed down the pace. Amani wanted more.

She must have verbalized her request because he asked, "You want me to let you come?"

"*Yes.*"

He shook his head. "The only way you're coming is if I'm inside of you."

Amani answered by wrapping her legs around his waist.

He laughed. "You're eager."

She was. The staff were gone for the evening, so they had the place to themselves. There was no fear of discovery or danger. They were free to explore each other freely.

"Wait, love." Cameron reached for his trousers and pulled out a foil packet.

"But we're married."

"And we haven't discussed children yet," Cameron responded. "Let's not rush things."

Amani nodded. She hadn't thought of that, and she should have, but she couldn't think clearly. "I just want you inside me."

"Your wish is my command."

Seconds later, she felt the head of his erection as he slid inside her. She exhaled. "God, you're so big." Although they'd already been together a few times, she was still new to this. "I can feel you everywhere."

"And you're still so tight," he murmured. His lips took hers in a low, slow kiss as he eased forward another inch, then another, until he was seated fully inside her.

"You feel *so good.*" Shudders racked Cameron's body and Amani was glad she could make him lose control too. He gripped her hips and began to move fiercely within her, rocking forward and backward, once, twice, setting a steady rhythm. His palms slid beneath her buttocks, lifting her higher to find the exact spot to give her the most pleasure.

"So good," she moaned, "don't stop." It was mind-blowing. She didn't know if it was because he was her husband now and was hers alone, or because the sex was just that good.

She clung to him, so that he could thrust harder and faster. Hot, white lightning radiated through her and her female muscles, as if programmed to obey, followed suit and contracted around him. Cameron was right there with her as a low growl escape his throat and he came.

When the tremors finally subsided, Cameron picked her up and carried her to bed and that's where she lay, her head on his chest until unconsciousness claimed her.

20

Their weeklong honeymoon was everything Amani could have asked for. Their mornings were spent waking up in each other's arms. Some mornings, they took breakfast on the terrace before going for a swim or lounging about. Other times, they stayed in bed and made love until they were both sweaty and exhausted and in need of a shower. Of course, showering together was the last thing they needed because the experience usually turned to a sensual one in which one or the other found themselves on their knees.

Amani found she enjoyed giving her husband oral sex. It wasn't something she'd been particularly interested in when she read it in her romance novels. However, she loved bringing Cameron pleasure. It was both humbling and incredibly satisfying. She no longer felt awkward about what to do in bed. Cameron taught her all the ways to please him and she was learning all the erogenous zones on her body that she never knew she had.

Every night with Cameron was a sexual awakening and now they were seated across from each other having a candlelight dinner on the terrace that the staff had prepared. They only had two more honeymoon nights left together. Then, it would be back to reality and the pressures of royal life. They'd stayed away from difficult topics that might cause an argument, but Amani knew they couldn't leave here without hashing a few things out. She didn't want to argue, not when Cameron's eyes blazed at her from across the table.

"Something on your mind?" Cameron asked intuitively.

She smiled. "How can you tell?"

"Your nose crinkles and your brow furrows," Cameron replied, taking a sip of the excellent vintage the chef had suggested for their meal. It was fruity and crisp and paired well.

"Well, we've had a great week thus far, and I don't want to mess that up, but I feel compelled to discuss our marriage."

"I thought we were doing well in that department."

Amani blushed. "You know that's not what I'm talking about. There will be a lot expected of us as a royal couple. Sometimes we'll need to attend events together and sometimes apart."

Cameron placed his wineglass down. "Sounds easy enough, but I'd like to limit our time apart. We are newlyweds after all."

Amani's heart kicked over in her chest that Cameron *wanted* to spend time with her. "You'll probably need to take classes on the history of Bahara to learn our customs as well as take protocol and comportment classes."

"I figured as much," Cameron stated.

She was glad this was going so well. "Most likely, they'll give you your own assistant to help you manage your daily calendar. I have one, but we have an arm's length relationship."

"Why?"

"I'm not sure I can trust her, which is why I've always kept Nadia and she's doubled as my maid and assistant."

Cameron frowned. "Then you should get rid of her. You can't have someone working for you that you don't trust."

"But it's unheard of."

"I don't care. When we get back, we'll find you a new assistant, one that you've interviewed and that meets your expectations."

Amani nodded. "Thank you."

She hadn't expected Cameron to be on her side. She was so used to being forgotten about altogether. As the third child to the throne and a woman no less, her feelings were often over-looked. It was a refreshing change of pace.

"You don't have to thank me, Amani. I'm your husband now and I will always look out for your best interests. Was there anything else you wanted to discuss besides the business of being a royal? Something more personal perhaps?" He raised a brow.

Amani swallowed. "Since we're on the subject. Earlier in the week, you mentioned waiting for children. Is that what you want?"

Rather than answer her, Cameron stood up and walked toward her. As it always did, her breath hitched, but she didn't protest when he pulled her to her feet and led her away from the table and the half-eaten meal to some low-end white sofas that faced the Mediterranean Sea. Once there, Cameron sat down and then pulled Amani into his lap so they were facing each other.

"I think we should have this discussion somewhere less impersonal than the dinner table," Cameron replied. "And to answer your question. Since marriage wasn't on the horizon for either of us until Khalil's edict, don't you think it's prudent we wait? Get to know each other better? Spend some time alone as a couple before we bring another life into the world?"

"Yes, of course," Amani replied. "Ordinarily, I would agree, but with Khalil unmarried and with me, married, everyone will be looking to me to produce the next heir to throne — that is until Khalil marries."

"Forget about what everyone else expects," Cameron snapped back. "It's about what you and I want and what's best for our relationship. I think that's time for just us."

Amani shook her head and just laughed.

"What?" Cameron asked harshly. He was frowning and Amani sensed he was upset because she was laughing at him.

"It's just that you're nothing like us. I suppose it's because you weren't raised like I was. It's been ingrained in me that I must always think of the crown first. I've never had the luxury of thinking otherwise."

"Well, I wasn't born royal," Cameron replied, his voice softer than it was before. "I'm doing my best to roll with the punches, but I'm not used to be waited on hand and foot." He motioned to the staff who were already coming to take away their plates. "It's going to take getting used to, but that also doesn't mean I'm going to be a pushover either."

"I get that," Amani said, "and I agree with you. I would like more time to develop our relationship. I don't even know your favorite color."

"Black."

"Your favorite food?"

"Soul food," Cameron answered, "when we visit my family in the States, I'll take you to my favorite restaurant."

"I'd like that," she replied. "When was your first kiss?" Since he was answering questions, Amani continued to press him for details.

"I was six years old," Cameron answered, "one of the girls in my kindergarten class said I was going to be her boyfriend and planted her lips on mine."

Amani couldn't resist a laugh. "Wow, even then, you made the girls go wild."

Cameron chuckled and shrugged. "Can I help it if six-year-olds fall for my charms? When was your first kiss?"

Amani's head lowered. How had this conversation turned back to her. "With you."

"Seriously? Not even when you were at college?"

Amani shook her head. "I was always surrounded by guards. Plus, no one ever moved me." *Until you.* To get the heat off of her, her next question rushed out of her mouth before she had a chance to think about it. "When did you lose your virginity?"

Cameron grinned and stroked her cheek with his palm. Amani couldn't resist closing her eyes when he did. "Oh, you want to get really personal."

She opened her eyes again. "Are you going to tell me?"

"I was sixteen," Cameron said, "Lauren was a year older than me and I'd been eyeing her. She was way out of my league, but she loved my eyes. Anyway, one day after school on the base where my father was stationed, and when her mother was gone for an appointment, she invited me over and introduced me to sex."

"How was it?"

"Honestly? I don't recall because it was over with pretty quick." At her bewildered expression, he laughed. "I didn't exactly last very long, not like I can now."

His voice had become raspier and, if Amani wasn't mistaken, she felt him swelling underneath her bosom. She looked at him from hooded lashes. "Is that so?"

"Oh, yeah. She had me over a few more times and showed me how to please her." Cameron shifted on the couch, until he was lying back against the pillows and Amani was draped over him. "How to abstain longer and how it could make the experience all the more intense."

Amani had to swallow the lump in her throat. "Sounds like you learned a lot."

Cameron's eyes darkened. "How about I show you what I learned?" His hands cradled both sides of her face bringing her mouth into contact with his, and then his lips claimed hers. When Cameron touched her she felt *alive*. More alive than she'd felt in all twenty-three years of her life. When his tongue swept across her lips demanding entry, she opened for him.

The kiss turned incendiary fast and had Amani climbing astride him. She pushed at the t-shirt Cameron was so found of wearing rather than the suits and button downs her family were so fond of. She lifted it over his broad shoulders. Then her hands swept over his biceps and onto his gorgeous chest and rippled torso.

She lowered her head and flicked her tongue across one of his nipples. When a low groan escaped his lips, she pressed open-mouthed kisses on his other pectorals. She loved his clearly defined muscles that was due to his relentless physical regime, but also it spoke of his pure, raw masculinity.

She would have reveled in him and gone lower, indulging in the hot, salty essence of him, but Cameron was pulling her up towards him in a slow lingering kiss, while simultaneously lifting the sundress she was wearing to her hips. He quickly snatched at her thong, ripping the thin fabric and tossing it to the floor. Then he reached into his pocket for a condom, slid down his joggers and sheathed his straining erection.

If he didn't want children, Amani would have to get on contraception so they could do away with the protection. She craved the fulfillment he could bring and wanted nothing between them. His tongue slid deeper into her mouth, taking possession like he always did. His hands pushed down the straps of her sundress, baring her naked breasts to him. When he skimmed the sensitive peaks with his hands, she moaned.

"Please, Cameron."

He didn't break the kiss. Instead, he slid his fingers lower to touch her intimately. He skated over her wet folds and she opened her legs wider for his teasing caress. Cameron took the hint and parted her so he could delve deeper with one finger and then two. She undulated against him. She wasn't ashamed to take her pleasure even though they were out in the open where any of the staff could see them. Instead, she let her husband caress her deeply, and when his lips left hers to suck on a sensitive spot on her neck, Amani came with a sharp cry that destroyed all her self-control.

But rather than let Amani take a moment to recover, Cameron grasped her hips and slowly lifted her down on top of his bulging erection. Amani took him deep inside her body and then leaned down to kiss him, but it was never just a kiss. Cameron made love to her mouth just like he did her body and it totally unbalanced her. She began rocking against him, slowly at first and then faster and harder as she found her own rhythm, but then Cameron took over, thrusting his hips upwards to meet hers.

Amani started to shake above him and then her orgasm struck and she convulsed around him. His name on her lips goaded him into his own release and curses escaped his lips as he pumped desperately up and into her. Even though they were still joined, Cameron wrapped his arms around her and Amani found herself relaxing against him.

How could she not have realized it sooner?

She was in love with her husband.

But he didn't love her back. Or rather, he refused to risk loving anyone. Something or someone had damaged him and Amani wished she knew why because it was holding them back from having an amazing marriage.

21

─────────

On their last day on the island, Cameron took Amani into a nearby village, a short boat ride away. He'd arranged a special day for just the two of them to explore the town with its monuments, churches, and shops and have dinner later that day in a restaurant on the top of a cliff. This would be their last private moment before he was thrust in the spotlight of being Prince Consort married to Amani Princess of Bahara.

All of the titles meant nothing to him. He didn't want them. If anything, he would take Amani and run. Cameron chuckled to himself at the thought. As if that would happen. Her brother had guards stationed all around the island. He was surprised they had the level of privacy they enjoyed at the villa, especially after last night's dinner turned into something way more.

Amani's innocent questions about his favorite color or favorite food had quickly shifted into something more sensual, something more passionate and he'd taken her right there on the sofa without removing any of her clothes save for her thong which thankfully he'd had the good sense to pocket before one of the staff found it.

The passion between them last night ignited and had been unexpected and highly erotic. She'd let him feast on those gorgeous breasts of hers while she'd rode him all the way to heaven. Starbursts had lit up behind his eyes as she'd swept him up in a storm.

Their lovemaking hadn't stopped there. He'd plundered her mouth as if she were a hidden treasure he'd found. Afterward, once upstairs in the bedroom, he'd rid her of the dress until she was naked and he'd feasted on her. He'd dropped to his knees, swept his tongue over her clitoris and drew pleasure from her until she'd shattered and cried out his name so loud, the entire house had to have heard her.

That was his Amani.

Beautiful.

Spirited.

Passionate.

Wait a minute. Had he just thought of Amani as *his?* He had. Because wasn't she? She'd never been with another man except him and she wouldn't be because they were married, but that's not the reason he'd thought it. He felt possessive about her and he'd never felt that way about another woman. Even with Monae, it had been more about a prior claim than feeling as if she was *his* woman. Amani was different. They fit together. It was like she was *made* for him.

Cameron shook his head. He had to stop thinking these romantic thoughts because they weren't going to lead anywhere. He didn't want to feel that sort of pain. He was caught up in his emotions because they'd been spending a lot of time together all week on their honeymoon. Of course, he might have feelings for her. He wasn't a robot.

He had to put things in perspective. Once they left this island and got back to normal every day duties and his new role as a royal, things would inevitably change. Then he might be able to view Amani as his incredible, sexy wife that he liked taking to bed.

Speaking of his wife. She looked H-O-T! She sat on the boat in a floral mini dress showing lots of thigh and her jet-black hair was down in soft waves framing her face just how he liked it. She wore minimal makeup and had diamond studs in her ear and, of course, she wore her wedding ring, *his ring*.

"Ready to go?" Cameron asked when the boat docked and he helped her onto the jetty. "I've quite the day planned."

Amani nodded. "I'm ready."

Cameron grasped her hand and led her to a red convertible sitting outside the door. She turned to him with wide eyes.

"Are we driving in that?"

He nodded. "Hell yes."

"And the royal guard agreed?" She glanced at the guards behind them.

Cameron snorted. "Not exactly, but they'll be following closely behind us. C'mon." He opened her car door and she slid inside. Several seconds later, he joined her in the driver's side. "Ready for a fun day?"

"Absolutely."

An hour later, after parking, they were walking through the cobble-stoned streets of the old town and holding hands as they went. The weather was at its best. The sky was an endless stretch of blue with a slight breeze taking the edge off the heat.

"This is amazing," Amani said, squeezing Cameron's arm. "I've never had freedom like this to walk like an average citizen. It's a real treat."

"I'm glad you like it." Cameron ushered her toward the old church he'd read about. They meandered through the large wooden doors and admired the architecture, artwork and craftmanship of the stained-glass windows and carvings inside. They talked about art and Cameron learned Amani had taken art history in college.

He was discovering more and more new things about her which is why he wasn't ready to start a family. Becoming a father was already a scary thought. He still had so many feelings he hadn't dealt with about his own situation, that having a family had to be pushed off as far as possible. Yes, he knew eventually, an heir would be needed, but in the interim, he and Amani needed this time to navigate their new, unplanned marriage.

Though if there was anyone he could have envisioned marrying, it was Amani. Not only was she beautiful and his match in the bedroom. She was incredibly intelligent. What she was able to accomplish with the Bedouin tribe and win their respect showed she had a lot to offer the crown, but they had to be willing to allow her to take a bigger role. Or she needed to demand it. She was more than just a pretty face.

"What are you thinking about?" Amani asked, coming over to him as he stood facing a statue.

He shrugged and grabbed her hand, pulling her into his embrace. "Just how talented my wife is."

Her brow rose. "Really?"

"You weren't daydreaming about this morning?" Amani asked and her cheeks flamed.

Cameron loved how she could still be embarrassed after the things they'd done during their week-long marriage. "As much as I enjoyed your mouth on me as I woke up this morning," he said, "I was thinking about how Khalil needs to realize what an asset you are. Yes, our marriage wasn't planned, but that doesn't mean you don't have great ideas. I hope he doesn't throw the baby out with the bath water."

"I don't understand. What does a baby in the bath water

have to do with my situation?" Amani inquired, looking completely flabbergasted.

Cameron released a loud guffaw. "It's a colloquialism."

Her mouth formed an 'o'.

~

THEY SPENT the remainder of the afternoon looking at some ancient ruins, before finally ending in town to peruse the shops. When Amani saw a bracelet she liked, she stopped to purchase it. It was simple, but she loved it all the same.

"I'll get it for you," Cameron said, pulling out his wallet, but Amani stopped him.

"That's not necessary." Then he saw a guard coming over to them and pulling out his wallet. "My allowance will cover it."

Cameron grasped the guard's card and handed it back to him. "I can buy my wife a damn gift," he said and handed the stunned clerk, his American Express.

After they paid for the item and walked outside, Amani spoke. Her eyes were rimmed with unshed tears. "I'm sorry, Cameron. I didn't mean to offend you."

"You didn't," he replied and even to him, his voice sounded strained.

"Yes, I did," she whispered, following him onto the pavement. "You're not used to the royal customs, but we don't pay for anything. It all comes with being royal and now that you're one of us, you won't have to worry about money."

Cameron's mouth firmed. "I've never had to worry about it at all, Amani. My family may not be royalty, but they do quite well and besides I've been taking care of myself since I was eighteen years old."

"Of course." Her eyes welled with tears again and Cameron felt like a heel for his harsh tone.

"I'm sorry." He pulled her to him, molding her to him until there was no room between them. He leaned his forehead down onto hers. "I'm still getting used to this royal thing, but that doesn't mean I can't buy my wife a gift. Okay?"

She nodded and he released her.

He inclined his head. "Let's go. We have a reservation for dinner at one of the best spots in town."

He grasped her hand and soon they were back in the convertible and he was whisking them to the top of the mountain to a restaurant with a killer sunset. Cameron had asked for the best table and they were led to one on the terrace with a view of the sea below.

"This is beautiful, Cameron," Amani said, "thank you."

"You're welcome."

The waitress came over and he ordered a bottle of their finest champagne. This was the last night of their honeymoon and he wanted to show Amani a good time before they went back to reality.

"To our last night," Cameron held up his flute and they toasted. He had no idea when they would have time like this again. If the previous seven months were any indication, alone time and privacy were now a thing of the past. Somehow, some-way, he had to carve out time for them. "Tell me about your childhood. What was it like growing up in the palace?"

Amani regarded him for a few minutes before answering. "Tough. Being a girl, I was often overlooked by my parents, by everyone. I wasn't the crown prince. I wasn't even the reject heir like Khalil."

"I'm sorry, Amani."

She shrugged. "Often, I was left with my governess or the maids because my parents, the King and Queen were busy grooming Malik. They didn't have time for a young girl who wanted attention and someone to play with her dolls. I was only trotted out during royal functions in which my presence was required as the dutiful princess."

"How did you manage to go off to college then?"

"Although Malik was the Crown Prince, I had a good relationship with my brother. He understood the value of a Western education because he had studied at Harvard. He convinced my parents to afford me the opportunity and since I was of little value to them as third in the line to the throne, I was allowed go away. Of course, with the proper protection. It was hard assimilating when I got there. I looked different. Talked different. I even dressed different. My roommate told me I was matronly and dressing like a schoolmarm. I immediately went out and bought some Western clothes, even a few pair of jeans."

Cameron grinned at her small rebellion.

"When I returned, I hoped to use my education and everything I learned and be of value to Bahara. However, my father passed and Malik became King. He primarily listened to the Royal Council and refused to hear anything his little sister had to say."

"That must have been difficult for you. To be seen, but not heard."

"It was. Until Khalil came and gave me a voice. But enough about me," Amani said. "I want to know about you. What was it like growing up for you?"

"Transient. Regimented," Cameron responded. "My father and my grandfather were both military men and they expected a lot from me and my brothers. Growing up my father was steadily achieving ranks and consequently we moved around a lot as he sought glory in his career."

"How high did he achieve?"

"He was a lieutenant colonel in the United States Army."

"I take it's that pretty high?"

"My grandfather is a three-star general," Cameron replied.

"So you and your brothers decided to follow suit into a life of service?"

Cameron nodded. "I think it had been so ingrained in us, we never thought about another path. It's just what the Mitchell men did."

"Did you ever want to do anything else?"

Cameron was silent for a long moment. It had been so long since someone asked him that. "Once upon a time, I thought I might play professional basketball. I was quite good in school and since I was so tall, I was a natural, but my father wasn't supportive of that dream, not when Caden had gone to West Point and Cage was killing it as a Navy Seal."

Amani frowned. "Killing it? What does that mean?"

Cameron chuckled. "It means he was doing really well. Excelling even when he'd been so bad at school. Cage was physical and the Seals suited him."

"And you? The Air Force suited you?"

"I learned to fly at a young age when one of the Army pilots on one of the bases took me with him. I became obsessed with flying planes until soon my obsession turned into my future. A future that is no more."

"Can you tell me what happened to end your career?"

Cameron's eye shuttered. That's the one thing he didn't want to talk about. "How about dessert?" He suggested when the waitress returned with their order.

Amani went with a chocolate baklava while Cameron opted for cheesecake with strawberries. If Amani noticed he'd expertly changed the subject, she didn't let on. Instead, they enjoyed the sinful delicacies along with some cappuccinos before heading back to the convertible and then a quick boat ride back to the villa.

After such a long day, Amani fell asleep along the way and that was fine with Cameron. It gave him time to reflect on the day and how easy it was to *be* with Amani. When he was with her, the anger and heartache of all he'd lost seemed to ease and become slightly more bearable. He was even starting to accept the fact he was now a husband.

What he wasn't ready for was the royalty part. He'd seen how other royals struggled and were constantly in the news. He didn't want that for himself or Amani. How he carried himself the next couple of months would set the tone for this royal life, but he also wouldn't be a pushover and give up his freedom entirely. There had to be a compromise and he would figure it out.

In the meantime, he would enjoy this last night with Amani. He would lose himself in her until the morning came and he was forced to return the real world.

22

___

Amani wished they could have stayed at the villa forever, but alas, they were in a helicopter on their way back to the palace. To rules. To decorum. All of which had flown out of the window over the course of the last seven days. She'd come to enjoy spending time with her husband and if she wasn't mistaken, Cameron liked their time together too.

It wasn't just about the sex, though they had mind-blowing, mind-bending sex on multiple occasions. But it had been their last night which Amani treasured most. Cameron had been romantic by organizing such an amazing day and candlelight dinner on the mountain. He followed it up by being soft and tender. His heated exploration of her body had made her body scream for release from the exquisite torture he inflicted with his mouth and hands, hell on every part of her.

Amani had felt treasured.

Loved.

She knew she was deluding herself. She was getting caught up in the moment because he exposed her to a whole new world of sensations. Cameron didn't love her. He never would. He told her he wasn't capable and she had to accept it. Even though her heart desperately craved for him to feel the same way she did.

During their week together, Amani had come to realize she was madly in love with Cameron, but he was closed off. It was maddening knowing no matter what she did, she would never be good enough. Like she'd never been good enough for her parents because she'd been born a girl instead of a boy. Amani knew her mother wished it so because she overheard a conversation one day between her mother and her maid. They hadn't known Amani was there, but the Queen made it clear, she wanted another boy to ensure Khalil would never be able to make a claim on the crown.

And it happened anyway.

Malik was gone and it was just Khalil and Amani left to carry on the Naseer name, though now her name was Amani Naseer Mitchell.

She would have to focus on being a good wife and making a life with Cameron the best way she could. Perhaps one day when she became a mother, she would have someone who would love her unconditionally.

"Are you all right?" Cameron asked, reaching for her hand across the tight space of the helicopter.

"I'm fine."

But would she be in a loveless marriage?

THEY ARRIVED BACK to the palace with much fanfare. It appeared everyone was thrilled to see them return. The staff were lined up to greet them, but it was Nadia who emerged from the crowd and Amani instantly relaxed.

"Your Royal Highness." Nadia bowed. "I hope the honeymoon went well."

"It did indeed," Amani replied.

"Omar agreed to allow me to show you both to your new quarters in the East Wing."

"Thank you, Nadia." Amani smiled at the other staff who bowed in deference to her and now to Cameron. She could tell he wasn't comfortable being treated like a royal, but he would have to get used to it. It was his life now.

Nadia chatted easily about the latest goings on at the palace and it kept Amani focused on something else rather than the tension radiating from Cameron at her side. Although royals weren't supposed to show a reaction of any kind, Amani couldn't help it and reached for Cameron's hand. He stared down at their joined hands and smiled at her.

A few minutes later, Nadia was opening the double doors to the most sumptuous suite of rooms. There was a large and airy living room, dining area, small kitchenette, a luxurious bedroom with one of the largest beds Amani had ever seen covered in a brocade of ivory and gold with dozens of pillows. There was a delightful master bath complete with a soaker tub big enough for two and a walk-in shower with lots of nobs. There were two offices, she assumed one for both her and Cameron.

"Thank you, Nadia."

"Is there anything you require, Your Royal Highness?" Why was Nadia being so formal? She always called her Amani when it was just the two of them, but she supposed things were different.

"No."

Nadia turned to Cameron. "His Royal Highness has requested your and Amani's presence in his office."

"Do you know why?"

"I would not presume," Nadia replied. "But I can only imagine it's to go over your official duties."

"Great!" Cameron managed underneath his breath. "We might as well go now before we're summoned," he said, turning to Amani.

He started for the door, but Amani whispered in Cameron's ear, "Now that you're a member of the royal family and not merely Khalil's friend, I would suggest, you address him as His Majesty and give a quick bow of the head."

He gave her a sideward glance. "Duly noted."

Within minutes, they were headed to Khalil's office and this time Omar was waiting for them.

"Welcome back your Royal Highness," Omar said. "I trust you enjoyed your holiday."

"It was lovely," Amani answered since Cameron remained stiffly at her side.

"His Majesty is waiting for you." Omar opened the door and Khalil rose to greet them from his desk.

"Your Majesty." Amani bowed first and she thought Cameron wouldn't oblige, but to her shock he repeated the words and gave a slight bend of his head.

"I see my sister has been teaching you our ways," Khalil said with a smile. "That's good, but you're going to need a crash course which is why I asked you both here."

"What did you have in mind?" Cameron replied.

"We have a big slate of events coming up," Khalil said and Omar handed them both a sheet of paper. "That's the list. We'll need you to divide and conquer some of them. You'll notice your name next to those you'll attend alone or as a couple. There's a handful we'll attend together as a family."

"It's a long list," Cameron stated.

Khalil shrugged. "Comes with the job. Omar has lined up for

you to take comportment and history classes to help you in your transition to Prince Consort of Bahara."

"When do I start?" Cameron inquired.

"Tomorrow," Khalil said. "As for you Amani, I have to thank you for your work with the Bedouin. Rafiq Al Tajir has agreed to the concessions I've made to help ensure their way of life. I think he finally understands I'm on his side."

Amani beamed with pride. "Thank you. I was glad to help. Is there anything else you need?"

"Actually...," Khalil's voice strayed and then Omar handed her an envelope. "I'd like you to review the deal I have with Hadir as well, about our imports. I'd love to hear your thoughts."

Amani nodded. "Of course. I'll get back to you right away."

"Is there anything else you need me to do, other than figure out how to jump through hoops?" Cameron asked.

Amani and Omar collectively gasped, but it was Khalil who smiled letting them know that although Cameron's role had changed, he hadn't forgotten they were once friends. Amani was glad of that.

"Yes. While you were away, there was a threat made against the monarchy. We believe it was some naysayers who are unhappy about your marriage, but we have to assume every threat is real which is why we're going to need you and Amani to stay close to the palace. No unplanned visits."

Amani could only assume Khalil was referring to their one night together in the harem, but that was water under the bridge. They were married now.

"I will protect Amani," Cameron replied.

"But you will also have your own protection," Khalil responded.

"Is that really necessary, Khalil? I mean, Your Majesty. I can take care of myself," Cameron amended.

"You're a member of the royal family and will be protected as such. We can only assume some factions expected Amani to marry someone titled."

"I'm aware," Cameron said through clenched teeth.

"Good. But I'm open to suggestions if you think your security detail needs improvement."

Cameron nodded. "If that's all..."

"You're dismissed," Khalil stated.

Amani noted Cameron raised his brow, but didn't respond to Khalil's obvious bait. Instead he inclined his head, offered Amani his arm and they left Khalil's office.

Once they were no longer within earshot, Amani said, "I'm proud of you. You handled that as well as could be expected."

"I'm not used to being *handled*."

"I think we all gathered as much, but you can do this, Cameron. You'll see."

Amani certainly hoped so because if they couldn't find common ground, her marriage was doomed to fail.

AFTER WEEKS of classes on the history of Bahara, comportment, and even how to dance the perfect waltz, Cameron felt as if he'd graduated and didn't need to have his hand held. He was even trying to soften his approach. He'd been raised in a military family. There was respect and honor, but not tact, diplomacy and charm. It was not something that came easily to him.

He was a pilot.

He knew how to fly a plane.

Or, rather, he used to, but those days were in his rearview. Instead, he was faced with endless engagements, dinners, parties and ribbon cuttings. The fake smile he learned to plaster on made his face sometimes hurt, but he managed not to embarrass himself or the royal family.

He and Khalil had a long way to go in mending fences, but he was seeing progress. Earlier in the week, Cameron had come down to the gym and upon finding Khalil there, they sparred like they used to and there was no animosity between them about Cameron sleeping with his sister. Though not much sleeping was happening between him and Amani.

The evenings were Cameron's favorite, a time when the job of being royal could be put to rest and he could just be himself. He and Amani often shared dinner in their quarters in the East Wing. Sometimes, they watched television or read a book and relaxed. Other times, they walked the gardens and moon gazed — though there had been an occasion, they'd snuck behind a column and he'd hoisted her against the wall and buried himself deep inside her. She'd been hot and ready for him and her sighs had only encouraged him to go faster and faster until he'd had to cover her mouth to prevent her screams.

It didn't end there. Once they were back in their suite, they were all over each other. Cameron never realized he had such a happy appetite for sex until the right woman awakened him. Amani stunned him with her uninhibited enjoyment of his touch which only made him want her more.

It's why he'd insisted she get on birth control. Although he understood the expectations for the crown of having an heir, he wasn't ready to become a father just yet. The palace doctor hadn't been happy about prescribing them, but Cameron hadn't cared. He'd been able to be deep inside Amani without any barriers. With every other woman, he always donned protection, but with his wife, they were free of restrictions. And Cameron had to say, the sensation was incredible.

He felt connected to Amani more than he had with any other woman. He told himself it was because she was *his*. Not just his wife, but he was the only man she'd ever been with or would be. He felt like a caveman ready to beat his chest and say 'Mine'.

Sometimes, he had to remind himself he hadn't *chosen* to marry her, but Amani wasn't smothering him either. She had her own interests and causes or she was helping Khalil with state matters. Often, he didn't see her all day until they were alone at night.

Today was one of those such days. They had separate calendars. Amani had a women's group meeting while Cameron entertained members of the Royal Council. He hated those stuffy dodgers. He sensed they were all angry he'd managed to snag Amani and they or any of their children hadn't. Cameron didn't trust the lot of them and would keep them at arm's length.

After arriving in the suite, Cameron showered, changed into his favorite jogging pants and a t-shirt and was playing a game on his phone when Amani arrived an hour later, looking as beautiful as ever in a multicolored plaid single-breasted jacket and skirt which reached her knees.

"Good evening, wife." Cameron greeted her by brushing his lips across hers.

Amani's eyes lit up at his words. "Hello, husband." She tried to move away, but Cameron pulled her into his lap until she was straddling him. He tossed away her purse and began removing her suit jacket.

"Cameron… I need to shower," she replied, when he began kissing her breasts through her thin camisole. "I've been in these clothes all day."

"I don't care." He grabbed the hem of the cami and pulled it over her head until her bountiful breasts were in front of him in a lacy bra. "I want you this way. All hot and a little bit musky."

Amani blushed. He loved saying naughty things to her because she still managed to blush even though they'd already been married over a month and he'd introduced her to all sorts of lovemaking.

He unclasped her bra and nuzzled his head in her bosom.

She held him to her chest and he turned so he could latch onto one of her turgid nipples and suck. She threw back her head and gave in.

THE FLICKS of Cameron's hot tongue on her breasts made Amani's entire body go taut. How did he always manage to make her raw with need?

Sliding against him, she began to rock her hips, needing to feel all of him against her. Her skirt began to rise until it was at her waist giving her husband easy access to deftly slip his fingers inside her panties and arrow straight to the place where she wanted him most.

She shuddered when his thick fingers parted her folds and began the quest to bring her to the edge.

"Cameron!"

"Yes, baby." His mouth was now locked on her other nipple while his finger was moving in and out of her. Lightning shot through Amani but she refused to go into the abyss alone, she reached beneath her to pull at his jogging pants and pull his straining dick out of his boxers. She wanted to eradicate the edgy feeling of need.

She pushed his hands away and with her underwear pushed to the side, she sank down on top of him. He was thick and hard and exactly how she liked him. She loved the incredible fullness she got when she was in this position. She gripped his broad shoulders and began to ride him.

Cameron met her stride for stride, his body taking a harder more insistent rhythm until they began to buck against each other. And then it came, a white-hot light that had her calling out his name and Cameron growling as his orgasm pumped deep within her. She fell forward onto his chest and he wrapped her in his embrace until their breathing slowed.

When she finally caught her breath, Amani eased up and away from him. Her chest was bare and she was still wearing her panties and skirt while Cameron was fully dressed. She watched him tuck himself back inside his jogging pants.

"Now, it's time I had that shower."

When Cameron started to move, she pushed him back down. "Oh, no. You stay there. I want to get freshened up, not end up on my back."

He smirked and Amani rushed off to the bathroom for a moment of sanity. When the door was closed, she leaned against it. It was getting harder and harder not to reveal she loved him. He was a demanding, intense, passionate, and insatiable lover, sometimes she thought, or, at least, hoped he might feel something for her other than lust.

Was she fooling herself?

She had no experience of love. Had certainly never felt or knew what it was like to be loved by her family except maybe Malik. But just because she'd never experienced love didn't mean she didn't understand what it felt like. She loved him. And every day those feelings got deeper and deeper. They'd intensified when he stopped wearing a condom and she went on birth control. Having him pulse inside her had been nothing short of mind-altering and made her long for a real, lasting connection between them.

She closed her eyes and remembered how gentle Cameron had been with the children when they toured the pediatric wing of a hospital that was being upgraded earlier that week. As he crouched down and admired the young boys cast and signed his name, Amani realized what a great father Cameron would make someday.

"I don't hear running water," Cameron said from the other side of the door. "If I don't hear it soon, I'm coming in."

Amani quickly rushed over and turned on the taps, stepping out of her ruined panties and skirt. She doubted she'd ever be able to look at the outfit again without thinking about the way they just made love on the sofa.

Maybe with time Cameron would come to love her and she would finally have someone who wanted her for her.

23

———

Buzz. *Buzz. Buzz.*

Cameron wished the incessant ringing would stop, but it wouldn't.

"Are you going to get that?" Amani croaked.

Cameron cracked open one eye. It was three a.m. in Bahara. Who would be calling him at this hour? He reached for his smart phone and swiped right. "Hello?"

"Cameron? It's Caden."

Cameron instantly sat upright, because he didn't like the tone in his brother's voice. "What's wrong?"

"It's Grandpa," Caden said, "he's had a heart attack."

"Oh, God!" Cameron sucked in a deep breath. "Is he — he still alive?" He felt Amani rise beside him and switch on the bedside lamp. Worry was etched in her chocolate brown eyes.

"Yeah, he is, but it's not looking good. Several arteries in his heart are blocked. They need to perform open heart surgery."

"Christ! All right, we'll be there as fast we can," Cameron said, but when he glanced up, Amani was already on the palace phone.

"Good. I wish we weren't meeting your wife under these

circumstances," Caden replied, "But you should come back, it's not looking good."

"We'll be there." When he hung, Amani was just finishing her call, but Cameron was paralyzed, sitting on the bed. His grandfather was such a strong and dominant force in their family, it was unfathomable to think he could lose him, but Carter was human.

"I've already spoken to Khalil," Amani said. "He's contacting the pilot to get the jet ready to go in an hour. That will give us just enough time to pack whatever we need. He's also calling Omar and Nadia to help us pack."

He didn't respond, so Amani came over to him and kneeled in front of him. She touched his cheek. "Are you okay?"

Cameron nodded. "I can't lose him, Amani. I can't lose another important thing in my life."

"You won't." She rose to her feet and sat in his lap, wrapping her arm around his neck. "He's strong, right? That's what you've always told me about him."

"Yeah."

"Then that's what we're going to believe, that he'll pull through this."

Suddenly, there was a knock on the door. He watched Amani rush over and open it. Omar and Nadia were on the other side wearing dressing robes.

"What can we do, your Highness?" Nadia and Omar asked coming to Amani's side as if he were an invalid and incapable of speech. Maybe he was.

Cameron left them and went to the walk-in closet and chose some of his old clothes when he'd been Cameron Mitchell, not Prince Consort Cameron Michell of Bahara, but placed a sports jacket over it. Then he went into the bathroom. By the time, he emerged out of the shower. Omar had his suitcase open and made good work of packing his luggage. Amani's was nearly done, too, as Nadia rushed around the room adding this and that with Amani's guidance.

"You need to get dressed, Your Highness," Nadia said, "We," she glanced in Omar's direction, "have got this."

"Of course," Amani glanced at Cameron and mouthed 'are you okay'? He nodded and she rushed off into the ensuite.

A half hour later, they were pulling up to the jet in a limousine and climbing up the steps. Cameron was anxious to get back to the States, to his family. He didn't know what awaited him on the opposite side of the ocean. He just knew, whatever it was, he had Amani by his side to help him face it.

Amani was nervous though she tried not to outwardly show it to Cameron. He had enough on his plate, what with worrying about his grandfather and whether he would make it through the delicate surgery.

It's just that she'd never been to the States.

She'd been out of Bahara and to her finishing school in Switzerland and often to Paris and other surrounding kingdoms near Bahara, but never to America. She saw it on television, read about it in books and in newspapers, but it had always seemed like a world away.

Not today.

She was going to Washington D.C. with her husband, where she would meet his family, the Mitchells, for the first time. She'd already had a dossier of each family member prepared for her awhile ago. She knew it was over the top, but Cameron didn't often reveal much about his family. She'd only skimmed the document for the pertinent facts so she was prepared and wouldn't seem as if she didn't know Cameron at all.

But did she know him?

Not enough for her liking even though they'd been married six weeks. She hoped he would open up and let her in, but he was like a tortoise, closed off, and it was hard to break through his outer shell.

She knew about Carter, Cal, Caden and Cage's military careers because that was public record. Cameron told her Caden was governor, but not much else. She'd read he had a wife, Savannah, a special needs son, Liam, and a daughter, Thea. His brother Cage and wife, Monae, recently had a son, Caleb.

She hadn't wanted to know much more because it would have been intruding on his family. The only thing she picked up on from the one FaceTime call they'd had with his parents was that his relationship with his mother was strained. He never spoke fondly of her. Amani had wanted to ask why, but she hadn't wanted to press unless the information was freely given.

And, now, she would meet them all and not under the best of circumstances. What would they think about her, the woman Cameron had been forced into marrying? Amani shuddered to think. All she could do was put her best foot forward and be there as a support system for Cameron should he need her. Maybe this adversity would bring them together and he would see the kind of marriage they could have if he was willing to meet her halfway.

WHEN THEY ARRIVED at the Ronald Reagan Washington Airport, after being escorted through customs, Cameron and Amani were taken to a private car where a driver was waiting to take them to the hospital where his grandfather's surgery was taking place.

Cameron was quiet on the drive to the hospital. His mind far away in another time in place when he'd been someone else. He remembered coming back to D.C. after completing the United States Air Force Academy, he'd been a pilot with a bright future ahead of him. He looked forward to making his family proud and continuing his family's tradition of a career in the military, just a different branch.

Today, he was coming back a changed man— that young kid with so much promise had been obliterated and in his wake, he was a husband and a figurehead for a small Middle Eastern island. He was a long way from where he envisioned himself to be.

He felt Amani's hand slide over his and he glanced up to find her eyes on him. She was always watching him. He wondered what she was thinking and whether he was living up to being the man she dreamed of when she decided to go to bed with him.

She offered him a tremulous smile. "How much further?"

Cameron glanced out of the window. "About a half hour."

She nodded and was silent, but didn't remove her hand. For the nearly thirteen-hour flight, she'd been quiet and kept to herself as if she didn't want to intrude on his pain. She'd tried to stay up when they'd taken off, but it was late when they'd been woken up out of their sleep. So when she fell asleep in the cabin, he unbuckled her seatbelt, wrapped her in his arms and carried her to the bedroom at the back of the plane. At least one of them could get some rest. He was too wired to sleep.

Throughout the flight, he kept in constant contact with Caden on updates about the procedure. The surgery was a success, now all they had to do was wait. His grandfather was currently in intensive care and would be in the hospital for seven to ten days depending on his recovery. All of the family was at the hospital and Cameron was eager to see them.

The Medstar Washington Hospital Center was a bustle of activity by the time they arrived. It was still visiting hours according to the lobby attendant who gave them badges and then they were taken by elevator to the fifth floor. Their security detail accompanied them. He hated the extra protocol that came with being part of the royal family, but it was unavoidable.

Cameron sensed Amani's nervousness at his side and reached for her hand. He understood. It was her first time meeting his family. The Mitchells were already a daunting clan and this was no social setting, but she'd never looked lovelier. She'd showered on the jet as had he. She was wearing a tank dress with a long duster cardigan while he sported jeans, a polo shirt and a sports coat as his ode to being a dressed down royal.

Exiting the elevator, they were walking down the hall, when he saw Caden and Liam walking toward him. He was relieved to see his older brother first. When Caden glanced up and saw him, Cameron broke protocol and quickly strode toward him. The hug Caden gave him was much needed. Cameron hadn't realized he'd needed one until the two men separated.

"You're a sight for sore eyes," Caden said, stepping back to take a look at him.

Cameron smiled. "So are you. I've missed you, bro."

"I've missed you too," Caden said.

"So have I," a slightly softer masculine voice said. Cameron glanced behind him to see his nephew. Liam had gotten taller in the nine months he'd been gone. He now almost reached Cameron's shoulders.

"You're getting taller."

"I know." Liam beamed with pride. "I'll be as tall as my dad and you one day."

"You wish," Caden laughed and then glanced behind Cameron. "And you must be Amani."

Christ! Seeing his family, Cameron had nearly forgotten his wife. "I'm sorry." He rushed to her side and he could see she was perturbed by the slight. "Amani, this is my older brother..."

"Caden," she finished for him and offered her hand which Caden ignored and wrapped his arms around her.

"Welcome to the family, Amani."

When they parted, a wide grin spread across her full lips. "Thank you."

"I'd like you to meet my son, Liam," Caden said. "My wife, Savannah, is at home with our two-year-old daughter."

"Nice to meet you." Amani inclined her head to Liam. "And I can't wait to meet my new sister-in-law."

Caden smiled at the comment. "Liam, say hello to your new aunt, Uncle Cameron's wife."

"Hello," Liam said, staring at Amani. "Where are you from? You don't look like us."

Cameron's hand came up to his forehead. Trust Liam to say exactly what was on his mind. Amani took it in stride and laughed good-naturedly.

"I'm from Bahara."

Liam frowned. "Where is that?"

"An island country far, far away in the Middle East," Amani replied. "Perhaps you can come visit one day."

"Can we, Dad?" Liam asked, looking up at his father.

Caden grinned. "Absolutely, son. I want to see the palace Cameron has been living in these days."

"Palace?" Liam's eyes grew large with excitement. "When can we go?"

"Soon. Maybe over the holidays or when school is out," Caden responded.

"How is Grandfather?" Cameron asked.

"Holding his own. He made it through surgery. Now it's just a waiting game. If you head further down the hall, the family's all there. I'm taking Liam home because he has school tomorrow."

"Of course," Cameron said. "It's good to see you."

Caden nodded and gave him a wink. "We'll catch up later."

He and Liam continued down the corridor leaving him, Amani, and the royal guard behind.

"I like him," Amani said. "He's very genuine."

"Yes, he is. C'mon you might as well meet the rest of the family," Cameron replied and started down the hall.

He had no idea Monae would be the first person to greet them halfway there. She was walking with a bundle in her arms and pacing the corridor. He hadn't seen Monae since he'd told Cage and Monae that he forgave them and was moving on. He knew she'd given birth to Caleb, her and Cage's son, but that was the extent of his knowledge. He was hoping to delay this meeting, but it appeared she would be Amani's first introduction.

When she saw him, astonishment crossed her features. She called out for Cage and then began walking toward him. His brother was right behind her and suddenly everyone who'd been in the waiting room was descending upon them.

The guards immediately each held up a hand to hold them back.

"It's fine, Ahmad. These people are my family," Cameron said and pushed past them with Amani by his side.

Monae arrived first with baby in hand, and with Cage just steps behind her. "Cameron, it's so good to see you."

She looked different from the last time he'd seen her. She still had a round, heart-shaped face, a button nose and almond-shaped eyes, but she'd grown out her asymmetrical bob until her hair reached her shoulders, while her figure was no longer petite. She had more curves thanks to the bundle in her arms.

"Monae." Cameron inclined his head. "This is my wife, Amani. Amani, this is Monae, my sister-in-law."

Amani offered her hand. "Nice to meet you." Monae was only capable of lending one hand with the baby in the other. Amani turned to stare at the brown-skinned child. "He's beautiful."

"Thank you," Cage spoke as he finally made it to the group. "It's good to have you back, Cam." Cage walked over to Cameron and gave him a one-armed hug which Cameron returned. His brother was just as tall he was, with beefy arms in a muscle t-shirt and cargo pants, closely cropped black hair, but his skin was dark brown just like their father's and Caden. When they pulled apart, Cameron could see Cage was equally surprised by his response.

"Is that my boy!" He heard his mother's voice, rather than saw her behind his brother.

Camilla Mitchell looked as put together as she always did, despite being in a hospital. Not a hair of her stylish pixie cut was out of place, her smooth, caramel skin had no lines and the tracksuit she wore didn't even have a wrinkle. How did she manage it?

"Mother." He hoped his tone was enough to keep her at bay, but it wasn't and she flung her arms awkwardly around him.

Time hadn't changed his feelings much, but it was Amani's hand on his arm which propelled him to hug his mother back. After, there was a sheen in her eyes as if he'd done something momentous. He merely tried not to be rude.

"Son." His father, Cal, strode toward him and Cameron met him halfway and genuinely wrapped his arms around his father's shoulders.

"I'm sorry, Dad. I wasn't here. How's Grandpa?"

"Holding his own," Cal responded. "And who is this pretty little thing?" he said, grinning in Amani's direction.

Cameron laughed. "I'd think you'd remember that I'm married now, Dad. This is Amani."

"You're a princess, should I bow or curtsy or something," his father asked, coming toward Amani.

She chuckled. "Absolutely not. You're family." He loved that she accepted his father's embrace.

His father gave Cameron an approving wink. "Where did Caden go?"

"He took Liam home," Cameron replied.

"Can we assume the hulks behind you, are your protection?" Cage asked, speaking again after quietly watching the interaction.

"Yeah," Cameron said.

"I still can't believe you're a prince," Cage responded. "I feel like I need to put your head in the dirt or something like I used to and remind you you're one of us."

"Try it and you'll regret it. I'm not as small as I was when I was kid and you and Caden used to pick on me."

"Oh, cry me a river." Cage rolled his eyes.

Their exchange lightened the mood. "Caden was able to secure us a private waiting room again," his mother said. "Perhaps we can go there?"

"Yes, my darling," his father, Cal, said.

My darling? Cameron nearly did a double-take. Had his father forgotten the lies his mother told for over three decades? Apparently, he had, because as they all walked to a waiting room down the hall, Cameron noticed his mother slide her arm through his father's. Well, he had been gone over half a year. What did he expect — that things would stay the same?

The waiting room was private and away from the public area, giving the family much needed privacy. Cameron doubted this was for his and Amani's benefit as royals. They left the guards outside the door to man the corridor.

"The hospital approved us using this place?" Cameron asked Cage.

"They do if the governor asks for it," Cage replied. "We stayed here when we were waiting on news of your accident."

Cameron stiffened. He didn't want to think about the accident or the heartbreaking news which came after it, but he was back home and there was no way around facing his past. Hell, Monae and Cage were standing together and staring adoringly at each other while holding their son.

Cameron turned away from the sight and walked over to a coffee bar in the corner. He set about making coffee while Amani ventured away from him and was chatting with his mother. He would have preferred his wife have no contact with the woman, but he couldn't very well make a scene.

He was pouring coffee when he felt his father's presence by his side. "Does it still sting?" he asked quietly and Cameron glanced up to see the direction of his gaze which was Cage, Monae, and their baby boy.

Cameron shook his head. "Not anymore."

"So I guess time does heal all things?"

Cameron stirred some half and half and sugar into his coffee. "I suppose. It was more the lies of omission and brother code that irked me. But who am I to judge since I did the same thing to Khalil."

"He's not your brother."

"No, but he's always felt like one," Cameron said quietly, "And I betrayed him with Amani."

His father looked over at his wife. "Doesn't seem to have turned out too bad for you. She's a beautiful woman and I can see she's besotted with you."

Cameron snorted. "I doubt that."

"I'm serious, son. She cares for you, of that, I'm sure."

Amani chose that moment to glance over and smile at Cameron and he felt his heart kick over in his chest. His father had to be wrong. He told her he wouldn't be able to offer her love, that he wasn't capable of it. He hoped she hadn't gotten her hopes up of his feelings ever changing. He still hadn't gotten over his mother's lies, though his father had. "Walk with me outside?""

"Sure thing." His father joined him in the corridor to walk as Cameron sipped on his coffee. One of the guards followed quietly behind them.

"You and Mom seem to be back on solid ground."

His father nodded. "We are, but it wasn't easy getting there. We went to therapy and it helped. Talking through all the hurts and fears got me to a place of forgiveness. I was hoping all this time, might have made you feel the same."

Cameron turned to regard him. "I don't hate her like I did before."

"That's a start, I guess," his father growled. "But I want more for you, son. So much more. I want you to find love and happiness like your mother and me, like even Cage and Monae, though they didn't start out on the right foot."

"I don't know, Dad. I don't think I'm cut out for love."

"That's the anger and hurt talking. Besides, you're married now to a beautiful woman."

"Amani knows where I stand."

"Meaning?"

"I told her what I am and am not capable of."

"And she accepted that?" his father asked incredulously.

"We didn't have much choice. I'm pretty sure Khalil might have locked me up and thrown away the key if I didn't agree to make an honest woman out of her."

"But, son. That's no way to live."

"It's the best I've got," Cameron responded. And it was. He was giving the marriage a hundred percent of his time and focus. He was a good husband to Amani and doing right by her.

So what if love wasn't part of the equation. Surely, he was doing enough?

24

"You should come home with us," his mother told Cameron once they sat in the private room for several hours. "I'm sure you're both tired.'"

"We are, but that's not necessary. We have a room booked at the Four Seasons. Besides which, we need room for the guards."

"I can make up rooms for them."

"Leave it alone, Mother," Cameron snapped. Several pairs of eyes focused on Cameron at his harsh tone. "I'm sorry, it's been a long day."

"Of course, I understand."

Cameron turned to Amani. "Are you ready to go? We should check into the hotel."

"Yes, please." Amani's voice was soft.

After they made their goodbyes, they were whisked away by a Cadillac Escalade to the Four Seasons where they would be staying for the duration of their stay. Cameron didn't know how long that would be. He just knew he couldn't, *wouldn't* leave until his grandfather was out of the woods and on the road to recovery. Plus, he wanted to spend some quality time with his family and let Amani get to know them.

"Are you all right?" he asked, when they finally made it to their suite. Amani had been quiet for most of the ride to the hotel.

"I'm fine," she said, taking off her duster cardigan.

"When a woman says she's fine, she never is," Cameron said, whipping his sports jacket off.

"And you would know what I'm thinking?"

"I wouldn't presume," Cameron replied, plopping down on the couch and grabbing the room service menu. The pastry he had at the hospital was horrible and he was starving. However, when he glanced up, he saw that Amani's arms were folded across her chest.

"Would you care to tell me what's going on with you and your family? I couldn't help but notice the tension between you and your mother, and you and your brother, Cage, and his wife."

Cameron tossed down the menu he was reading. Was she trying to pick a fight with him because he wasn't in the mood? "I don't want to talk about that."

She rolled her eyes and swept pass him to open her luggage. "You never do."

"What's that's supposed to mean?"

She spun around to face him. "Exactly what I said. You know all about my family, but you never want to open up and talk to me about yours."

"Have you ever thought it might be too painful for me to discuss?" Cameron asked. "Or that it's hard for me coming back here? I had a life before you, Amani, a good one, but it blew up in my face and I'm living with that the best way I know how."

She released a long sigh. "I know that losing being a pilot hurt you, but you can have a good life, Cameron, without it."

"Can I?" he inquired.

At her sharp intake of breath, Cameron realized he'd hurt

her with his words, but he couldn't take them back. "I'm going downstairs to the bar. Don't wait up."

"I didn't plan to."

Cameron stormed out of the room with one of the bodyguards following directly behind him. He couldn't even have a fight with his wife or be alone with his thoughts without someone shadowing him. It drove him crazy.

He was silent on the way to the bar which was thankfully still open. He slid into one of the booths and ordered a whisky neat. He needed something to take the edge off. Being here was both an elixir and a fire starter. He loved his family. He did. He just wasn't sure if he could trust them — at least not all of them.

Once upon a time, they'd meant everything to him. And now, well, he had a family of his own with Amani. A woman who both thrilled and exacerbated him at the same time. She was always pushing him for more, just like she did before they slept together, which changed the trajectory of his life forever.

Although Cameron didn't regret being with her, he wished he would have thought about the consequences of his actions before allowing his impulses to take over. He didn't know how to make this right with Amani or that he could ever give her the kind of marriage she wanted. And if he couldn't, what did that mean for their longevity?

THE NEXT MORNING, Cameron woke up hornier than ever. He and Amani had gone to bed angry. Something they'd never done. After a burger and a couple of drinks at the bar, he'd returned to their room only to find her sound asleep. He wanted to wake her and squash this ridiculous argument. He knew he could do it by seducing her, but that wasn't right either.

He'd gone to bed without spooning her. Usually her back

was against his chest and her butt was nestled in his crotch, not last night. She'd slept as far away as she could on the king-size bed as was physically possible without falling off. When he'd woken up, she was already dressed and looking beautiful and poised while he felt grouchy.

"Good morning," Amani said cheerily, too cheery for him.

"Morning," he responded, climbing out of the bed and heading toward the bathroom.

"I've already eaten, but I took the liberty of ordering breakfast." She followed him inside and watched him brush his teeth "I called your mother and your grandfather is awake this morning."

Cameron frowned as he rinsed with mouthwash. "You spoke with my mother?"

Amani nodded and handed him a towel. "Yes, she was kind enough to give me her phone number."

He heard the accusation in that statement which was that he hadn't. He ignored it as he wiped his mouth. "That's good. I'll get dressed and we will go over right away."

"I figured as much. The guards have the car at the ready."

Twenty minutes later, they were on their way to the hospital. Cameron didn't like the atmosphere between them and told the guards to stop the car and get out.

"Is there something wrong?"

"Yeah, I don't like this tension between us, Amani." When she remained silent, he continued. "There's a lot of history between me and my family that I don't talk about with anyone."

"Not even Khalil?" she asked quietly.

Damn, she had him there.

"That's different."

"Ha," she sniffed and turned to face the window. "You can tell your best friend, but not your wife. That's good to know, really warms my heart."

"Damn it, Amani. Don't be this way."

She turned to face him and there were tears glistening on her eyelids. "I get it. I'm good enough to fuck, but not good to enough to talk to." She rolled down the windows. "We're ready," she told the guards.

Cameron was too stunned to speak. He'd never heard Amani say a word out of turn, let alone use foul language. And she'd just put him in his place and he didn't like it. He didn't like it at all.

~

As she sat in the back of the Cadillac Escalade, Amani was fuming. Never in her life had she spoken so foully, but Cameron brought it out in her. How dare he act as if he was put out because she was giving him the silent treatment.

He friggin deserved it!

His 'I don't want to talk about it because it's too painful was a load of bullshit. There! She'd thought it, but not spoken the word. He could tell Khalil, *her brother,* about what was going on in his family, but not *her,* his *wife,* the woman sleeping in his bed every night? Not that they did much sleeping. She made it so easy for him to keep her at arm's length because he was her first love, her only lover. She had no idea how to process all of the emotions she was feeling. So Cameron used sex to keep them from growing and becoming more intimate and talking to one another.

No more.

She wasn't going to make it easy for him to keep her out in the cold. She was going to demand he give her more, tell her the truth. From the tension radiating off him beside her, he didn't like it one bit.

Tough luck.

They arrived at the hospital shortly after the stop and headed inside. Cameron didn't bother holding her hand like he did yesterday and Amani kept hers wrapped around her purse. When they reached the private waiting room, the Mitchell family were all gathered. Amani recognized all the faces, except this time, there was a new one. A beautiful woman.

She was nearly Amani's height with hair the color of chestnuts and smooth hazelnut skin. She had on an animal print shirtdress which hugged her figure. She greeted her with a warm smile. "You must be Amani. I'm Savannah, Caden's wife."

Amani smiled back at her. "Yes, I am, and it's good to finally meet you. Where's your daughter?"

"In daycare," Savannah said, "I wanted to come and be here for Caden and Carter. You haven't met him yet, but the patriarch of this family is quite a character. He's all bluster. Deep down he's a pussycat. Wait until you meet him."

"Oh, I can't wait," Amani responded. After greeting everyone, she returned to sit next to Savannah. There was an aura about her that Amani could trust. She was certain that there was something going on with Cameron, Cage and Monae so she was giving them a wide berth.

"Is everything okay between you and Cameron?" Savannah inquired.

"Pardon?"

Savannah shrugged. "I don't know, I just sensed some tension when you both walked in and you went in different directions."

"With our royal duties, we're used to working a room." At Savannah's raised brow, Amani chuckled. "Okay, so we had a disagreement earlier. Well, make that last night."

"And it carried over into the morning?" Savannah inquired. "That's not good. If I could give you a piece of marital advice..."

"I would love some," Amani responded. "My mother passed

away and well I don't have anyone I confide in back at the palace other than my maid." She could tell Soraya, but for some reason she couldn't bring herself to tell her best friend about the issues in her marriage not when Soraya was blissfully in love.

"Never go to bed angry. Hash out whatever differences you have before you go to sleep. Otherwise, they'll only be compounded in the morning light."

Amani nodded. "He doesn't make it easy, Savannah."

"Men never do."

"He's stubborn and refuses to let me in. Last night, I guess I just lost it and told him how I really feel."

"Good for you. Don't keep it in or it'll only build resentment. You told him how you feel and what you need. It's up to him to step up to bat."

Amani's brow furrowed. "Step up to bat?"

Savannah chuckled. "It's an American phrase that it's up to Cameron to make things right between you."

"I agree, because I'm not backing down."

Not this time. She was done kowtowing to the men in her life. First, Khalil with his demands which she'd done because he was her king and sovereign, but not Cameron. He was her husband and, by God, he would give her the respect she was due.

"Grandpa!" Cameron stared down at his grandfather in the hospital bed with tubes sticking out of him. He hated seeing him like this. In his mind, Carter Mitchell was fearless and invincible, but seeing him here in this bed, made Cameron realize he was human just like the rest of them.

"Cameron, is that you, my boy?" his grandfather whispered.

"It is." Cameron nodded and reached for his hand, taking

the older man's frail hand in his. How was it that he'd only been gone less than a year and it looked as if his grandfather had aged overnight.

Although he was six feet five inches and broad in stature with warm brown skin, his hair seemed to have turned white overnight.

"I'm so glad you're back home," his grandfather said. "I feared Camilla and that granddaughter-in-law of mine had run you off."

"I'm made of stronger stock than that, Grandpa."

"You're a Mitchell, of course, you are." Carter started coughing a bit and Cameron reached over to the bedside table and grabbed the water cup and put the straw to his grandfather's lips. Once he'd taken a sip, Cameron set it back on the table and took a seat.

"I hate that this damn surgery is the reason you're back home instead of celebrating with that pretty new wife of yours. I saw the picture and videos and she's a stunner. No wonder you couldn't keep it in your pants. Where is she by the way?" He raised his head as to look for Amani.

Cameron softly pushed him back down on the bed. "Rest, Grandpa. Amani is here."

"Why isn't she with you?" He wisely surmised as his dark eyes studied Cameron.

"She's in the waiting room."

"A wife should be by her husband's side."

"Well, Amani isn't too happy with me at the moment," Cameron replied.

"Oh yeah, what'd you do, boy?"

Cameron laughed. "Why does it have to be me, Grandpa?"

"Because we men are always in the wrong," Carter said, "when your grandmother was alive, I just took the 'L' sometimes just to keep the peace. You know the saying, happy wife, happy life."

"I hear you."

"I want to see her," Carter said. "Go get her."

"Right now?"

"No time like the present."

Cameron stared at his grandfather incredulously and when he didn't budge, he rose to his feet and left the room. How could he deny his ailing grandparent? With his tail tucked between his legs, Cameron went back to the waiting room.

Amani was seated beside Savannah. The two women were seemingly becoming fast friends the last couple of hours. She'd even chatted with his mother, though he noted she spoke very little to Monae. Was she picking up on what he was putting down?

Cameron walked over to his wife. "Amani." Her eyes were cold when she glanced in his direction. "My... my grandfather would like to meet you." Suddenly, her eyes turned warm like they used to be for him.

"I would like that very much." Amani stood. "Savannah, I'll be back." She followed Cameron as he led her out the door.

Once they were no longer within earshot, Cameron whispered. "I know you're upset with me, but my grandfather..."

She stopped midstride and glared at him. "I don't need you to tell me not to upset your grandfather. He's in a hospital bed!" Then she spun around and stalked to the elevator. Cameron had no choice but to follow behind her.

She stayed several inches apart of him in the elevator which made Cameron want to haul her into his arms and make her forget about this argument. The elevator dinged and he walked out. Instinctively, he reached for her hand to show her the way. She glanced down at it at first, but to his joy, she took his outstretched palm and Cameron breathed a sigh of relief.

They walked down the hall to his grandfather's room. Cameron knocked on the door and they stepped inside. At first, it appeared Carter was sleeping, but then he popped open his eyes and they grew large at seeing Amani.

"Ah, Princess Amani." His grandfather held out a fragile hand.

Amani dropped Cameron's hand and immediately rushed over to his grandfather. He accepted her small hand and brought it to his lips. "It's such a pleasure to meet you, Mr. Mitchell. I'm so sorry it's under these circumstances."

"Me and you both," his grandfather replied, "but you— you're absolutely stunning. I can see why my grandson is so taken with you."

Amani smiled, but she didn't agree.

"Will you be staying for a while?"

"Absolutely," Amani responded. "Our place is here with you until you're better."

His grandfather beamed at her words. "You're such a treasure. Isn't she, Cameron?" He glanced over at him.

Cameron was staring at her too because despite being angry with him she was making a real effort to get to know his family. "Yes, yes, she is."

Perhaps Amani wasn't asking too much for him to let her in. He didn't have to tell her *everything*, but he could open up and be less guarded. She was right that he was keeping her at a distance because he was. Because if he got too close, allowed her in, he might lose his head and fall head over heels for her. And he already cared deeply for her, more than he should.

25

––––––

The ride back to the hotel was tense and Amani didn't like it. She didn't want to be upset with Cameron but he wasn't being upfront with her. Even his family could sense things weren't right between them and Amani wasn't going to be the one to change that. If Cameron wanted their relationship to be better, he would have to put forth an effort.

Amani stared out of the window at the passing sights of D.C. as if it were the most amazing thing she'd seen when Cameron spoke. "I'm sorry."

"For what exactly?"

"It's not easy talking about my past, my family and everything that went wrong here," Cameron responded.

She nodded, waiting for him to continue.

"When we get back to the hotel, I'd like to try and explain."

Well, that was a start, but seeing was definitely believing, so Amani would see how the night progressed before getting her hopes up.

True to his word, once they were alone in their suite and had changed, Cameron into sweats and Amani in a sleepshirt. She typically slept naked because they had such an active sex life, but not tonight, though she had removed her bra for comfort. As if he knew, Cameron's eyes zeroed on her nipples which poked through the shirt, but he didn't say anything. He merely walked over to the wet bar in the room, made them a drink and handed her a glass of dark liquid. Amani crisscrossed her legs and sat across from him on the sofa.

Cameron wasted no time and blurted out, "My father is not my biological father."

Amani spurted out her drink. "Ohmigod!" She was about to get up to wipe the excess liquid, but Cameron pushed to his feet before she could and rushed to the bathroom. He returned with a towel and Amani wiped her face and blotted her now soiled shirt.

"Were you serious?" she asked after a moment passed.

Cameron nodded. "I grew up believing Cal was my father. Yet, I always wondered why I was so fair-skinned as opposed to my brothers who share my father's darker complexion. I figured it must have been some recessive gene."

"How did you find out?" Amani inquired. She didn't want to push, but he'd just dropped a bombshell.

"After the accident that ended my career, I was in need of a blood transfusion. My family all tried to donate and when my father did, that's when he was informed there was no biological way he could be my father. Of course, I knew none of this until I woke up and found out the career I devoted my life to was over. Can you imagine? I was grappling with a huge adjustment only to find out my mother had lied to me my entire life."

"Who is your father?"

"A former military man who passed away. She had an affair with him while my father was deployed."

"That explains why your relationship with her is so strained."

"Apparently, my father has forgiven her and I get it. They were married for forty years and he loves her."

"And you don't?"

"I don't know what I feel for her right now other than anger and disgust. Growing up, she always held us to such high standards when she's a liar and a cheat. Do you know she kept Caden and Savannah apart?"

Amani gasped. "She did? How?"

"They met when Caden was at West Point and she paid Savannah to leave. She had no idea Savannah was pregnant at the time, but she made her feel as if she would never be good enough for Caden. It took them over a decade to find each other again and it cost Caden ten years with his son."

"Wow! I had no idea. She seems so genuine."

"It's all a charade and fake. Just like her," Cameron replied, taking a sip of his drink.

"Cameron," Amani placed her tumbler on the table, "you can't hold on to this anger you have toward your mother. It isn't good for you or her. You have to find a way to make peace with this."

"Why?" he asked, staring at her.

"Because it's only hurting you in the process. It's eating you up inside and I suspect it's why you don't believe in marriage anymore. I bet you did before this discovery."

He rolled his eyes. "Don't try and psychoanalyze me, Amani. You wanted to know about my past. I've told you."

Amani sighed. "I understand she hurt you, Cameron," she scooted closer to him, "made everything you believed a lie. But she does love you."

"She doesn't know the meaning of the word. If she did, she would have confessed sooner and not made me live a lie."

"I'm not making excuses for her. I'm just asking you to look into your heart and see if you can find a way to forgive her so you can move on. Besides, one day, we might have kids of our own and I would like them to have a relationship with their grandmother."

"We don't have any kids, yet."

"That hasn't stopped you from practicing on making them," Amani responded with a smile.

"I don't see you complaining. In fact," Cameron placed his tumbler beside hers and pulled her into his lap and Amani let him because she missed being in his arms, "I think you've rather liked all the practicing."

She *loved* being with Cameron, that was the problem. When they made love, she felt close to him as if they were joined not just in body, but in mind. She felt unique when, for the majority of her life, no one had ever made her feel special. Certainly not her parents. At times, Khalil, but with Cameron she felt everything. She didn't feel lonely. Instead, she felt *craved*. She wanted that again. When he lifted her nightshirt over her head in one fell swoop, she let him.

He wasn't gentle. He kissed her as if she were the oasis he'd been searching for in the desert and she kissed him back. Within seconds, his clothes disappeared just as quickly as her panties and they came together with an intensity Amani had never felt before.

When his lips moved from her mouth, lower past her breasts and abdomen until he could bury his face between her thighs, she cried out when he dragged his tongue over her slick flesh. She bucked when he focused his attention on the bundle of nerves that was the source of her pleasure and she grasped his head because she couldn't get enough. Neither could he because he held her against his mouth and ravished her with his tongue, teeth and fingers. When her body began to shake, he shifted positions, rising up so he could widen her legs with his thighs. Then he placed the thick head of arousal at her slick entrance and flexing his hips, he thrust deep, finding her center.

"Yes, yes…!" she moaned. She hated being this needy, but she would take whatever Cameron was willing to give.

His hazel eyes pierced hers with raw desire and pain. Now that she understood his story, she would give him whatever comfort he needed. If that meant cracking herself open to reach him, she would. Once Cameron was inside her, she grabbed a hold of his behind and tugged him harder against her.

She poured herself into their lovemaking, undulating against him as his big hands braced her hips and he rode her. She gloried in the way she could make Cameron feel. When blinding white light flashed behind her eyes, she gave into the feeling because Cameron was a part of her. She didn't know if he felt the same, but it was the price she was willing to pay for the man she loved.

"It's so good to spend time with you, Cam," Caden said when it was just the two of them alone at Cameron's bachelor pad a week later. His grandfather had been released from the hospital and into their parents' care. Camilla and Cal had gone all out and had the upstairs guest suite and adjoining room outfitted for Carter and a full-time nurse to ensure he received the best care.

Cameron and Amani had decided to stay on for a little while longer. Amani understood that he had to be sure his grandfather was out of danger before he felt comfortable enough to get on a plane halfway around the world from his family.

He was, however, packing up his condo because his life was now in Bahara. He would be selling the place as soon as he could find a buyer. Caden had already put him in touch with a realtor who thought it would sell faster if they could stage it by Cameron removing personal items. Amani was spending some time with Savannah and his niece so Cameron asked Caden to come by and help him out.

"It's good to hang with you too," Cameron replied, placing some old video games into a storage bin. Some of this would be shipped to Bahara. The others he would donate. "It's been too long since you and I had some real one on one time together."

"Something on your mind?" Caden asked, as he placed some linens into an empty box. "I was surprised you didn't want to bring Amani here instead of the hotel."

"Security felt the hotel was much safer than my condo."

Caden shrugged. "There is that."

"I remember giving you such a hard time about running for governor and how bad it was living in a fishbowl," Cameron started, "now I know exactly what it feels like."

"I can't imagine being Prince Consort of a tiny nation is easy."

"Hell, no!" Cameron said, and reached for a beer he'd opened early. He took a long pull. "It's an endless array of events. Our social calendar is never empty. How do you manage being governor and having a wife and two kids?"

Caden laughed. "It's not easy. It's a balancing act and Savannah and I make every effort to ensure we have time for ourselves and Liam and Thea."

"My nephew is handsome as ever," Cameron said. "And, Thea, she's just an adorable two-year old." He'd stopped by a few days ago to meet the beautiful brown-skinned baby who stared up at him with Caden's dark eyes.

"Adorable, yes? But she's in the terrible twos and is running me and her poor mother ragged."

"But you're happy?" Cameron asked.

A broad smile spread across his brother's lips. "Absolutely.

Wouldn't have it any other way. How about you? Do you foresee any children in your and Amani's future?"

Cameron rolled his eyes. "Being royal, there's always talk of heirs, but I'm not in any rush. As you know, this marriage was not planned. We need time alone, just the two of us getting to know each other."

Caden nodded in understanding. "But matrimony appears to suit you. You and Amani seem to be a good fit."

Cameron grinned broadly. "I have no complaints."

"I wasn't talking about sex, Cameron. Other than first couple of days when there was a decidedly chilly note in the air between you, you seem to have good communication and the pictures and videos make it seem like you're of one accord."

"We are."

"But?"

"There's no 'but'," Cameron responded, "I guess, the only thing I worry about is Amani developing feelings for me if she hasn't already. She was a virgin when we met and, well, I just don't know if I can get there Caden."

"Not now? Or not ever?"

Cameron gave him a sideward glance.

"I see. Does Amani know how you feel?"

Cameron nodded. "She knew I wasn't a proponent of marriage before we were rushed down the aisle. I've been as honest as I can be without hurting her."

"I don't know if it's possible not to, Cameron. You're married and you're basically telling your wife, you'll never love her. It's like you've got one foot in and one foot out the door."

"That's not true," Cameron said. "I've done everything that's been asked of me. I've been a good husband."

"A husband who doesn't love her. You're in a tough spot. Perhaps you can get a quiet divorce in the future so Amani can marry a man who *wants* to be with her."

The thought of another man with Amani made Cameron physically ill. For all intents and purposes, she was *his*. He felt proprietary.

"You don't like that thought, huh?" Caden asked. "Have you ever considered your feelings for Amani might run deeper than caring and lust?"

Cameron shook his head. It was the one question he was running away from because he was afraid of what the answer might be.

26

"Should I be nervous about a family dinner?" Amani inquired. She didn't have anything to compare to because meals in her family were an event or a royal affair.

Cameron shook his head. "No, I don't think so."

"That doesn't sound reassuring," she responded, smoothing down her dress. She hadn't known what to wear and had called Savi, Savannah for short. Savi had told her to dress casually, but Amani didn't have much in her repertoire.

As a princess, she didn't do casual. Instead, she had Nadia order an outfit from a nearby shop. The bags were delivered earlier and included a houndstooth mock neck sweater dress with a leather jacket and booties. It was the coolest thing she'd ever worn. Cameron whistled at her when she twirled in her ensemble.

The last couple of weeks, she'd enjoyed getting to know Savi as well as Cameron's mother Camilla, even though Cameron was still standoffish towards her. Amani understood his hurt feelings, but she was trying to bridge the gap. When Camilla suggested a family dinner like they used to have, Amani jumped at the chance, especially since Camilla said they hadn't had one in over a year. Amani assumed after Cameron's accident those meals had ceased.

"It'll be fine," Cameron said, patting her knee. "If my mother knows what's good for her, she'll be on her best behavior."

"She's not a child, Cameron."

"No, she just lies like one."

Ouch.

Amani wasn't sure if their relationship could ever be salvaged, but she would try because if Cameron and his mother were on speaking terms... Surely, that boded well for their relationship?

They arrived at the Mitchell family compound, a beautiful estate an hour outside of Baltimore. There was a car as well as a similar SUV parked which Amani assumed was Caden's as governor because there were several guards surrounding the home. As they exited the vehicle, the royal guard convened with them while Amani and Cameron walked inside.

Camilla greeted them at the door looking beautiful in a red faux-wrap dress with a belt cinched around her middle. His mother was a stunner and didn't look a day over forty. Amani could only wish she would age just as gracefully.

"Welcome." Camilla pulled Amani into a hug, but Cameron was already passing by her to enter the living room where the rest of the family were gathered.

"Give it time," Amani replied.

Camilla gave a half-hearted smile. "It's been a year and he still hates me."

"He's hurting."

"I know and I want to make it better, but I can't if he won't let me."

"I agree," Amani patted her arm and followed Cameron inside.

Carter was seated in a plush recliner. He was looking better each time they saw him. He still had a head full of white hair, but there was color in his caramel cheeks and his eyes were full of life instead of drawn.

"Granddaddy." Amani came toward him and kissed either side of his face. He'd asked her to call him Granddad and since she didn't have one, she jumped at the chance.

Carter practically beamed. "Now there's a greeting." He glanced at Savannah and Monae. "You two could learn a thing or two."

"Sure, Grandpa." Savannah pointed her finger at Amani with mock indignation. "Don't be making us look bad. He's a hard one to please."

Everyone laughed. Amani made the rounds, greeting her father-in-law, Caden, Liam, and even little Thea who bounced up and down on her father's leg, desperate to get off his knee and run around the room. She eventually made it over to Cage and his wife, Monae. Admittedly, she hadn't made much of an effort to get to know them, something bothered her about their interaction with Cameron. It seemed forced and so Amani was on her guard, but good manners required her to greet them.

"Good to see you both again," Amani said, offering Cage and Monae a smile.

Cage was holding the baby, so it was Monae who rose to greet her and gave her a quick hug. "You too. Have you been acclimating to the States?"

Amani nodded. "I have. It's quite different here from Bahara. More open. More opinionated, especially the evening news."

Suddenly, she felt Cameron's arms wrap around her waist. "Monae." He inclined his head at his sister-in-law and walked over to Cage. "Is that my nephew?"

Cage offered a smile. The first genuine smile Amani had

seen in all their interactions. "Yes, he is. Would you like to hold him?"

"I would," Cameron replied.

Cage rose and placed the bundle in Cameron's bulking arms. "Caleb, this is your Uncle Cam." Monae came to Cage's side and whispered something in his ear.

Amani sensed this was a big request and again wondered what was going on between Cameron and Cage? He'd held Thea several times, but she'd never seen Cameron holding Caleb.

Was this what it would be like if they were to have their own child?"

"It's good to see him and Cage mending fences," Savannah said from Amani's side.

"Would you care to enlighten me on what happened?"

Savannah didn't get the chance to answer because Camilla announced dinner was ready. Cameron handed the baby back to his brother, came over to Amani's side and led her to the dining room.

Whatever happened between Cameron and Cage, Savannah knew about it which meant everyone at this table was in on it except for her. Cameron hadn't shared *everything* with her. He'd only told her enough to keep her off his back. And guess what? He was right. After he told her the secret about his paternity, Amani stopped questioning him which is exactly what he wanted. He told her half-truths and she'd fallen for it hook, line and sinker.

Amani fumed on the inside, but she was used to not showing what was going on in her head or her heart. You could never let the public see you sweat and she certainly wouldn't in this instance. She graciously sat down at the elegantly appointed dinner table and listened to the Mitchells' conversation while she planned her next move.

SOMETHING WAS WRONG.

Sitting beside Amani at the dinner table, Cameron sensed her anger. No one else could see it because she was practiced at being royal and giving them her princess persona. It was what she was doing now. She hadn't responded this way when they'd come to the house earlier. What could have happened in that short time? She'd spoken with his mother, grandfather, made the rounds and ended with Cage and Monae.

Damn.

Had someone said anything?

He hadn't wanted to share with her the single most embarrassing moment of his life which was finding out that his former girlfriend fell for his brother after they'd barely broken up. He felt foolish and though he was no longer upset— what was done was done. He also didn't broadcast it.

However, something irked Amani and he wanted to know what it was. "Everything all right?" he inquired.

She nodded, but he knew she was lying because he knew her. He'd spent the better part of six months watching her and the last few months, they'd been as intimate as two people could be. He would get to the bottom of it. He wanted her to be happy with him and his family.

"Do we seriously have to go through this again?" his father asked and Cameron tried to pay attention to the course of the conversation.

"What's going on?"

"I'm running for a second term," Caden responded.

"Ah, yeah, I remember those days," Cameron replied. "If I recall, I was against the first term. You had a rocky road."

"We did," Savannah added. "The press was less than kind as

we were getting our footing around becoming a family, but that's all changed. We're in a different place now."

"And I'm older," Liam chimed in. "I can help."

Caden patted Liam's shoulder. "If you're up for it, then you can absolutely help, son."

Liam lit up like a Christmas tree.

Cameron missed these moments and vowed to make visits home more often.

"I was still in the Seals," Cage said, "so you're going to have to walk me through all this campaign business."

"Oh, you'll get a crash course," Cameron said with a laugh.

"You're lucky because you'll be oversees," his grandfather joined the conversation, "the rest of us will be putting in the heavy lifting."

"Not you, Dad," his father said. "You'll be recovering."

"It won't take me that long. I'm as strong as an ox," Carter stated.

There were several laughs at the table and the meal continued in much the same fashion, but Cameron was aware of the tension emanating from his wife by his side. He couldn't wait for the meal to end so they could talk and clear the air.

Amani waited until Savannah came out of the powder room before she grasped her wrist and pulled her into the nearest room. She refused to be deterred.

"Amani! What's going on?"

"Why don't you tell me, Savi?"

Savannah sighed. "If this is about what I think it is, you should be talking to your husband and not me."

"He won't be straight up with me, Savannah, and I need someone to be." Amani paced the floor. "I'm tired of living in the dark. Everyone," she motioned in the direction of dining room, "knows what's happened except me. Please, I need you tell me the truth."

"You're putting me in a bad spot, Amani. Caden, not to mention your husband, will be very upset with me for getting involved in your marriage."

"I know something happened with Cameron, Cage and Monae," Amani stated. "I feel it in my gut. The only thing I can think of is... did they both pursue her and Cage won or something? There are definitely bad feelings there, though it appears they are trying to move past it."

"Something like that."

Amani could see Savannah was hedging her bets.

"You shouldn't be asking Savannah to reveal family secrets, you should be asking me," Cameron said from behind them.

Before she spun on her heel to face her husband, she saw relief across Savannah's features. "I'm sorry, Savi. Can I talk to my husband alone?"

Savannah didn't speak, she just escaped as quickly as she could and closed the door behind her.

Amani inhaled deeply, trying to calm the anger boiling inside her. "Well?" She folded her arms across her chest. "What the hell happened between you, Cage and Monae?"

Cameron rubbed his hand across his head and walked over to the window. "I never wanted to get into this."

"Clearly..." Amani responded.

He turned around to look at her. "Cage stole Monae from me."

Once again, Cameron dropped a bomb on Amani and she was stunned silent.

"Monae and I dated for over a year. Cue Caden's wedding and the two of them meet while we're dating. It's my understanding they clicked, but didn't act on their attraction. In the interim, I wasn't ready to get serious and signed up for another contract with the Air Force which Monae wasn't happy about because she was ready to settle down so we broke up."

He paused and she spoke. "Go on."

Cameron inhaled deeply and then continued. "Cage comes along newly retired from the Navy Seals and they start seeing each other unbeknownst to me until I find them fucking at my parents' estate in Martha's Vineyard. Neither of them bothered to tell me, they were seeing each other. But none of that mattered much because I was injured in the accident shortly afterward. Cage and Monae married, had a baby in short order and here we are. There you have it. All the secrets in my family. At least the ones I know of."

Amani digested all this information. "So let me get this straight, your brother went after a woman you dated?"

"Yes."

"And you were angry?"

"What do you think?" Cameron said. "The last family meal, we brawled and we haven't had one since."

Jesus Christ! This was worse than she could have ever imagined. No wonder Cameron wanted nothing to do with love, commitment or marriage. Other than Caden and Savannah, his examples were seriously flawed, but worse than that something else niggled her as to why Cameron wouldn't open up and let her in.

She knew she shouldn't ask this question, especially if she didn't want to know the answer, but she had to know. "Do you love her?"

Cameron frowned. "Love who?"

"Monae!" Amani's voice rose despite herself, even though asking the question broke her heart into tiny pieces.

"Of course, not! Monae and I are over. She's married to my brother, for Christ's sake!"

"That means nothing if you've never really gotten over her and their betrayal."

"I have," Cameron huffed. "I forgave them."

"Have you? Because from where I'm sitting it doesn't look or feel like it."

"How dare you?" Cameron hissed. "You have no idea what it feels like to walk in my shoes. You've been sheltered in a lily-white palace all your life. I was betrayed by two of the most important people in my life, my mom and my brother at the exact same moment. I'm allowed to process it how I see fit."

"How dare I? I'm your friggin wife," Amani said, picking up on American speech. "I asked you to be honest with me. Instead you give me half-truths? Why because you didn't want me to know that you're still harboring feelings for Monae? It's why you refuse to have a real marriage with me, why you won't let me in."

He shook his head. "That's not true!"

"Yes, it is." Tears coursed down Amani's cheeks and her entire world crashed around her. "And if you don't know that, you're lying to yourself. And I refuse to stand here another minute and be lied to or made a fool of."

She started toward the door, but Cameron beat her to the door. "Don't you dare walk out on me!"

"I can and I will."

"Damn it, Amani! I have given you everything I'm capable of. Isn't it enough that I've given up my life, my home to be with you in Bahara."

"Because you were ordered to do so, out of duty and obligation not because you *want* to be with me."

"I don't *want* you? I think I have more than proved how I can't get enough of you, sweetheart."

Amani shook her head. "Of course, you would boil this all down to sex, but it's so much more than that."

"What is it about then?"

"I L-O-V-E YOU, CAMERON!" she yelled.

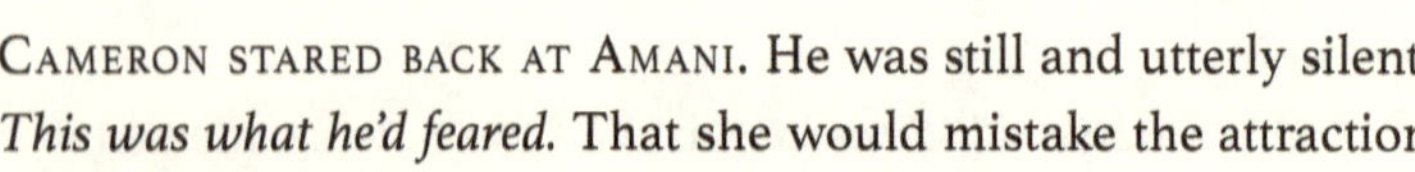

Cameron stared back at Amani. He was still and utterly silent. *This was what he'd feared.* That she would mistake the attraction they felt for one another as love.

"Amani…"

"Don't you dare." Amani held up a hand. "If you attempt to tell me I don't know how I feel, I will scream."

"Okay, okay." He had to tread lightly. "I'm the only man you've been with and we've been very intimate. It's bound to stir up feelings."

"Unrequited feelings?" Amani asked. "Because that's what we're talking about, Cameron. Your inability to *feel* anything, be it for me or your mother."

"Don't bring Camilla into this."

"Why not? You blame her, Monae, and every woman, for their failures!"

"No, I don't."

She cried, "Yes you do. You need to truly forgive them and move on before it consumes you."

Damn this woman! From the very first moment, he saw her, she'd been burrowing deeper and deeper into the places he never let anyone else in. He'd bared himself to her and still she wanted more.

"This is because I can't say the words back that you want to hear," he rasped bitterly. "I told you from the start what I was capable of, Amani. I warned you this wasn't a love match."

"Yes, you warned me not to fall in love," Amani responded. "Yes, I recall that conversation. You took pains to spell it out loud and clear. Somehow I thought we could work through your issues, build a future beyond the great sex and you would finally see we could be good together."

"Everything has been going great. You're the one trying to change the terms." He wasn't about to start kowtowing to Amani's demands.

"No, what I'm doing is telling you that I refuse to spend the rest of my life, settling and certainly not for second best when you're still carrying a torch for your ex."

His face slowly hardened and his hazel eyes bored into hers. "What are you saying?"

"It's over. We're done!" Tears streamed down her cheeks and a bolt of anguish and anger shot through Cameron in equal measure.

"You're done? I didn't ask for any of this. I just wanted to do the right thing for you, for the throne, because Khalil demanded it."

"I don't need your pity or your guilt," Amani said, "I want your love and if I can't have it all, then I want nothing at all."

"Use me and discard me. Is that how it's going to be? What will Khalil say?" He was reaching for straws, but the thought of losing her sent a chill through his veins. Besides, she *pursued* him until he was so weak he'd given in, but deep-down Cameron knew that wasn't the truth. He'd developed feelings for Amani and had come to care for her in ways he never had and that scared him.

He refused to go down that road again and feel that kind of pain if things didn't work out. He already feared he was losing himself in her especially when he held her in his arms as they slept. Sometimes he would pretend he was asleep until he heard her soft snores because he'd come to crave her so desperately.

"I don't care," Amani replied, "this is my decision. I'm no longer under the illusion you will ever grow to love me and, as such, I want a divorce." A sob nearly escaped her throat, but she closed her hand over it and hurried from the room.

Cameron fell backward against the desk in his father's study and watched her retreating figure. He didn't chase after her. What could he say? What could he offer except amazing sensual pleasure? Certainly not the one thing she wanted most in the world.

L-O-V-E

That damned word had just ruined his life for the second time.

27

"Thank you, Khalil," Amani said when her brother agreed to charter a plane to get her back to Bahara. The royal plane had gone back weeks ago when she and Cameron decided to prolong their stay until his grandfather was on the road to recovery. However, upon rushing out of the Mitchell's family home, past Savannah's regretful expression and Camilla, Cage and Monae's shocked faces, she fled to the Escalade and demanded the royal guard bring her back to the hotel.

Cameron's family heard every word she said because she hadn't necessarily been quiet. Not when Cameron was beating around the bush. She'd forced him as well as herself to look in the mirror and see that their marriage wasn't going anywhere. They'd always been on borrowed time, but she hadn't been able to see that. She'd given Cameron her body, soul and mind.

Cameron had stolen her heart and she doubted it would ever be reclaimed.

"Of course, I owe you a plane ride and a lot more, Amani," Khalil said. "I should never have forced you into marrying Cameron. I thought I was doing the right thing."

"You were wrong."

"I know and I can't say how sorry I am. I honestly thought Cameron would grow to love you because I can see he genuinely cares for me."

"I'm just a warm body in his bed, Khalil, nothing more."

"No!" Khalil responded fervently. "I don't believe that. I've seen Cameron with other women and he was different with you. I thought... I thought...well, I guess I was wrong. This is all my fault."

"It's mine. I made the decision to sleep with him which started a chain of events I couldn't stop. All I wanted was for someone to love me. Is that too much to ask?"

She deserved a man who was head over heels for her. She wanted a man to look at her with love and affection the way Caden looked at Savannah. Even Cage stared at Monae like she was the most beautiful woman in the world.

Amani wanted love, but she wouldn't have it with Cameron.

He was a broken man. A man who refused to let go of his past hurts to embrace a future he could have with her.

"Of, course not," Khalil stated, "and I love you, sis. I swear. You're my family."

"I love you too."

They ended the call soon after. It was time for her to go. It didn't take long for Amani to pack her luggage because she practically tossed everything into the suitcase in a hurry to be out of the room before Cameron returned.

Within an hour, she was on her way to the private airstrip where a plane was fueled and ready to take her back home. Back to the palace. *Alone.*

She knew Khalil was more upset than he let on, but instead of blustering like he did the night he discovered she and Cameron had slept together; he actually listened to her reasoning why her marriage needed to be dissolved. If Cameron was amenable, she and Khalil discussed waiting six months before announcing they'd part ways. It would give the palace public relations time to come up with a plan for the fallout and allow Khalil to get ahead of the Royal Council.

She buckled herself into recliner on the small jet, along with two of the Royal Baharan guards, while the other two guards stayed behind with Cameron. Although, he may not want them, he was still considered a Prince of Bahara and, as royalty, required protection. As the jet taxied down the runway, Amani allowed the torrent of tears to come.

CAMERON STARED out the window of his parents' home with his fingers clenched around a coffee mug. He couldn't believe it had only been a couple of days since Amani left D.C., left him.

When she told him she was leaving, she'd meant it. Arriving back at the Four Seasons, he'd found the room cleared of all her things as if she'd never been there, but he knew otherwise. Her perfume still lingered in the room and he'd decided to come to his parent's.

Instantly, he wanted to call her back because despite the things he'd said about Khalil backing him into a corner, Cameron had agreed to the marriage. He was enthralled with Amani and would miss her.

Her beautiful smile.

Her laughter.

Her intelligence, vivaciousness and passion.

He assumed marriage would be a chore, but it hadn't been. He enjoyed getting to know her inside and out. They'd been partners and well suited not just in the bedroom but in sharing their royal duties. They fed off each other and Cameron found he was good at being a prince, at helping people.

Wasn't being in the Air Force about service to his country? He'd just been serving Bahara.

"Well, you really messed that up," his father's voice rang out from behind Cameron.

Cameron turned around and glared at him. "Dad..."

"Don't, dad me," his father replied, walking into the kitchen. He went straight for the cabinet and pulled out a mug and poured himself a cup of coffee from the carafe, Cameron had made. "You broke Amani's heart."

He didn't need his father telling him that. He knew and it gutted him. Cameron released a long sigh. "It wasn't my intention." He'd never wanted to hurt her. Yet, he didn't want the glow in her eyes that she had for him to go out as the years passed and then grow to cool indifference.

His father regarded him for a moment and sipped his coffee. "Nevertheless, you did. How are you going to fix this?"

"I'm not."

"What do you mean? Are you honestly going to let that wonderful woman slip through your grasp?"

"If I can't give her the love she needs," Cameron answered, "then yes."

His father shook his head. "You're an idiot!"

"Probably, but I'm doing the right thing. I'm giving her the freedom of choice, to find the man of her dreams."

"And you're sure that's not you?"

Cameron didn't answer. He couldn't because he wasn't sure. One minute, he felt relief because he was back home and could do his own thing, like spend time with the family. He'd already spent a couple of evenings at Caden's.

Then there was the rest of time, when he felt utterly alone. The nights were especially difficult because he loved holding Amani and spooning her curvy bottom against his groin. She was his match in the bedroom and he loved her exuberance.

But Amani wanted more than he was willing to give, so as much as it pained him, Cameron wasn't that man. "Yes, I'm sure." But his words were a lie.

He might very well be her dream man and if he were, he'd made the biggest mistake of his life.

"It's GOING to be okay, Amani," Nadia rubbed her back as Amani lay crying in bed. Ever since she returned to the palace, *alone a week ago,* she had retreated to her suite.

Her suite.

Not the one she shared with Cameron in the East Wing. She couldn't bear to be in those quarters without him. Memories of Cameron would haunt her everywhere she went and it was bad enough just making it through the day.

Every day she woke up, Amani hoped that today would be the day, Cameron realized he'd made a mistake. He would come home, beg her forgiveness and tell her he was desperately in love with her and then they would live happily ever after. She should never had read so many romance novels. If she hadn't, she wouldn't be hoping for something that was never going to happen.

Cameron didn't love her and never would. She was deluding herself if she thought otherwise. It just hurt so much. It physically hurt and she hadn't been able to leave her bed for the last week. She cried all the time and had more than one emotional meltdown with Nadia. Thank God for Nadia, she'd been a lifeline because Khalil hadn't known what to do.

He'd been waiting for her as soon as she arrived at the steps of the plane. Khalil had immediately pulled her into the biggest and longest hug she'd ever received from her own family. It had felt so good to be held. She'd broken down in his arms and to her utter relief, he lifted her into his arms and carried her to the limo. Amani didn't even remember the ride to the palace. She just remembered waking the next day in Bahara without Cameron and the tears started flowing and hadn't stopped since.

Amani lifted her head and stared at Nadia. "I'm sorry."

"Why?" Nadia asked. "It's not your fault. Prince Cameron is in the wrong here. He should have treated you better."

Amani smiled. Nadia was always in her corner. "Thank you."

"Are you ready for a shower? Or how about a bath?" Nadia inquired. "I can prepare your favorite."

"A bath sounds lovely," Amani replied.

A short while later, she was covered in bubbles and reclining her head against the soft pillow. Nadia really was a godsend. Amani couldn't make it without her. It was difficult to be without Cameron because he'd made her feel special.

No one in her family had ever done that. She'd always been treated as an afterthought because she was a woman and not the second son, her father the King and her mother had hoped for. No one had ever shown her any sort of affection. Was it any wonder she fell for the first man to show her some? Maybe Cameron was right — she was infatuated with him.

Her heart rejected that notion as soon as it came into her head. She'd found a sense of wellbeing and a sense of purpose when they were together. And every night he'd take her to heaven with his lovemaking. They had an active sex life and one she would miss.

And that's when it hit her.

Amani sat upright in the bathtub.

"Amani? You look stricken," Nadia said. "Is everything okay?"

"Nadia, can you hand me my phone?" She was almost afraid to ask, afraid to look.

Nadia left the bathroom and several minutes later she returned carrying Amani's smart phone. With shaking hands,

Amani grasped it from her and went to the calendar. She swiped this way and that and counted the weeks since her last period.

Dear God!

She hadn't had one since before she left Bahara. That was nearly six weeks ago.

Her hand flew to her mouth. "No, no, no, this can't be happening."

"Amani, what is it?"

She was afraid to say the words aloud for fear they were true, but then Amani thought about how she'd felt the last week, tired, drained. She glanced down at her breasts that now seemed noticeably larger and more sensitive.

Oh, God, she was going to be sick. She bolted upright and Nadia quickly wrapped a towel around her which Amani tucked around her bosom before rushing off to the toilet. She made it there in enough time to relieve the contents of her stomach. Nadia was such a sweetheart and held back her hair.

When she was finished, Amani sat on the cold tile floor and tears slid down her brown cheeks. "Nadia, I need a pregnancy test, but it has to be a secret. No one can know. Can you do this?"

Nadia nodded. "Of course, *princess*. I will make it happen."

"Thank you." Amani feared what the test would say. Her period was already late and with the other symptoms she was having from being emotional to the sensitive breasts and now morning sickness, she was all but certain what the results would say, but she needed confirmation before taking the next steps that would determine her and quite possibly her baby's future.

28

———

"**G**randpa, it's so good to see you on your feet," Cameron said when he stopped by the family compound to check on his grandfather. It had been over a week since Amani left and he was still in disbelief that she'd actually left him and he was here in the States alone, without her.

He was doing his best to act as if he was unaffected, but it wasn't true. Every day, a voice had been growing louder and telling him he made a mistake letting her go, but Cameron forced it down. He didn't want to do love and marriage. He was disillusioned by what he'd seen and experienced. First, his former girlfriend choosing his brother over him after she claimed to want to marry him.

Then finding out that his own mother cheated on his father and had him, only to keep both of them in the dark for over three decades. How can you claim to love a person if you continually lie to them day in and day out? Cameron didn't believe real love was possible even though he might have seen evidence of it in how Amani was with him. He chose not to accept it because he feared it would bite him in the ass like it had already done.

"My boy." Carter rose to greet him from his chair out on the terrace. "It's good to see you."

Cameron accepted his embrace and sat down with him on one of the wicker chairs.

"What's the word from your doctors?" Cameron inquired, giving his grandfather the once over. His color had returned and he appeared to be getting back some of his strength based on how he was moving about the house.

"I'm doing well," his grandfather said. "I'm recovering nicely from the open-heart surgery."

A smile crossed Cameron's features. "That's great news!"

"Yes, it is, but let's not beat around the bush here, Cameron. Why are you still here without Amani?" His grandfather always cut to the chase. He didn't mind calling his grandsons or son out if the situation called for it.

Cameron had been dreading this conversation. "Amani decided to go back to Bahara."

"Why?" he pressed.

"Because I couldn't give her what she wanted."

"Couldn't, or *wouldn't*?" his grandfather pressed.

Cameron shrugged. "Does it matter?"

"Hell yeah, it does," he bellowed. "You're being a stubborn and foolish goat and letting the best thing that ever happened to you get away because you're angry about your past and the hand you were dealt. Get over your damn masculine pride, Cameron and go get your woman."

"Grandpa…..."

"Don't you, grandpa me. I know what I saw and that girl loves you and I suspect you love her too. So why do you refuse to admit it?"

Cameron shook his head. "You're wrong. I care for Amani, but that's as deep as my feelings go."

"That's not what I saw. I saw two young people in love. And I get that you're scared. It's not easy for us Mitchell men to be vulnerable. We've had to be strong to fight for this country. But you also have to be strong enough to admit when you need someone. And you need Amani."

Did he need her?

He certainly missed her smile. Missed her exuberance and zest for life. He'd seen a lot more than she had of human nature and was more jaded, but she grounded him and made him want to look at the bright side.

But need? He was self-sufficient and lived his life on his own terms - until he met her. How had that suddenly changed in just a short amount of time?

"Well, boy?" His grandfather was waiting for an answer. "What are you going to do?"

"I don't know, Grandpa." Cameron hesitated to take further action.

"What is holding you back?" His grandfather continued to press him. "Fear, shame, pride? She knows everything that transpired now. She knows about your mama, about Monae. I assume you've told her about the accident which ended your career and still she stayed by your side."

Cameron shook his head. "I wasn't always forthright with Amani. I told her about the accident and finally Mama, but we hadn't discussed what happened with Cage and Monae. She thinks I might still be hung up on Monae because I said I didn't want love, marriage or commitment."

"Is that true?"

"Hell, no!" Cameron wasn't holding a torch for his sister-in-law. That ship had long since sailed.

"You know, Monae loves Cage. And now that they've had a child, I'm sorry to tell you, boy, that isn't going to change."

"I know, but Amani thinks otherwise."

"Then you make her believe," his grandfather said. "You're a smart enough man to know how. You can't let this rift and divide go on. The longer you're away from her, the more she'll think she can live without you. Do you want that? Do you want her with another man?"

"No." Amani was his. He knew it was crazy to feel so possessive of her, but since the start when he was just her bodyguard, they'd had a strong connection which only intensified once they were married.

"Then fight for her. Don't give up on love, Cameron. I would give anything to have your grandmother back, to have another day, another week, another year with her. She was taken from me much too soon..." His voice cracked and Cameron reached across the short distance and touched his grandfather's arm. Carter rarely got emotional. He was always so tough, so it was good to see he could be real.

"Thank you, Grandpa. I've heard everything you said and I promise to take it all to heart."

His grandfather patted his knee. "That's good, my boy. Don't let a good woman like Amani go."

Cameron knew that too, but as much as he wanted Amani, he also knew, he couldn't go back to Bahara unless he was offering her *everything*. She was right when she'd said she deserved love and unless he was prepared to give her his heart, she wouldn't take him back.

It was all or nothing.

Amani stared at the two blue lines on the pregnancy stick and covered her mouth with her hand. She was hoping against hope that she was wrong, but there were several sticks lined across the sink in her suite in the palace. They all said the same thing.

She was pregnant.

With Cameron's baby.

In another life, she would have been thrilled to be carrying a child with the man she loved, but this wasn't that circumstance. She was estranged from her husband who *didn't* love her and was still harboring feelings for his ex-girlfriend, turned sister-in-law.

What the hell was she going to do now?

Extracting herself from her marriage wouldn't just be difficult, but an uphill battle. Her country, the royal council, even Khalil wouldn't accept her being a divorced princess having a baby. The divorce was already going to be a hard enough pill to swallow, but a baby, an innocent baby?

Amani's hand immediately flew to her stomach where a tiny life was growing inside. A life she and Cameron created together. It may not have been love on his part, but it had certainly been love for her. And she loved this baby even though the timing and circumstances were inconvenient.

"Princess?" Nadia was staring at back her with grave concern. "Are you okay?"

She was far from okay, but now there was no more doubt. Amani would have to be strong to protect herself and her baby. The right thing to do would be to inform Cameron he was going to be a father. He may not love her, but she suspected he would love their child. And that pained her.

Why couldn't he love her back? This would be so different if they were in love and looking forward to this pregnancy. But that wasn't where she was and she would have to accept that.

Amani closed her eyes and breathed in. She would have to tell Khalil. She already knew his answer. He wouldn't want her to go through with the divorce, not until the baby was born and maybe not even then. A child was a gamechanger.

Her brother's reaction, however, shocked the hell out of Amani.

"I'm so sorry Amani." Khalil pulled her into his arms. "I should never have bulldozed you into marrying Cameron. This travesty is my fault."

Amani pushed away from his chest and looked into her brother's ebony eyes. "No, it's not. Cameron and I made a choice that has brought about a consequence, a beautiful consequence."

"An heir to the throne," Khalil added.

Amani nodded.

"How do you want to handle this?"

Amani was surprised by Khalil's response. She assumed he would be issuing orders and making demands such as getting Cameron back on the first plane to Bahara.

"If it's all right with you, I'd like a few days to think about this. Figure out what I want to do."

"Of course. In the meantime, I'll contact the palace doctor to confirm your pregnancy and ensure you receive the very best care in the interim. I'll ensure its kept quiet until you give me the word on how to proceed."

"Thank you, Khalil. Your support on this means a lot."

"I should have been a brother to you three months ago instead of being a King."

A smile curved Amani's lips. "You're new to the role so I think I can forgive you."

"And you're being too kind. I was a complete and utter ogre."

"Yes, you were," Nadia quietly said, behind her, and Khalil turned to stare at her, but didn't reprimand her about talking to her King that way. Instead, their eyes connected for the briefest of moments and Amani wondered if something was going on between them that she didn't know about, but surely Nadia would tell her if that were so?

Nadia quickly spoke again. "My apologies, my King. I spoke out of turn."

"You did, but I appreciate how loyal you are to my sister. She needs someone that she can rely on and that hasn't been me these days. But I promise you that will change going forward, Amani. No matter what you decide."

Amani's brows furrowed in consternation. "Are you sure about that? Cameron is your friend. You go way back."

"And you're my family."

She'd never felt more loved or cared for *ever* than she did in this moment. Khalil wasn't behaving like the monarch of the Bahara. He was acting like a brother and that meant the world to her. "Thank you, Khalil. I love you."

"Love you too, Amani." He pulled her into one final hug and retreated from the room.

"That went better than I expected," Amani said after Khalil had gone.

"Yes, it did," Nadia replied. "I had no idea the King would be so understanding. It's a big surprise."

"And how are you and the King?" Amani inquired. It was nice to think about someone other than herself.

"Khal— I mean His Majesty and I have no relationship."

Amani raised a brow.

"We don't. I merely helped him out when his maid was gravely ill while you and Cameron were away. Nothing more."

"I see." Amani wasn't sure she believed Nadia because her cheeks were flushed red, but she let it go. She had bigger issues to face which was what she was going to do about this pregnancy. She was afraid to tell Cameron because he'd made it clear he wasn't looking for love and marriage, but then Khalil had pressed him into doing the right thing. She could only imagine how he would react if she were to tell him she was carrying his baby. He might feel forced into coming back to Bahara because it's what he *should* do and not what he *wanted* to do.

Amani didn't want that. She was more than capable of raising this baby alone if she had to, but she wasn't sure she could leave Cameron out and have him estranged from his child.

She was more confused than ever on which direction she should go. She just knew whatever decision she chose, one of them was going to lose their dream.

29

"I'm surprised you wanted to include me," Cage said, when he arrived to the running field to find Cameron and Caden already assembled.

"You're my brother. Of course, you should be here," Cameron responded, lacing up his running sneakers.

Cameron wasn't surprised Cage felt this way. Although he'd made his peace with Cage and Monae's marriage, he hadn't exactly rolled out the red carpet or gone out of his way to spend time with him either. After speaking with their grandfather, Cameron was trying to change that. Carter was right. It was high time he put the past in the past. *Permanently.*

When Caden asked Cameron to attend one of his normal morning runs, Cameron inquired if they could ask Cage to come. Caden had been surprised, but eagerly agreed. The track had been cleared by Caden and Cameron's security team, so they had the entire place to themselves.

"We have to move on and start healing this family," Caden said, jumping into the conversation, "Cameron took the first step and you're here, Cage, to take the other."

"I want that too," Cage responded, "It's why I gave you your distance to come to terms with how everything went down with me and Monae. I'm not going to apologize for finding the woman I was meant to be with, but I apologize for hurting you and not being upfront with you about my feelings."

"I appreciate that, Cage," Cameron said while doing a few squats, "But we don't need to rehash the past."

"Don't we?" Cage asked, bending his legs to stretch his quads, "Because your wife seems to think you're still hung up on mine."

Cameron frowned. "You know that isn't true."

Cage chuckled. "I do. But I'm not who you need to convince."

"Amani took it all out of context," Cameron replied.

"That's because you didn't tell her," Caden responded. "If you had been honest with her from the jump, she wouldn't have leapt to the wrong conclusion."

Cameron nodded. "You're right. I know that."

"Then you know, you need to high-tail your ass to Bahara and get her back?" Cage asked, "because that's what you should be doing instead of talking to us. But if you need us to pound some common sense into your head, your two big brothers," he glanced at Caden, "are happy to oblige."

"I've heard all this before," Cameron said, "Grandpa gave me an earful the other day."

"Doesn't look like you're heeding his advice," Caden replied. "What's holding you back?"

Fear.

"I don't know if I'm good enough for her," Cameron said. "The only reason she married me was because her brother forced her to. And, yes, she may have grown feelings for me, but I'm a broken man. I'm not who I used to be."

"No, you're not," Caden said, "but so what if you're not a fighter pilot anymore. You're more than your rank and file, Cameron. You always have been and always will be. Besides which, I saw some of the footage of you as Prince Consort of Bahara. You were thriving in the role."

Cameron gave an awkward smile. "Don't you think you're laying it on a little thick, bro?"

"Not at all," Caden replied. "I know what I saw. You were born for this. You're a leader and you're fulfilling your destiny in another role."

"Yeah, all of that," Cage motioned to his big brother, "you know Caden has a way with words much better than I do. He's a politician, after all."

The three of them all chuckled.

"Yeah, well, someone had to be referee between the two of you," Caden replied, looking back and forth between Cameron and Cage.

"We weren't so bad," Cameron said.

"You were terrible," Caden responded, "And as the oldest, I have always had to look after you even when Dad was deployed."

Hearing about the deployment, it suddenly occurred to Cameron that Caden could know something. "Do you ever remember another man coming around when Dad wasn't there?" Cameron asked.

"Cam..."

"What?"

"I thought we were moving on and wiping the slate clean," Caden replied.

"How can I do that when there's so many unanswered questions?"

"Then talk to Mom," Cage came toward Cameron. "Get whatever it is you have to say off your chest so you can bury this anger and move on to be with your lady."

"It's not that simple."

"It's exactly that easy," Cage responded. "I know what it's like to be scared of letting love in because you're afraid of getting hurt. I was afraid because I never felt love from Dad. I always thought Caden was the golden boy and you were Dad's favorite. I know what it's like to be afraid of loss. I know because I saw my best friend Griffin die, but Cam, if you don't, you're going to let a good woman like Amani slip through your fingers. Make peace with Mom, only then will you be worthy of Amani."

Cameron cocked his head and stared at Cage. He was stunned by his brother's fervent speech. "I thought Caden was the eloquent one, but that was pretty good."

Cage shrugged. "What can I say? When the moment calls for it, I can come through in a clutch."

They all laughed once again, but even after their hour-long run and subsequent breakfast at a nearby diner, Cameron couldn't forget his brother's advice. Were they right? Was settling things with his mother the key to making him feel ready to go back to Bahara and claim *his woman?*

AFTER SHOWERING and dressing at the hotel which he'd returned to within a few days of Amani leaving, the Baharan royal guard were driving him to the Mitchell compound. Cameron had called ahead to be sure his mother was home. She'd been surprised to hear his voice, but delighted he wanted to visit.

Cameron wasn't sure how this meeting was going to go, but he was willing to try. He couldn't stay in this limbo forever. He needed to move on with his life and his mother was the key.

He punched in the code for the front door and walked inside. He called out and she appeared several seconds later. She was usually immaculately dressed, but today she was dressed down in jeans and a simple white tunic. However, her short hair was stylish slicked down and she wore no makeup.

"Is everything okay?" Cameron inquired. He was used to her being more put together.

"I'm not sure," his mother replied. "Am I going to be your punching bag today? If so, I didn't see the need for makeup if I was going to cry it all off."

Damn. Was he that harsh? Cameron supposed he was. He had a right to be. She'd lied to him his entire life.

"Let's go sit down." She motioned him toward the living room and took a seat on the sofa while Cameron sat down in a high-backed chair opposite her.

"I assume you have something to say?" his mother asked. "Whatever it is, just say it."

"Who is he?" Cameron asked. "Who's my father?"

"Cal Mitchell is your father."

Cameron sucked in a harsh breath. "Let's not play word games, Mom. Yes, I know Cal is my dad. Who is my biological father?"

"Why do you need to know this?" she inquired. "What good will it do?"

"It will give me the closure I need."

His mother lowered her head and held her face with both hands. "I promised your father I would never speak of it again."

"That was your promise to your husband, but I'm your son and you owe me this," Cameron responded, "you owe me the truth since you let me spend and build my entire life on a lie."

When she glanced up, tears glistened in her eyes and she reached into her jean pocket and produced a handkerchief. "It was one night, Cameron. Like I told you before, it wasn't a grand affair. I was lonely and missing your father and I messed up."

"I need to know, Mom. I have to," Cameron said. "I need to deal with this so I can move on and quite possibly save my marriage."

She nodded as if she understood, but she was silent for

several beats and Cameron wondered if she was going to tell him, but then she whispered, "I slept with his best friend, Mike Robinson."

"Ohmigod! Uncle Mike!" Cameron said. He remembered the fair skinned man who was a big part of their family and his father had no idea that his friend was the one who had slept with his wife? "Did Mike know?"

His mother shrugged. "If he did, he never said anything and I certainly wasn't about to. It was a mistake which we both deeply regretted as soon as it was over. He went on to marry his wife and your father came back."

"But Mike didn't, not after his last deployment in Iraq," Cameron said, staring at the tears stained on his mothers' cheek, "If I recall, he was killed in action."

His mother nodded. "I was so relieved and I know that's an awful thing to say, but it was like our secret died with him and no one would ever know."

"But then I got in the accident and needed a blood transfusion."

"Yes, and the truth came out at the worst possible time when we didn't know if you were going to live or die," his mother cried, sniffing into her handkerchief.

Cameron absorbed this information and consequently he felt as if a weight was being lifted off his shoulders. When he saw his reflection in the mirror previously, he'd never seen Cal in himself. Now, he knew who he looked like and could put the pieces together in his family tree, his biological one. Yet, knowing Mike was his father changed nothing. Cal Mitchell was his father and always would be.

"Thank you," Cameron said. "Thank you for telling me. I know Dad didn't want you too, but he had no right making that decision for me. I deserve to know the truth for myself and for my children if I have any. We have to know our medical history."

"Oh, my goodness, of course," his mother teared up again, "I never even thought of that. I was only seeing how all of this affected me. I know I hurt you, Cameron, and I can never express how deeply sorry I am. I should never have lied to you or your father, but I didn't know what else to do. I didn't want to lose him."

"You haven't lost me." His father stated from behind them and Cameron watched him stride into the living room. "Not now and not ever." He pulled his mother into a hug and placed a soft kiss on her lips.

The love in his father's eyes was evident and was damn near embarrassing that he could love his mother this much that he was willing to forget her indiscretion and years of lies. Was love truly that powerful?

It was.

Because he had been fighting his love for Amani this entire time. He had pushed it down because he didn't think he was worthy of Amani or could ever love her the way she was meant to be loved. He was wrong. He had the capacity for love because he'd been shown it each and every day by his parents. And each and every day he'd been with Amani.

She was the purest, sweetest thing that had ever happened in his life. And even though he'd tried to bury his pain behind his work and in their passion, Amani had seen beyond that. She'd seen him, *loved him.*

And he missed her. With every shared laugh, every caress, every moment they spent together, he slowly began to let her in. He tried valiantly the last couple of weeks to vanquish any feelings he might harbor for her, but it was a losing battle. She was his air and until he saw her again he wouldn't be able to breathe.

"I have to go!" Cameron said, pushing past his parents who were still embraced, so much so they barely noticed.

"To get your wife back, I presume?" his father inquired, lifting his head.

Cameron nodded. "If she'll have me."

He'd ruined things royally and now he had to make amends. He had to convince Amani to give him another chance. But how? How could he explain that finding out he wasn't who he thought he was, had fucked with his head? How could he explain that losing his career and the life he thought he might have had threw him off course and made him vow to never love or commit to anything or anyone?

He prayed she would forgive him and if she didn't, he would spend the rest of his life trying to convince her otherwise.

30

———

The morning sickness was not getting any better, in fact, Amani would say it had gotten worse. She'd already had to cancel several engagements. If this continued, people would begin to suspect something was amiss. According to Nadia, there were already rumors, she and Cameron's marriage was in trouble because it had been two weeks and he hadn't returned. She was running out of excuses as to why he hadn't returned to Bahara. She would have to make a decision soon on what to do.

As for her emotions, they were worse than ever. Often she would burst out into tears for no apparent reason. Surely, she couldn't cry forever? At some point she was going to have to find the strength to move on, pick up the threads of her life and make a new one. The thought of a life without Cameron made her nauseous.

But she was going to prevail, today was the first day she'd felt some semblance of normalcy. She'd been able to tolerate some Baharan tea and crackers which thus far hadn't decided to come up. Nadia had already helped with her hair and makeup and now she stood, poised and ready to attend another opening for a girl's school, much like the one she'd opened months ago when Cameron was still her bodyguard.

"How do I look?" Amani asked Nadia, posing. Nadia had been able to cover the dark circles under her eyes from lack of sleep and wishing Cameron's arms were wrapped around her. The dress was hanging off her a bit. She'd lost a few pounds, but the palace doctor told her it was normal and had given her some nausea pills yesterday which seemed to be working.

"Much better, princess," Nadia said. "Are you ready to face the world?"

Amani nodded. She'd been hiding in her suite of rooms for weeks and it was time to come out of hiding. As they walked the corridors of the palace, members of the Royal Council and several from the court, stopped to speak to her and say how happy they were to see her.

She kept her head up even when one of them mentioned Cameron and asked when he was returning home. Nadia quickly gave the same excuse of his ailing grandfather, but that was getting old and she knew they wouldn't be able to use it for much longer.

A chauffeured car was waiting for Amani outside the palace and she slipped in along with Nadia. She glanced out the window, willing the tears to stay away.

"It's okay," Naida said, brushing her hand over Amani's. "You'll figure it out. If you have to raise this baby alone, you will have help. You have me."

Amani turned to Nadia. "Have I ever told you just how much you mean to me? You've always been quietly by my side, in my corner, supporting me, holding me up. I've never said thank you because royalty is just supposed to expect loyalty from their subjects. But you're more than that, you're my confidante and my very best friend."

Nadia touched her chest. "Thank you, Amani. Your words mean a lot."

"They were long overdue to be said."

They spent the rest of the ride in silence until they arrived at the school, but to her surprise, she wasn't the first royalty there. Cameron stood waiting on the steps.

"Did you know he was going to be here?" Amani whispered as if he could hear her.

Nadia frowned. "Of course not, I would have told you. He must have come of his own accord."

How dare Cameron just show up out of the blue after all these weeks without even a phone call? It was just like him to be so high-handed and think he could get away with it. Any other time, she would tell him exact how she felt, but as she exited the vehicle, they had an audience.

He knew that.

Is that why he planned this entrance?

"Amani." Cameron bowed when she approached and lifted her hand to his lips and brushed a soft kiss across it.

"What are you doing here?" she whispered under her breath as she turned so they could smile for the cameras.

"I'm here to win you back."

CAMERON WAS certain all of Bahara would want to know what he said to produce the stunned expression on Amani's face that would surely grace tomorrow's papers. She tore her eyes away and they both walked up the steps and into the building.

He'd been afraid to go straight to the palace for fear Khalil might turn him away and refuse to let him see Amani. When he tried reaching out to Khalil, all of his calls had been steadfastly ignored and none of his texts *read.*

He'd known then it was going to be an uphill battle.

Coming here today was a preemptive strike. By making himself visible again as Prince, Amani or Khali wouldn't be able to ignore his presence. Ideally, he would have loved to have gotten Amani alone so they could talk, just the two of them and that's exactly what he intended to do. He'd already arranged with the guard to ensure the other car with Nadia in it would be returned to the palace. He needed his wife alone and, bless her heart, Nadia was protective and would guard her against him.

As it was, as they walked through the school and admiring all the hard work from the construction company and the staff, Amani was keeping herself at a distance from Cameron. He understood. He deserved it. He'd hurt her, but he was here to fix what he'd broken, if she'd let him.

They continued touring the school, chatting with students and taking a pictures until it was time to give a short speech. Cameron lent a helping hand to Amani as she climbed the dais. The school was near and dear to Amani's heart because she was eager to see more education available to women in Bahara. She wanted to see other women be given the same opportunities she'd been given.

Amani's speech was flawless as always and when it was finished, it was time for the ribbon cutting. Cameron stepped closer to Amani and placed his hand over hers to help cut the ribbon. He felt her shiver and understood because he felt the same way. Whenever he was within a few yards of her, a scalding heat raced like molten lava through his veins.

Just as quickly, the cutting was over and once the formalities were concluded, they started down the hall. "I was hoping we could talk," Cameron said.

"Now isn't a good time," Amani responded once they reached the double doors to exit.

She was going to make a run for it, Cameron was certain of

it, but he wasn't going to let her. He'd made some provisions of his own. Amani quickly descended the steps and glanced around for her car.

"Where's my car?" She turned to Cameron. "Did you have something to do with this?"

His limousine pulled up to the curb and Cameron reached for the door. "Get inside, Amani."

She stood with her feet planted on the sidewalk and Cameron thought he might have to lift her in, but then a camera flashed. He saw the second she realized fighting was futile with the press nearby and slid inside, Cameron joined her in the backseat and closed the door, locking them in.

Once inside, the subtle scent of her perfume, light and floral with notes of jasmine, reminded him of just how much he missed his wife.

"I assume you set this up to get me alone?" she asked.

"I did."

"Why?" Amani inquired. "Why did you come back?"

"I missed you," Cameron answered honestly and truthfully. He wasn't going to hold back the truth from Amani, not anymore. He owed her that and whole lot more. He owed her his heart.

Amani glanced out the window. "This isn't the way back to the palace."

"No, it's not."

"Are you kidnapping me?"

Cameron chuckled. "Something like that. I just want some time alone for us to talk with no interruptions."

"The time for that came and went."

"Do you really believe that'?," Cameron asked. "Are you saying it's over between us?"

Her answer was silence and Cameron took it to mean there was still a chance. Ten minutes later, they were pulling up to the airfield where the Baharan helicopter was waiting to take them back to the summer villa. The place where they'd been the happiest. Cameron had thrown around his weight by calling the pilot and demanding he have the helicopter waiting and it worked.

Cameron opened the door and climbed out, but Amani was ruthlessly staring out of the window. "Are you going to get out or am I going to have to carry you?"

The withering look she gave him told Cameron he'd better not dare and then she was sliding out of the limo and walking to the helicopter. She didn't say a word to him. She merely put on the headphones and stared out the window as the helicopter lifted them up into the air.

"Amani..."

"Don't..." she said over the roar of the helicopter.

He would have to leave his groveling for later. The ride seemed interminable, but eventually they landed a half hour later.

Once she was on solid land and the helicopter was lifting off the ground, she turned on him. "Why did you bring me here of all places?" She motioned to the villa.

"It's because we were happy here. And it's where I realized I was starting to fall in love with you."

AMANI SHOOK HER HEAD. She couldn't believe what Cameron just said. "You don't mean that. You told me you don't have faith in love, marriage or commitment."

"I didn't," Cameron replied, "because so much happened to me last year that it hardened my heart against all the things I once believed in. But let's not talk about this out here, can we go inside?"

She nodded. What else could she do? He'd just thrown her for a loop by showing up in Bahara after two weeks of no contact. He pretty much ambushed her at the school opening and planned a scheme to get her away from the palace and onto the helicopter. If she was honest, a slight bit of hope was starting to seep in on why Cameron would take such drastic action.

What did it all mean?

She didn't know, but followed him as he walked inside the villa to the living room. It was just as beautiful as before except then she'd been thrilled to be alone with Cameron to explore the chemistry between them. Memories of how intimate they'd been here were littered throughout the house. Everywhere she looked, she could see her and Cameron laughing in the kitchen. Her and Cameron swimming in the pool. Cameron spreading her out on one of the poolside loungers and having his way with her.

Amani blinked and tried to erase the images and turned to face him. "All right," she folded her arms across her chest in a protective measure. "Talk."

"I knew you were remarkable, Amani, from the moment I met you," Cameron murmured, "Being your bodyguard was a special kind of torture because every time you looked at me, my heart started in my chest. I did my best to ignore you and push down any feelings I might have for you, but it didn't work. I was weak for you."

"That's all just physical, Cameron."

"You're right. And it started that way," he admitted, "but the more I got to know you and see how much you cared about your country and your people I was more enthralled. How you convinced the Bedouin people to come over to Khalil's side was nothing short of epic, but you made the impossible possible."

Amani smiled. "Thank you." He didn't have to say it. It was nice to feel validated. For years, no one in her family cared and so she'd created a protective shell around herself to prevent herself from cracking. Only Nadia knew the self-doubts she had about whether she could be of any use to the crown.

"I mean it, you're amazing, Amani. And I wasn't able to resist you, not just physically. Though the night we spent in the harem was nothing short of spectacular. It rocked me to my very foundation. It was a one-of-a-kind experience that I'd never shared with another woman. I felt so connected to you."

Although she had nothing to compare Cameron to, Amani had known intrinsically that what they had that night, she'd never find with another man. It's why she hadn't fought Khalil harder on his demand that they marry.

"But then Khalil found out about us and rather than face what happened between us, I allowed him to use marriage as a shield to protect myself, protect my feelings."

"Why?"

"Because I didn't want to risk getting hurt again," Cameron responded. "And I know you think my reticence toward love and marriage is about Monae choosing Cage, but you're wrong. It did make me see how much people were willing to risk for love, but I'm not harboring feelings for her. If nothing, it made me envious and jealous she found love with Cage and not me."

"Then why didn't you tell me about her? Why did you keep it from me? It made me think . . ."

"I didn't want to be with you?" Cameron finished. "Well, you're wrong. There's no one else I want to be with, but you, Amani. But my mother's deception after all these years, lying to me and my father and calling it love was twisted. It messed with my head and made me think love wasn't real but just an illusion."

"And now? What's changed?"

"I've made peace with my mother. She and I had a long talk

and I expressed my anger and hurt. I told her I needed to know who my biological father was."

"Did she tell you?"

"She didn't want to, but I had to know where I came from and what my medical history is. Not just for me, but for any future children we might have."

Amani's heart constricted. *For any future children we might have.*

Cameron had no idea that children were no longer a prospect in the future. It was happening now. He was going to be a father. She had to tell him, but not yet. She didn't want to interrupt his revelations. He needed to get off his chest everything that had gone unsaid for far too long.

"She shared with me that my biological father was my dad's best friend, Mike, whom I knew. He was a friend of the family."

"Ohmigod! That's awful. Your dad must be so upset," Amani responded.

"Honestly? I don't think he knows because he asked my mother not to share the identity. Said it didn't matter to him because he's my father."

Her eyes welled with tears. "He is. It's clear how much Mr. Mitchell loves you."

"I know," Cameron said, "besides which, Mike was killed in action years ago. He's dead."

"Cameron, no!" Her hand flew to her mouth.

"It's for the best, Amani. No way would I have had a relationship with the man. I would never do that to my dad. But I will make some inquiries about his family if nothing else than to find out my medical history and know who I look like."

"Of course, as you should."

"What all of this means is that I've come to realize I have to let go of the past and my hurts and fears. I have to embrace what's right in front of me and that's you, Amani. I didn't just fall in love with you here. I am in love with you."

"No, you can't be!" She shook her head. She was afraid to believe it. No one in her life other than Khalil and Malik had ever truly loved her.

"I know, sweetheart. I fought it tooth and nail. I thought keeping you at arm's length and acting as if our lovemaking was just sex, but it was a losing battle. After all the protective barriers I'd put up, being with you made me feel exposed and vulnerable so I pushed you away. The last couple of weeks have been torture, it made me see that life wasn't worth living without you in it. I love you Amani and I'm asking for your forgiveness for not realizing this sooner. Can I please have another chance to be your husband?"

Amani was in stunned silence over the way Cameron basically flagellated himself over the past to prove to her he was ready for love.

Should she believe him?

Could she risk her heart for love?

31

For the first time in his life, Cameron was scared. He had no idea what Amani was going to say. She was just standing there looking at him with tears streaming down her cheeks.

He couldn't lose her. He had to fight for her.

"I've never had someone want me," she whispered. "Someone to really and truly just want *me*."

"I do, Amani," Cameron walked over to her and wiped the tears from her cheeks with the pads of his thumbs. "I want all of you and I offer you all of me. My head, my heart, my body, my soul, however you want me."

"Cameron... I—I missed you so much."

Her words were all Cameron needed to wrap her in his arms. He grasped both sides of her face and looked into her beautiful brown eyes and knew he'd come home. "But do you still love me?" Cameron asked. He had to know he hadn't lost her.

"Yes, I love you, Cameron. As if it were possible to ever stop. I love you with every part of my body and my soul," Amani said. "I have and will always be forever yours."

Cameron leaned down and took her lips. He pressed

desperate kisses to her lips. When he lifted his head long enough to look at her, he said. "I love you, Amani. I wasn't sure I would ever be able to say those words to any woman again, but I can. But I'm a changed man. You changed me. I not only want to say them, but I could keep on saying them."

He kissed her again this time. It was a soft kiss, sweet and tender because he would cherish what he had with Amani for the rest of his days. He wanted to go on kissing her and perhaps take this somewhere more private but Amani wouldn't let him.

"You spoke words from your heart and now I need to," Amani said.

"Go on."

"I was enamored with you as soon as you arrived at the palace, but you had a protective fortress around yourself that I was determined to penetrate. I kept pushing you because I sensed how great we could be together and I was right. When we became lovers, the passion between us was so powerful, the fire so intense that I welcomed going up in flames. I didn't think about the consequences of our actions. I just wanted you."

Cameron smiled. He loved Amani's honesty and fearlessness. She hadn't been afraid to show him how she felt.

"I didn't fight Khalil when he commanded us to marry because I didn't really want to. I put up the obligatory front. I was afraid you might never feel for me what I suspected I was feeling for you after the night in the harem. When you agreed to the marriage, I hoped in time that you would fall in love with me."

"And I did, my sweet." He pressed her palm to his mouth and peppered her with kisses.

"I'm so happy because I have some news to share."

"Oh, yeah?" He asked with a smile, "And what might that be?"

Amani grasped Cameron's hand and led it to her stomach. "I'm pregnant. You're going to be a father, Cameron Mitchell."

His eyes grew and she wondered if he might faint. "What? How? How far along?"

Amani laughed heartily, but her eyes were ablaze with love. "I think you know the how and I'm two months along."

How could he not have known? As he looked at Amani and finally took note of her breasts, they had increased in size.

Amani was pregnant.

This remarkable, beautiful woman was going to have his baby. It seemed almost unreal. He knelt before her and hugged her hips to him so he could kiss her stomach. He would love and protect Amani and his baby for the rest of his days.

Amani rubbed his head and then pulled him to his feet, then she melted into him, her lush body so pliable and lovely in his arms again. He breathed into her hair and his nostrils flared as he caught her scent, a scent he would never tire of because she was his.

He looked down at her. "I love you, Amani. You've made me the happiest man alive." Then he was kissing her, their lips meeting in a dance older than time. He lost himself in her and in the life they created together.

When they finally pulled apart, it was Amani who grasped his hand. "Come with me." Cameron took her hand because he would follow her anywhere.

ALL OF HER dreams were coming true. Cameron loved her and was excited about the baby. It was everything Amani could have hoped for and more. Once the door was closed to the master bedroom of the villa and it was just the two of them alone, she threw herself into his arms and kissed him with unfettered passion that set them both afire.

They worked quickly to dispatch their clothing, feverish for the connection they shared. Of love. Of family. Eventually, they fell backward onto the bed and when Cameron finally thrust home, Amani cried out with utter joy. She hadn't realized just how much she missed being with Cameron until she'd been deprived of his kisses, of his touch. But not anymore. They had a lifetime to love each other.

They moved together in harmony – fast and frantic, urgent as if neither of them could believe this was real and they were together again. But they were—their bodies were locked together as one. Her moans and his groans echoed through the room, mingling with the rhythmic sounds of their panting breaths as their bodies contacted.

The combination of it all was sublime and drove Amani into sensual overload. When she looked up into his hazel eyes, she knew Cameron loved her because he was giving up his control and allowing her to see he was cracked open and vulnerable. She saw the pleasure in his eyes and it made the experience all the better.

He maintained steady, impossibly sweet strokes as she clutched him to her sensitized breasts. When her climax struck, she shattered around him, her inner muscles spasmed in powerful waves and stars burst behind her eyes. She heard Cameron's primal groan seconds later as he sank on top of her and they collapsed together in a heap of sensual bliss.

They hadn't gotten here the conventional away, but they were partners, who loved each other and were committed and that's all Amani could have ever hoped for.

Cameron stared at his beautiful wife and four-year-old son, Cassius. He'd kept the time-honored tradition in the Mitchell family of naming their son with the letter C and couldn't be happier. He was even more so because Amani just had their second child, a daughter, Amira, and his family was here to celebrate her baptism. The festivities had taken place earlier that day in the family chapel and now they were all gathered in the courtyard where he and Amani shared their first kiss. It was a special place for them because it was there, Amani once told him that she'd known he was the one.

He knew Bahara didn't follow the Christian custom, but Khalil had understood his and Amani's need to stay true to some of his family traditions. And so, the entire Mitchell family had been flown to Bahara for his little girl's big day.

Liam was beside himself with learning all about the palace and required Cameron give him a personal tour while filling him in on the history. Meanwhile, Thea, Caleb, Colton and Chance, Monae and Caleb's other sons had been running around driving the poor staff insane. Cage wasted no time knocking up his sister-in-law in quick succession. Three boys in six years had to be some sort of record.

Meanwhile his parents, Cal and Camilla and his brother Caden and Savannah looked as in love as ever. Cameron and Amani had arranged for each of the couples to have spa treatments and flower baths in their suites.

"Did you see your grandfather?" Amani asked moments later, coming to him on the terrace as the family laughed and talked in the courtyard. "He was blustering about us going overboard, but he didn't mind when one of the chambermaids offered to bathe him if he wasn't up for it."

Cameron laughed and planted a hand on his forehead. "Oh, lord!"

Amani chuckled along with him. "It's fine. Maybe a little action might be good for the old man. You know, keep him young."

"Amani!"

"What?" She shrugged. "My relaxed attitude is all because of you, ya know. You ruined me."

"Did I?"

"In the best way." Her mouth lifted to his invitation and her hand went to the back of his head, urging him to kiss her. And he did. He cradled the back of her skull and covered her mouth with his. No matter how hard he tried, he would never be able to kiss her enough, hold her enough or fill her deeply enough to stop the need he had for her.

When he finally lifted his head, Cameron said. "You know you have my heart, right? It's yours."

"I do and I'm keeping it," Amani responded, "because you're all *mine*."

If you enjoyed

Guarding His Princess
By Yahrah St. John

Look out for the first two books in the Mitchell Brothers trilogy:

Claimed by the Hero
Seducing the Seal
Available now!

BOOKS BY YAHRAH ST. JOHN

__Mitchell Brother Series__

Claimed by the Hero

Seducing the Seal

Guarding His Princess

__Chicago Nights__

One Magic Moment

Dare to Love

__Dirty Laundry Series__

Dirty Laundry

Can't Get Enough

__Stand Alone Novels__

Never Say Never

Risky Business of Love

__Hart Series__

Entangled Hearts

Entangled Hearts 2

Untamed Hearts

Restless Hearts

Unchained Hearts

Chasing Hearts Pub Date

Captivated Hearts

ABOUT THE AUTHOR

Yahrah St. John is not just an author; she's a symbol of ambition and resilience. A Chicago native, now Orlando-based, she's an award-winning romance writer of forty-eight published books with a career spanning 20 years. Her books, filled with tension and sensuality and drawn from a well of personal strength, have earned her accolades and a loyal readership. When not writing, Yahrah is succeeding in her other roles as a pioneering property manager while traveling the world and pursuing her latest passion, travel vlogging. Visit www.yahrahstjohn.com to explore more of her world and her work.

amazon.com/Yahrah-St.-John

facebook.com/YahrahStJohn

instagram.com/yahrahstjohn

pinterest.com/yahrahstjohn

youtube.com/yahrahstjohn

bookbub.com/authors/yahrah-st-john